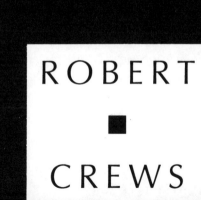

ROBERT

■

CREWS

Other novels by Thomas Berger

Thomas

ROBERT

■

CREWS

Berger

William Morrow and Company, Inc.
New York

It is the policy of William Morrow and Company, Inc., and its imprints and affiliates, recognizing the importance of preserving what has been written, to print the books we publish on acid-free paper, and we exert our best efforts to that end.

Library of Congress Cataloging-in-Publication Data

Berger, Thomas, 1924–
    Robert Crews : a novel / by Thomas Berger.
       p.   cm.
    ISBN 0-688-11920-4
    I. Title.
PS3552.E719R62   1993
813'.54—dc20   93-19004
                                                                         CIP

Printed in the United States of America

First Edition

1   2   3   4   5   6   7   8   9   10

BOOK DESIGN BY LISA STOKES

To John Hollander

1

■

IT STOOD TO REASON THAT BOB CREWS, who hated and feared any kind of flying, would be drunk in the little private airplane being flown by his old college room-mate and so-called friend Dick Spurgeon. The other two passengers were a tall, thin man named Comstock, whom Crews had never met or in fact heard of until ten minutes before boarding, and the jowly Jack Beckman, who had some kind of business connection with Spurgeon. Crews had encountered Beckman now and again at the latter's social events and very likely had insulted him on one or more occasions, for Beckman had greeted him coolly this morning. Though Crews had no particular memory of such offenses, he was well aware that he could behave outrageously when drinking—and he *was* drinking most of the time.

Crews needed no airplane to be drunk. He was usually in that condition anywhere on the ground after—originally it was after six P.M., but as the years went by, the line of departure was moved ever earlier, to teatime for a while, then after lunch, finally coming to a tentative stop at high noon. Unless emergency conditions prevailed, as now, he had thus far held the line against drinking in the morning, which was done only by hopeless alcoholics.

Given Crews's disdain for his old roommate, his distaste for

7

flying, and a total lack of interest in anything he had ever heard about trout fishing, one of Spurgeon's countless favorite sports, he might well have wondered why he was a member of the party at hand. And though he did not pose such a question, because having lived with himself so long he was not obliged to, his answer would have been to the effect that one ought to do something as the season turned warm, and such an enterprise as this was as good as anything else. There was nothing to keep him in town. Having lately endured his third divorce, he was in fact without a current home, unless a shopworn residential hotel could be given that name. While Spurgeon was becoming a force in big-time city real estate, Crews had managed to squander all his own father had left him.

Beckman now climbed aboard, the light aircraft vibrating under the imposition of his considerable weight. He squeezed himself into the copilot's seat, and he was welcome to it. Crews was on the left, in the rear. He would not have looked forward to a flight of hours while trapped in a side-by-side with Spurgeon.

While Comstock and Spurgeon were speaking together on the ground just outside, Crews took the opportunity to tip another gout from his flask of vodka into what remained of the coffee in the cup thoughtfully provided by his host, a role that, as usual, Dick played to the hilt: the coffee was the special breakfast blend supplied by his gourmet purveyor and poured from the thermos that accompanied an outsized wicker basket which presumably carried some version of lunch, to be eaten during the flight to Spurgeon's fishing lodge up in the north country.

Just as Crews was in the act of dosing his coffee with vodka, Beckman turned and looked at him. But Crews made it a point of pride never to apologize for taking a drink in whatever circumstances. He now pushed the dull-silver flask at the other man and made an exhortation of the meaningless sort associated with drinking for effect. "Have a head start."

Beckman snorted, his fleshy under-chin wobbling. "At eight in the morning?"

Crews snorted back. "Suit yourself." He flipped the cap shut,

on its hinged arm, and secured it in place, then returned the
flask to a side pocket of the old seersucker jacket he had chosen, along with a pair of chinos and battered rubber-soled
moccasins, as a costume for fishing. Spurgeon had promised to
provide all the tackle needed, but he had groaned in chagrin
when Crews appeared in this attire. "Christ, Bobby, we're
going up into the bush, not for cocktails at the Fog Cutter."
But in a moment he was snickering again. Crews for him had
become the provider of comic relief, the flunky who in an earlier age would have worn multicolored tights and belabored
people with an inflated pig's bladder. Crews could assume
that his devoted friend had long since defined him for Beckman's uses. *What does he do? He drinks. And gets married a
lot. Father was J. C. Crews, you know. The lawyer? Left him
well fixed, but women have got all his money. I have had to
help him out. Known him since college. Got a sense of humor,
you can say that for him.*

Spurgeon to Crews was a pretentious ass. The "bush" happened to be, judging from photographs, a handsome fishing
lodge, professionally decorated by an expensive practitioner
and equipped with every contemporary gadget including com-
puter and fax machine, all powered by a private generator
sufficient, one gathered, for a small city. Crews had not yet
been there, but on the video of the exterior, the place was so
large it looked like a resort hotel. To be sure, the lake on which
it was situated might well be thirty miles from the nearest
village, which supposedly consisted of only a general store and
a few attendant shacks, but as always Spurgeon could call on
a staff of retainers, in this case a number of local Indians, all
of the same family, who maintained the lodge in working condition whether anyone was using it or not, and served as
guides, handymen, and even cooks, when the owner and his
guests were on the premises.

There was apparently an indeterminate number of these
folks, who might be father, mother, brothers, or cousins, according to Spurgeon, including a teenaged girl that he sug-

gested Crews might want to nail if he got desperate during the weekend and if he did not insist on a bed partner perfumed by Chanel rather than pickerel: this was the sort of abuse Crews had to endure from his old roommate and as a good sport find funny. The fact was that while he admittedly drank too much at times, he had never considered himself inordinately lecherous, not even back in the old days when irrespective of the alcohol in his system he could perform consistently between the sheets, and even then he had never had a predilection for adolescent girls, who were far too vain and demanding.

His taste was rather for married women, wives who needed some relief from insensitive husbands like Dick Spurgeon. To be sure, Crews could sometimes be outrageous at this endeavor. Once he had enjoyed Denise Spurgeon below while Dick was up at the boat's wheel, pompously lecturing on celestial navigation to Margo Hines, Crews's joke date: Margo had sex only with other females. On this three-day sail, she and Crews kept to their own bunks. Denise, of course, was in on the hoax and probably enjoyed it most. Her dislike for her husband very likely exceeded Crews's own, but people persisted with Spurgeon, obnoxious as he was. Because he made a go of whatever he undertook, which in adult life meant money.

Crews had never made a dollar in his life, and while he sometimes reflected on this fact with what was supposed to be a proud defiance, he was well aware that he was therefore at a disadvantage in a vulgar world, especially since squandering so much of what he had been given, and not only by way of his wives. International law enforcement was presumably still looking, or making a pretense thereto, for the criminal trustee who had absconded with the funds that were left. In reality Crews saw no possibility of his earning a cent throughout the rest of his existence and lacked in further relatives to die and leave him one.

Comstock now came aboard the aircraft and lankily stepped past Crews to sit down in the seat on his right. He immediately and prissily fastened the seat belt, then caught Crews's eye, which the latter had been too slow in trying to withdraw, his reflexes not being what they once had been.

"Supposed to be some bumpy weather up ahead," Comstock said.

Jesus Christ. Crews gulped the rest of his spiked coffee in one swallow and, regardless of Comstock's presence, refilled the mug with pure vodka. He selfishly recapped the flask without even making an insincere offer to either of his fellow passengers: it was all but empty anyway.

It was Beckman who responded. "Dick's a master pilot. We've got nothing to worry about. He wouldn't go at all if there was any real trouble." He nodded at the control panel and the windshield that was too high, Crews was wont to notice, to see anything through—except maybe another airplane a certain distance above. There was little about flying that tended to give the confidence implicit in the material details of a car, the visible brake pedal and gear selector and the sure sense of a solid surface under the tires. Crews's driver's license had been taken away for life, though in none of his crashes had he hurt any person but himself.

"I know," Comstock said, chortling no doubt to dramatize his lack of concern. He was answering Beckman but pointing his long chin at Crews, presumably for confirmation. "Else I'd haul my butt right outa here, right now." He sported a floppy canvas hat, with ventilation grommets large as quarters at various places in the crown. He wore a field jacket and matching pants, and short laced boots. Beckman's somewhat similar jacket had no sleeves and was thus a vest. Except for Crews, they were all dressed as if going to the front in some guerrilla war. Spurgeon encouraged that sort of display. He was himself decked out in the ultimate in posh safari gear, in what must be the latest of trendy colors, a dark khaki very near but significantly distinguished from green, and furnished with all manner of straps, buckles, and zippers. His headgear was, however, a tan cap of the baseball genre except that the bill was overlong and vulgarly covered with tan suede.

Comstock was still leering at Crews. Spurgeon's friends invariably expected others of presumably the same ilk to be comparable toadies.

Crews asked irritably, "What in hell is he *doing* out there?"

"Aha." Comstock was the sort who relished an opportunity to enlighten the baffled. "He's balancing the luggage. There's a baggage compartment in each wing. The weight has to be more or less equalized on both sides, so the plane will fly on an even keel."

A mixed metaphor. Crews had gone to a preparatory school of old-fashioned standards, including those of grammar, and still retained a few traditional phrases associated with Western culture: dangling modifiers, the subjunctive mode and passive voice, not to mention, from the wider range, benevolent despotism, the (whichever number) Law of Thermodynamics, the Rump Parliament, and scraps of notable verse, e.g., "bird thou never wert," "say not the struggle naught availeth," and an old ballad about someone named Lord Randall, who ate poisoned eels.

Comstock grew more companionable. "Dick tells me you're in—art?"

Crews glumly took a drink from the cup, which action Comstock chose to interpret as the response of modesty, and he added, "Says you're really talented."

Crews was approaching the state in which, at certain social gatherings and sometimes even in public places, he flagrantly insulted others. He made no allowances for those likely to retaliate violently. He was no coward when the adversaries were human. He would take on anybody of any size, brandishing fists which might well not launch a punch, let alone land one, before their owner was flat on his back and often bleeding from the mouth. Three of his teeth in the left front were artificial, and his nose had been reconstructed twice, though one time this had come about through another mishap while behind the wheel of a car.

"My daughter Cary's going in for art," Comstock went on,

12

"and intends to head for an M.F.A. next year. She's in her senior year at—"

Crews tuned out, having an uncharacteristic impulse toward prudence. If he was to spend a weekend in this man's company, it would not be sensible to make an enemy of him so early on. Instead he sipped more vodka as Comstock continued. Yes, he had had some small talent, as people had assured him from time to time when he was a schoolboy, but the simple truth was that when he got old enough actually to see what he looked at, it was obvious that he could never approach the masters whose works overwhelmed him (a roster extending from Cimabue to Matisse, but nobody of more recent vintage, if only because he had not gone to a museum or gallery in years). There were those who told him this was no acceptable excuse to quit. Crews understood quite early in life that the way to quiet one's advisers is apparently to agree with them, to which there can be no rejoinder but an impotent smirk. His only ghost of a true regret was in disappointing his mother, or rather her memory, her untimely death having come in his last year of college. But he was twenty-one at the time, a man by any legal standard. Thinking back, he felt only a rotten sort of gratitude for the excuse: surely he would have turned out as badly without it. She had framed and hung the Conté crayon "Head of a Lady," a work of his fifteenth year, where she could see it from her sickbed. In an excess of what he believed grief over her death but what he later recognized as his earliest example of self-loathing, he smashed the frame and shredded the drawing.

"Are we ready to rumble?" It was Spurgeon, boarding at last. In the service of his lifelong quest to be a regular guy (which unfortunately seemed to work with a lot of people, e.g., Beckman and Comstock), he had through the years employed the idiom currently in yahoo vogue: at the moment, it was probably taken from some contact sport, perhaps professional wrestling.

Speaking of which, Comstock was the perfect model of a pencil-neck geek. He now broke off the monologue about his daughter and her career aims to cry a phrase so long out of date that it should have appalled the trendy Spurgeon. "And *away* we go!"

Before taking his seat, Spurgeon looked at Crews. "How about you, Bobby? Bet you can't wait till we get upstairs."

Crews shot him with a forefinger. "You bet." He had never given Spurgeon the satisfaction of hearing of his fear of air as a medium of transport and had been amazed the first time he was needled about it. It had taken him all of three minutes to realize that Dick had surely got the information from Michelle, who had been so comforting to Crews once on a commercial flight that he had subsequently made her wife No. 2. This was back when such female functionaries were still called stews. Of course she quit the job when they were married, but kept all of her former colleagues as friends, including one who was subsequently caught by the DEA on an incoming flight from Caracas with a stash of coke behind the built-in mirror in her makeup case. Michelle also remained close with a pilot who was discharged from the airline for drunkenness but was immediately hired by some tramp carrier and worked with a forged license. Crews had no sympathy for this kind of drunk: an honest one stayed unemployed. Also, as it turned out before long, Michelle was defiant about continuing to go to bed with this guy. Yet she managed to take Crews for plenty in the divorce, if only because he could match her outrages two for one, any old day. All in all, his memories of Michelle were fond ones. She had a natural ebullience, beyond the synthetic stewardess act, and the most beautifully shaped nostrils he had ever seen on a human being. She was too good-natured, however, to believe the negative had any fundamental status in the way things ought to be, and thus had little sense of humor. She was actually hurt if Crews, as was his wont, gave her a joke gift at Xmas before presenting the real one, e.g., a sheepskin-upholstered toilet seat.

Crews drained the cup while Spurgeon was starting the engines. The trouble with always being drunk is that in case of emergency you can't *get drunk*. Perhaps drugs worked, but

Crews had ever observed a personal prohibition of them, seldom taking even an aspirin. He was restrained by a horror of addiction. You could pollute your life that way.

The engines were making a maniacal noise, and the craft under him felt as insubstantial as a construction of matchsticks. While emptying the mug, he bit its rim, but the clash of teeth against china, usually skin-crawling, was reassuring now. Had he sufficient strength, he could have leaned forward, put his hands around the headrest, and throttled Spurgeon, so taking all energy from the airplane, a device of great immanent power but purposeless without human direction. Remove the pilot and what was left was junk. But this should have been done long since, certainly before they were rolling down the runway of this suburban airport. Crews's timing had been deranged for years. He was now diverted by anxiety as to where to find his next breath. His nose was sealed, and his mouth congested with a large ball of spongy matter, which he identified as his tongue only as his head was pressed back and his chin elevated by an unnatural force inimical to life. The takeoff was in progress even before he could adjust to the taxiing! He tried to distract himself with indignation but failed and was abandoned by every feeling other than terror as the little winged box and its frailer cargo were hurled into the sky.

The engines were not so obstreperous once cruising altitude was reached, but it was still too noisy for conversation, as Crews was pleased to believe when he made the transition from heart-stopping crisis to the routine dread of being suspended thousands of feet in sheer air, while being heavier than it and thus abrogating every physical law that could be confirmed by the body: even a buoyant boat made of tons of steel, containing its own nightclub and swimming pool, made more apparent sense. He was never apprehensive on water, regardless of the weather or the size of the vessel. If it was large enough to have a bar, it was there that he defied vertigo no matter how high the seas ran beyond the portholes. On smaller craft he might well offer to lend a hand, though a captain like Dick Spurgeon became even more obnoxious than usual when under sail, and Crews's footing was hardly surer on a wet deck than it was ashore. If he went overboard it was usually though not always by accident. He swore that Ardis, his first wife, pushed him at least once. Technically speaking, she was the only well-born woman he had ever married but also the foulest-mouthed and the only one whose capacity for liquor approached his own. Ardis's choice of men had continued to be poor even after she divorced him: her second husband was an impoverished Italian nobleman who, so went the malicious story, was wanted in his homeland on a charge of having sexual congress with underaged boys and whose title was bogus.

Comstock proceeded to challenge the theory that the ambient noise would rule out conversation in the cabin. To do so required his leaning as near Crews as his seat belt permitted and raising his voice.

"Heart's always in my mouth in these little puddle jumpers."

Funny how this expression of a shared fear instantly altered much of Crews's aversion to the man. He nodded vigorously at Comstock and even smiled in the off-center style that dated from the time of the worst of the several wounds his jaw had sustained from steering wheels and fists. He felt allied to a fellow sufferer, even one with whom he had had nothing else in common. But even under the best of conditions (if such could be imagined), he did not consider words an adequate means of expression for any emotion deeply experienced. For example, so far as anyone else had ever known, he had not mourned for his mother. Because he never told anyone of his grief, he was believed to have none. It was assumed that what was never spoken of did not exist. But he believed he was being loyal to his feelings by concealing them from others, or misrepresenting them through rudeness.

So he said nothing to Comstock, but did produce and offer the flask.

Comstock patted himself on his gaunt chest. *"Don't use the stuff. Health reasons."*

Yet he would travel by puddle jumper. Crews himself never failed to astonish his doctor and, he knew, to disappoint him with a blood pressure that, despite all, was never too high, and neither were his cholesterol and triglyceride counts, nor did he ever show a symptom of cirrhosis or any of the other deplorable systemic effects of excessive drinking. He would not have seen a doctor at all were it not for external damage. To placate the trustee (what a joke: that was the one who later decamped), he had once been interviewed by a psychiatrist, but made short work of that practitioner by insisting he lacked utterly in what was essential for a change of ways: viz., the least wish to be sober.

Comstock was swallowing dramatically, with a jaw even more elongated. He cried, *"Ears hurt? Mine are killing me. I forgot gum."*

If by now, as was being proved, alcohol had lost its efficacy as a fear-killer, one thing could be said for it: Crews's inner ears were not affected by the ascent. Once again he offered the flask to Comstock, and in view of his new partiality for the man, went so far as to lean as near him as the belt permitted and shout, *"It really works. Try it: too little left to hurt you."*

But Comstock fended the vodka off again. *"Got a wife and three kids."* For the second time he tapped himself pectorally.

Crews was aware that some people had that kind of idea about booze. That one sip to steady the nerves or relax the inner ear could lead to the utter destruction of an animal large as a human being. It took a lot to ruin a life, on which subject he was surely the best authority on board.

At that moment the plane struck a bump, and clutching the bottom of his seat should this be the first in a series, he sought distraction by staring at Comstock, but was disappointed when he saw no evidence that the other had registered the impact with what could be imagined as either a gaseous boulder or, worse, a pothole, which, being in the sky, had no bottom all the way to the earth. Huge commercial aircraft sometimes met such and fell helplessly straight down for thousands of feet in a shaft of vacuum, seat belts breaking and all loose objects, including passengers, pressed against the cabin ceiling. Crews was perversely fascinated by the details of all miscarriages of air travel, just as when a child he was addicted to the movies that were certain to give him nightmares. Now he regretted not having taken the seat alongside the pilot, because in that position he could at least have been aware when Spurgeon talked on the radio and got warnings of oncoming thunderclouds in which the little plane could be hit by lightning, exploding into fragments that the wind would distribute across several counties below. Or watched as Spurgeon, in the grip of a heart attack or stroke, steered into a mountainside of sheer granite.

He shook the flask. The engine noise obscured the sound of the sloshing liquid, but his fingers were sufficiently sensitive to gauge the vodka that remained as not much more than a fluid ounce. If he finished it now, and rougher weather was encountered later on, he would have to resort to the bottle in the duffel bag he had, against Spurgeon's objections, insisted on bringing into the cabin. However, he had not been able to keep it close enough to reach while seated. Along with the big wicker picnic basket, it was stowed in the rear, not far away, but to get there would be especially hazardous in the rough air to survive which he needed the vodka in the first place. Here was another of those absurdities of the kind that as an undergraduate and still a reasonably good student he assumed was confined to the history of philosophy (how could you prove without looking that an object was there when no one was looking at it? etc.), but that had proved so characteristic of his life at large. For example, the only way he could have endured thinking about giving up alcohol was to drink more of it.

He leaned toward Comstock. *"I guess we're hitting that rough stuff?"*

The other smiled faintly and shook his head in the floppy-brimmed fishing hat. *"Naw. Long way yet."*

The worst thing about this information was that it made Crews not only realize the little bump was so insignificant that Comstock, by his own assessment no hero, had failed to register it, but also admit to himself that the real turbulence, which after all he had encountered back when one or another of his wives had forced him to travel on big airliners, was massively more than this minor thud, which was probably only the retraction of the landing gear.

Comstock was staring at him. *"Didn't mean to upset you. Dick just told me we might run into a few bumps: knows I get queasy. If you expect what's coming, a lot of things aren't so bad."*

Now that there was no danger, Crews returned to his earlier disdain for the man, which was intensified by hearing this sophistry. As if anything bad was made good by learning it was on its way! He never looked ahead, unless of course obliged to do so by his companions. But in fact such people were always at hand. And whose fault was that? Yet he could not stand to be alone, without a distraction from himself. In such a situation he invariably became occupied by thoughts in which the desirability of suicide was countered by a conviction that he would do a bad job of any attempt: use a gun that jammed, hit the wrong vein when slashing the wrist and just make a nonlethal mess. Yet he could not bear the thought of anything so certain as leaping from an upper floor or plunging in front of a speeding car.

It must have been at this point that, in spite of all, he fell sound asleep. True, he had drunk more than usual at this time of day, after staying up all night, drinking, rather than even consider going to bed and trying to get up early. It was also the fact that fear bored him after a while, and when it was particular, must give way eventually to a general lack of hope that was soporific. Sleep is good, said the German poet, and death is better, but best of all is never to have been born.

The last cannot really be considered if one is alive to think on the matter, and thus far he personally seemed incapable of doing away with himself. Which by default left sleep.

It was while sleeping that, as he remembered later, he felt the onset of the promised rough air and realized that it was not so hard to take unless one awakened: the reverse of the situation with a bad dream, in which at the heart of your terror is the fundamental sense that you can escape it by waking up. He could not be touched by what was real so long as *he* was not, and vice versa. This seemed an all-purpose formula that could not be challenged. Thus he slept harder as the turbulence grew worse, and the more violently the aircraft was agitated, the more gratifying his immunity became.

How long the rough sky lasted was irrelevant, for time and sleep notoriously lack a common standard of measurement and are given to attempts to hoax each other, but it could have been the calm air that woke him. He had been slumping within the security of the seat belt. He now reassumed the tension of consciousness, straightening his spine, and discovered, with a hand to his mouth, that he had lately drooled. Embarrassment for him was rare nowadays, but this was one of the few effects that might evoke it. Another was pissing in his pants, humiliating even when done in private, but he looked down now and saw that at least he had spared himself in that regard.

Comstock was staring at him woefully. *"Sorry."*

"For what?" The general noise seemed louder than before, requiring them to raise their voices even further.

"I almost upchucked."

Crews shrugged. Comstock went on, in his oblivious self-concern. *"Thought we'd never get out of that alive."*

Ahead, Spurgeon seemed to be speaking on, or at, the radio, but Crews could not hear what was being said, which anyway would probably be in the jargon of flying. Beckman's face was turned, frowning, toward the pilot, an arrangement of features that emphasized the folds of his jowls. Beckman was the sort of man in whom you could see the boy, in his case a stocky

20

youngster already getting a gut at age twelve. Spurgeon, however, was fitter today than he had been when in college, but he worked harder at it. He had installed a home gym in the country house, and when in town was dogged about working out at his club. He had also become a crank about what he ingested. The thermos of coffee, for example, was provided for the others: he drank none and had long since given up animal protein.

That Crews had not wet his pants while sleeping through the turbulence was very well, but he really did have to go now.

He leaned at Comstock. *"Know how much longer?"*

Glancing at a wristwatch that it was a relief to see conventional and not adorned with push buttons and ancillary dials like Spurgeon's aviator model, Comstock unfastened the belt so as to lean as far forward as he could and cry the question at the pilot, to whom at his angle he had access.

In a moment he was back, shaking his head in the floppy hat. Crews could see that Spurgeon was still occupied with the radio, yelling at it now (though still incomprehensibly) and tapping at the control panel. Beckman's frown had grown darker.

Remembering these moments later on, Crews told himself that he had probably known, in his blood, that the process by which the plane would crash was underway, for he took an utterly uncharacteristic care to put in order the few things at his command. He checked the seat belt; he tightened the cap on the flask in his pocket; he rubbed the remaining sleep from his eyes.

But on the conscious level he was as yet unstirred. In the absence of information as to their time of arrival, which he assumed would be at some little local airport from which they would then travel to the fishing lodge by Jeep, he could make no rational calculations as to when to fetch the half gallon of vodka from the duffel bag behind the picnic basket. This matter had its medicinal aspect. Unhappy experience had demonstrated that if the alcohol in his system fell below a certain level, he got sick as a dog that had gorged on tainted meat, and had an equivalent reaction. Teetotaling Comstock might have come near retching because of the turbulence, but a Crews who had sobered beyond a certain point was dead sure to vomit all over the place. That such a place might be within the confinement of the cabin of a small airplane was an unpleasant possibility. His companions should be grateful that, though admittedly degraded, he was in several important respects still a responsible citizen.

All this while the others were showing an ever more marked sense of crisis, though none was dramatic about it: this came back to him later on, after the terrible event, with greater force and more detail than at the time, when owing to his personal state he took it as unremarkable, for another of the phenomena associated with addictive drinking is that the emotions of others lack validity: they seem either to have none or to be flagrantly counterfeiting some. Of course, he could see not Spurgeon's face, but only that part of the back of the pilot's capped head that was visible, in the high-backed seat, and Beckman, who alternated between staring out his window and then at the instrument panel, but now had become careful about looking at Spurgeon, and the ashen-jawed Comstock, with his stricken eyes—all these should have had another significance for a Crews not so dehumanized: say at sixteen, when he got several A's in his studies, ran cross-country, and had a living mother. But the contemporary specimen was not wont to make any but malicious observations of his fellows, and so far as he was superficially concerned, the airplane was cruising confidently along the highway of sky (which he still preferred not to look out at), and even the sound of the engines, so noisy earlier, had gone. Then too he was preoccupied by the stress on his bladder.

It took a while before he realized that the diminution of noise was due to the apparent fact that the engines were no longer operating. But not even then did he assume that the craft was in terminal trouble. He had finally made the decision that if he could not soon urinate, he would get his mind off the matter by having more to drink, had unfastened the seat belt and risen to go for the bottle in the duffel bag at the rear.

By chance he noticed Comstock's face as he went past him: retroactively, days later, he recognized that the man was looking at death and was blind to all else. In the next instant Crews was pressed against the back of the seat he had only just left.

The airplane was plunging. Contrary to legend, a crisis does not bring immediate sobriety. Terror reduced to nil his already diminished capacities. He prayed at the top of his voice, but could not hear himself. There were no sounds inside the cabin, and even the rushing air outside had gone mute. His head felt an internal pressure that under other conditions might have made him scream, yet even when he discovered that it was surely due to the index finger pushed into each ear, he could not withdraw them and listen to the noise of his dying. In previous thoughts on methods of suicide (a routine subject of his musings), he had wondered what took place in the minds of those who leaped off buildings so high that many seconds passed before the impact with the earth. Or did consciousness quickly go to black? His own situation was different: he had not made the decision to take his life, nor was he falling on his own, naked to the air.

He was now concentrated on what would happen to his body when the plane reached earth. He kept his ears plugged and squeezed his eyelids shut and locked his jaws. He brought his knees against his chest. He incessantly cried out to God.

The descent could not be measured by the means available to his impaired senses—it was both interminable and begun and finished between two heartbeats—but simultaneous with its completion, existence converged on him centripetally. He was simply and instantly extinguished, with only a millisecond in which to wonder gratefully at the total lack of pain.

2

■

HE WAS CRUELLY RECALLED FROM THE comfort of the void. His need for breathing had returned, but he could not breathe with a nose and mouth that failed to function. His head hurt badly, and something had happened to one of the fingers that had been in his ears. He struggled to free his ankle from unreasonable bonds.

. . . The reason he could not breathe was that he was under water: the cabin of the airplane was filled with it, a truth at which he arrived by using senses other than sight, for it was too dark there to see anything but dim shapes, unidentifiable blobs. He tried to rise above a preoccupation with exhausted lungs and remember where he had been in relation to a possible exit. There had been the door up front, but was there an emergency exit? The window, through which he had avoided looking once they were in the air, with his dread of heights: where was it now? Had the plane turned on its side? He could identify nothing. He groped and pushed and fought the murky and seemingly gelatinous element in which he was immersed, and he kicked and clambered. Then, without understanding how, he was suddenly free of whatever had detained him, but he was obviously still within the general enclosure of the sub-merged plane, and the need to breathe had become crucial.

With his remaining physical strength and a savage resolve

to survive, he pounded at something and kicked at something else, a bulky but yielding barrier that obstructed his way— later on, he realized that it had been the body of one of his late companions—and pushed strenuously in the direction of a paler area or phase of the viscous medium that held him, which seemed as if about to solidify, trapping him in an agony that would be eternal: never would he die, but neither could he take another breath.

All at once, when hope was gone absolutely, he broke through the surface of the water. He spent the next eternity in gulping air, drinking air and puking it out, chewing more, spitting and swallowing. When finally he could remember to open his eyes, he stared at the heavens, a blueness that was empty directly above him, but at the limits of his peripheral vision—there was some reason he could not move his head— the edge of a cloud could be detected, unless it was rather some damage to the corner of his right eyelid. Obviously he was floating on his back. Whatever movements he made to keep afloat had to be instinctive, for he was consciously pre-occupied with an awareness that he was not immediately threatened with death. He could breathe free air. He was no longer imprisoned in and by an alien, hostile element. But life had become a privilege, having lost its claim to being a right. He had no resistance left. Had he been in rough water he would not have had the strength to stay up.

Before rolling over, he had to conquer an obsession that he could not move his head because his neck was broken. When he decided to take the chance at last, for the reason that he could not stay permanently where he was, and got away with it, he became so bold as to lift his chin and try to see where he was situated in the universe. He was stoically prepared to find only a vastness of water, but in fact within fifty yards was a clear beach of what seemed pale sand, beyond which rose a dense forest of dark green.

Only now did he belatedly register how cold the water was. The light clothing he wore provided no defense. He felt as though bandaged in ice. He swam for the shore, but despite a frenzy of directions to his muscles, they could hardly function. It was all he could do to keep afloat, let alone make any gain. . . . Yet eventually he recognized that somehow the beach was slowly getting closer, and could only believe that God was moving it toward him, showing mercy to the feeble. When at length the water grew shallow—to him it seemed rather that the bottom rose to meet his knees—he continued to make the movements of swimming, now the paddling of a little child or dog, until there was not enough liquid remaining to provide any lift to his legs, and even then he lay awhile in what was left of the lake, wet sand, for now that it had done its worst without destroying him, the water seemed friendlier than the unpopulated shore, and he had even become habituated to its chill, so that it was remembered as warmer than the air.

What he least wished to do was climb to his feet and walk. At this moment, now that he had survived, he saw no value in surviving. Had he perished he would now be a comfortable nullity. . . . What kind of man was he? It was obvious that only he had escaped from the submerged aircraft. All the others were still aboard. Some or all might, like himself, not have been killed, but were trapped within the fuselage, not yet dead but soon to be unless quickly extricated.

He pulled himself to his feet. Something had happened to his knee: it could not bear its share of his weight. He shivered violently in the slight breeze that felt like rather a winter wind. He limped toward water deep enough for swimming, but when there was only enough of it to cover his toes, he passed out—which event he learned of only when he came to, so much later that the sun, high overhead when he first gained the beach, had sunk almost to the horizon. His body was so sore generally that trying to change its position brought him pain, and his knee throbbed. He dragged himself from the wet sand up into the dry. He had a sense of having vomited while unconscious, given the rawness of his throat and the taste that remained in his mouth along with gritty sand. The side of him that had lain in the water was soaking. He struggled to expose it to what was left of the day, for the sun had dried him elsewhere.

There could be no question of his swimming out and diving to the plane now. In his state of semidelirium, it even seemed that he had already done so and found nobody on board, a mystery that his weary mind could not cope with. He tried to take refuge in his state of damage, which was worse than those resulting from his car crashes or fistfights, for it partook more of soul than of body, and had to do with fundamental considerations that were at once unbearable but not to be denied. Had he left the others to die? Thus was he tormented, in and out of consciousness, throughout the night, which physically was bad enough, the temperature of the air falling rapidly as the sun sank without drying his wet half, and spiritually it was desolating.

He managed at last to scoop up the surrounding sand, which retained some faint warmth from the sun, and from both sides to push it over his body so as to constitute the sort of burying-alive of which his latest previous experience had been at age nine or ten with his mother at the beach. In the simulated grave he survived the night. But he had no mental peace and did not sleep so much as continue fitfully to pass in and out of a coma in which he was dead to any feeling but anguish.

When first light arrived he tried to convince himself of the necessity of meeting the day. It was convenient to remain supine while imagining that one had performed one's duty. He had often done the like as a boy, without harm except perhaps when, at too advanced an age, he still indulged himself with the dream that he was peeing into the toilet while actually wetting the bed. Considerate of the maid, a recent Irish immigrant, he had balled the sheets and dropped them in his bathtub. Dealing with the mattress, however, was beyond his competence. Mary Frances did not inform on him but did provide a plastic mattress cover, demanding reimbursement for it from his allowance, which she claimed was larger than her wage, though he could never verify that assertion, for his father handled all money matters—to be precise, had the secretary do it, whoever filled that bill at the moment, for they were periodically changed so that his father at any given time had a young woman to minister to his professional and sexual needs.

Lying in the cocoon of sand now, Crews found it comforting to suppose that it had hardened overnight into a kind of sarcophagus inside which he would eventually mummify, simply dry up, shrinking into a state that would at last be irreducible, the spirit having long since fled to the afterworld and the population of inquiet souls who wander on the shores of Avernus.

They were all of them dead: his mother and father, his late companions in the airplane, everybody in the world, just look and see whether anybody was visible on this sunny morning in the sand beside the lake. But the three most recent dead were under water and decency and honor and respect for life demanded the recovery of the bodies. No one remained to perform such service but himself. There could be no further shirking of responsibilities, no further flight from humanity. He was trapped now, unless he would truly forsake life: his bluff was being called.

He struggled out of the mold of sand. There was not a centimeter of his flesh or muscle or bone that did not rage against being brought so rudely into motion. It was not that he could not walk: at first he lacked the ability to crawl. When pressed to the sand his knees felt as though the skin had been flayed from their caps; they could never support his weight. He had every reason to stay put. Nobody would think less of him for not moving. Nobody would know he had not moved. Nevertheless he was in feeble motion, first by snakelike writhing; then rising, in pain, to his knees; finally erecting himself, stripping off his clothes, and managing to stagger the few steps into the lake.

When he was in deep enough, the buoyancy of the water relieved him of most of the impediment of his body, and he swam to the place, which he identified by instinct, where the plane had crashed and sunk, and after filling his lungs dived for it. But he had not done this sort of thing since he was a teenager. Nothing functioned as it should have, neither his stroke nor his kick, and at first he could retain only enough breath to get within sight of the wreck and back to the surface, even though the roof of the craft was only about ten feet down.

But after many dogged attempts, rising to the air, gulping, gasping, heaving after each, he succeeded at last in reaching the submerged fuselage, the door of which was open, perhaps as a result of his escape, which he did not understand as it happened and so could not remember now as more than a burst of desperation. The plane had come to rest on the level lake bottom, its body seemingly intact though up ahead the nose was smashed in and the wing nearer him was conspicuously cracked.

Though the water was pellucid, he had difficulty in habituating his eyes to it, and the light was poor inside the cabin, from which, when at last he was able to reach and penetrate it in one strenuous dive, his importunate lungs forced an almost immediate return to the surface.

Unless he rested more, his mission was hopeless and would only provide another corpse for the lake. He kicked up to the surface, where he rolled over and floated on his back, using his old childhood ability to remain buoyant with only the occasional flutter of hands. He had been so much better than his cousins at that trick: Johnnie couldn't float well at all though being a powerful swimmer, and Sandy could do so only with an agitation of limbs. They said *he* was kept up by a head made of cork, with no room for brains, and they pummeled him for it when they all left the pool. Johnnie, or Jack as he had begun to insist he be called, who at fourteen was the oldest, soon tired of this sport and, with one more slap at Bobby's face, ran across the lawn in his wet trunks, but Sandy dashed into the poolhouse, where she subsequently ambushed him from one of the dressing cubicles, wrestled him to the tile floor. He got an erection from the abrading of her mobile belly. At thirteen she still had no visible bosom, which was his almost exclusive sexual interest at almost twelve years of age, because no other difference between female and male was consequential and apparent when the subject was clothed. In those days Crews, an only child, had yet to see a person of the opposite sex in the nude, except of course in photographs, and had only a theoretical sense of what was concealed beneath the vee of hair in the female groin. Breasts made much more sense. He was embarrassed to get hard against Sandy, who to him was a kind of boy, and rolled away, but her writhing abdomen was soon right back on him. These many years later, he could still remember her angry red face. Why was she mad, when it had been all her own idea? After a while she leaped up, stripped off her suit without entering the cubicle, and went to shower. Crews just lay there for a while, waiting for his ardor to relax: he had yet to be capable of a physical orgasm. In later years, Sandy married a surgeon and became mother of three. As the result of a contretemps at one New Year's Eve party, Crews was banned from their home for life.

He was not going to be able to retrieve the bodies from the airplane single-handedly. He could not stay underwater that long. Search efforts must be already in progress: Dick had been shouting into the radio prior to the crash. Those in authority would certainly have been apprised of the plane's position. And just how far into the wilds had it flown? Insofar as there remained any real wilderness in the age of space satellites which could presumably zero in, from on high, to see minuscule details on earth. He told himself that it would be no time before help arrived, even though the crash had occurred probably in the early afternoon of the day before and nobody had come looking thus far. From the sky the area would be much more vast than when represented on a map, and in this kind of terrain, *his* lake might well not be unique.

Spurgeon may have been shouting into the radio because it had ceased to function properly, in which case his position might not have been known. The wait for a rescue might be somewhat longer than one would project on the basis of normal expectations. Crews was striving to be realistic, after many years of refusing to confine himself within standard reality, for that is what he was provided by drink: an alternative to the tedium others called life.

Having given himself an irrefutable excuse for making no further attempt to bring up the bodies of his late companions, Crews dived again and again to the wreck and tried to do just that. Eventually he was able to remain there long enough to determine that on the impact with the water the instrument panel had been smashed back to crush and imprison the men in the front of the cabin. In back, Comstock was bent over a seat belt with a buckle that when located proved to be locked fast and could not be freed with unassisted fingers, nor was there an available means of cutting the impervious webbing.

Crews had begun with too few physical resources to exhaust, but if endurance was a matter of sheer will, force was not. He was simply too weak to deal with the problems at hand. He did have the presence of mind, on his final and otherwise ineffectual dive, to scoop up from the compartment behind the rear seats every object with a reachable strap. Some of them floated against the ceiling.

Impeded by his burdens, not all of which were buoyant, he had only enough remaining strength to swim to the beach and collapse prone on the sand, the sun hot on his bare back. It felt benevolent. Had he still been drunk—a state in which some effects were blindingly swift, but others lingered interminably, and these were no standards but those of caprice—he might have stayed interminably and suffered a severe burn. But now he was unaccountably conscious of threats to his well-being. His skin was in the spring mode, white and vulnerable. He put on his clothes, even unto the seersucker jacket. He had no shoes, having lost them in the frenzy of his escape from the plane.

He examined the objects he had towed, on their straps, from the airplane. By now the water had ceased to drain through the wickerwork of the big picnic basket. He was interested to see, on unfastening its top, that the interior was stacked with watertight plastic containers and another thermos that, by the heft of it, still held coffee.

The other three prizes consisted of his duffel bag, a long cylindrical hard-leather case that no doubt contained a segmented fishing rod, and a sizable box covered in olive-green fabric and belted at each end in leather: surely a tackle box. The fishing equipment was of little value to him, but the extra clothing in the duffel might be of use after it was dried. An examination of its contents disclosed that he had forgotten to bring along extra footgear. The absence of toilet articles, however, was not a surprise: he had been out of toothpaste and his old toothbrush was a disgrace. If drugstores were in short supply in the neighborhood of Spurgeon's rustic lodge, then the host could be counted on to supply such needs.

He *had* brought along an electric razor in a padded box and a can of spray deodorant, and there was probably a comb tucked away someplace, though it was not in evidence at the moment. The spray can, when looked at particularly, turned out to be of antiseptic, not deodorant, but would be more welcome if he cut himself before being rescued. The razor was useless at the moment, but then he had no reason to shave so long as he was stranded. He unzipped the case and drained it, but closed it without looking into the little mirror affixed to the inside of the top lid. For years he had had nothing to learn from staring at his own face.

The remaining contents of the duffel bag were not what they should have been for a weekend anywhere, crash aside, consisting of the half-gallon jug of vodka and too much underwear and socks and too little else, for example sweaters, of which he had neglected to bring a one. When packing, a five-minute event, he had apparently mistaken a couple of navy-blue T-shirts for heavier clothing. Two more knitted polo shirts of the type he was wearing and a pair of blue jeans comprised the only garments for exterior wear.

He spread the wet clothes to dry on the sand and inspected the contents of the plastic boxes from the picnic basket. The food proved to be the sort that some gourmet catering service deemed appropriate for four men on a fishing trip: little sandwiches of goat cheese and dried tomatoes; Cornish-hen drumsticks; vegetable pâté and sesame-seeded crackers. Probably these things were to be snacked on during the flight and never intended as a proper lunch. But they were a potential source of nourishment and might serve a purpose if he had to wait much longer for rescue. He had not eaten a bite of anything in recent memory, and was still not hungry, but he forced himself now to chew on a triangle of goat-cheese sandwich. He also sipped some coffee from the thermos; it was still faintly warm. Immediately he was nauseated, but with self-discipline not only kept down what he had eaten but continued to masticate until he finished the sandwich. He was suddenly aware of being dehydrated, and poured himself more coffee and drank it all.

He could see no evidence that any other human being had ever visited this place. But they had hardly been flying long enough to have reached uncharted wilderness, if any such even existed on the continent. Beyond that wall of Christmas trees, it stood to reason that civilization was not too far away, in some form or another. Had he possessed footgear, he might have done worse than choose a direction and hike toward it—if rescue did not come soon, that is. He had to consider the possibility that his position was not known, owing to the failure of the radio. It was now almost a full day since the crash. Could a searching plane have flown overhead while he was buried to his face in the sand?

Crews was trying to use a brain that had been pickled in alcohol too long to be instantly radiant when teetotaling. The flask had disappeared from the pocket of his jacket: he would not search the fuselage for it. The half gallon of vodka, in its plastic jug, had easily survived the disaster, surrounded by the soft clothing in the duffel bag. Crews had planted this vessel in the sand. He had neither taste for it nor horror of it. He was interested solely now in what would serve him, and alcohol, whatever it had done for him elsewhere, held no promise.

His pressing need at the moment was for a means of attracting the attention of any airplane that might fly over the lake. A big smoky fire would do it, but he had nothing with which to start one. He decided to make a horizontal sign on the beach, using the branches of trees. He had forgotten his bad left leg until he started to walk toward the forest. He had been immune to pain when in the water, or simply distracted, but could move on land only with gritted teeth and frequent rests.

When he reached the trees, he had nothing with which to cut the larger branches, ones large enough to be conspicuous from the air, and the minor extremities of the evergreens proved too elastic to be easily snapped with his limited strength. These trees, which he assumed were generically pines, seemed not to have the readily available dead limbs natural to their distant deciduous relatives, according anyway to his dim boyhood memories. Furthermore, if you did locate a brown branch, what usually came off to the pull was only the moribund needles rather than the shaft.

But finally he was able to move an armload of materials from the forest to the widest area of the beach and begin to spell out, in letters he hoped were large enough to be seen from the air, the word HELP. Halfway through the job, he ran out of branches and had to return to the trees for more. The pain in his knee was worsening with use. He favored it awhile by hopping along on his right leg only, but stepping on a pine cone with a foot clad only in a cotton sock, he lost his balance and fell. Now the instep of his good foot was sore, and in clawing out as he went down, he managed to wound his right hand on impact with a sharp twig on the floor of the woods.

Before completing the distress sign, he unscrewed the cap and with his left hand hoisted the heavy half-gallon container and splashingly disinfected the wound with vodka. Now that he had not drunk any for an entire twenty-four hours, he discovered that the liquid did have a faint smell: very medicinal, repulsive to him.

Making the sign was much simpler than exploring the wrecked airplane, certainly less taxing than the dives and swimming out and back, yet he found it tired him, what with the extra expenditure of energy required to avoid further hurt to his left leg and his right hand. The latter impediment, though no doubt temporary, was the more inconvenient. He had never been able to do much with his left, not even eat in the European way without switching the fork after cutting the meat into morsels. In school he had boxed some, but was hampered by this constitutional inability to give his left hand its due. Now he was stuck with it.

When the HELP sign was at last completed, however, he doubted that even five-foot letters could be seen from very high in the air. A much more conspicuous signal was needed, but he had exhausted his strength by now, and his leg hurt him so much that he groaned aloud. Judging from the position of the sun, it was already late afternoon. He still had no taste for food and felt internally ill, no doubt as a result of the sudden withdrawal from alcohol, but knew he should eat something more for his survival. So he munched on a Cornish-hen leg. No doubt it had been marinated in wine and herbs and carefully broiled, but he was insensitive to all tastes at the moment, despite his new ability to smell, or think he smelled, the normally odorless vodka. He tried to avoid thinking about how long it might be before rescue came. It was clear that he would not soon be able to hike out, in stocking feet and with a bad leg, to the nearest human community, even if one was relatively close by. And he could spare no more immediate concern for the bodies in the airplane. Until help arrived, self-preservation must be his obsession.

He had to find refuge again before darkness came. The sun, which he had taken for granted his life long, was now the sole available source of light and heat, and gauge of time and direction. As it sank toward the treetops on the far shore of the lake, he looked for alternatives to the sand burial that had served on the previous night but was unattractive to him now, if only in the moral sense: determined to survive, he could not afford the connotation of interment. If defiance was part of this determination, then what he defied was what he had been before the crash. Destroying oneself had a point only under conditions of civilization. The situation was otherwise when your adversary was nature.

But digging in made sense. He had no tools with which to build much, and no strength to drag back and forth to the woods for materials. After a while he found the pair of plastic cups that nested under the cap of the thermos. Using one as a trowel, he scooped out in the sand a shallow cavity long enough to hold his body. If seeing it as a grave was out of the question, it could be called a burrow or slit trench or the cellar of the structure to come. In the course of this project he soon discovered—or remembered, for he had dug in sand as a child—that there are physical laws ordaining how far you can dig down perpendicularly before the walls of a hole threaten to cave in altogether. Sand in volume has its natural conformations; a cupful on a level surface forms a miniature dune. Therefore he scooped to a depth of no more than a foot and graded the sides of the depression into natural slopes, not walls.

Given the season, he had enough clothes to survive another night, but he cursed himself for neglecting to bring along extra shoes. In collecting the branches for the HELP sign, he had picked up solefuls of pine needles, some of which pierced the weave of his socks to prick his feet. At the moment he could think of no better countermeasure than putting on a second pair of socks over the first. Were he faced with the need to walk far, and if his leg permitted such, he would have to fashion some version of footgear from the materials available, but it was premature to think of that eventuality, as well as being defeatist.

They might come for him at any time, though no more to-night; he had to accept that fact as dusk approached, and he worked, as well as he could with a wounded hand that hurt more than his knee, to make a better shelter of the shallow trench. To spare his leg, he crawled to the distress sign and pillaged branches from it and erected them, stems embedded in the sand, around the rim of the trench. Across their tops he tried stretching the empty duffel bag, which was supposed to be waterproof but even when flattened out was only wide enough to protect his head and shoulders. However, the thick canvas proved too heavy to be supported by such slender uprights. After reerecting the latter, he constructed a flimsy roof of whichever garments he was not wearing, mainly extra underwear. The result was not in the least water-resistant should rain fall—the T-shirts would grow more weighty when wet and probably pull the structure down on him—but until then it would provide a ceiling under which one could enjoy the illusion anyway of being less at the mercy of the elements. The sense of irony that had become Crews's dominant emotion toward his fellow men could serve little purpose in this realm of the literal, where you made the most of what you could get and were grateful for it.

Before retiring for the night he once again scanned the shoreline for signs of humanity. He had of course been doing as much, periodically, since crawling from the lake after the crash, but what he could discern of the rest of the shore was as deserted as his own patch. It was a sizable body of water, perhaps a mile across in the part he could see, but his view was limited by a headland in the middle distance on his side of the water. Perhaps he was on a kind of bay, and just beyond the headland lay a village full of people.

He was startled by the sound of a splash and looked just in time to see, in what little light remained, a strand of silver glide beneath the surface of the lake. He knew so little of nature. He had never been a Scout. His swimming had been done always in pools and private areas of beach, not the sort of thing from which you learned to identify species of wildlife or edible plants, or anything of use in his current plight. How helpful it would be if he could make fire! Not only would night be less bleak, but by day smoke would be the most effective way of making his position known. Surely rubbing two sticks together was done only in cartoons. Then there was something called flint and steel. Flint might be found in the woods, when he could walk better—if he could recognize it—and perhaps something of steel might come from the electric razor.

He had enough food for another day and a lakeful of pure water, and he had a rudimentary shelter for the night, so long as the weather stayed clement. After a day of more physical labor than he had done in years, or ever, he was ready to sleep. He was morally pleased to have drunk no alcohol since the crash—and the vodka bottle was still planted there in the beach, untouched—but in body if anything he felt much frailer than when he had been drunk. He would probably not have damaged his hand if he had not been sober when he fell. Once, in the old life, he had tumbled down a length of concrete steps without sustaining a bruise, and while he had received damages of the face in his car crashes, there had been no lack of policemen and medical personnel to assure him he was lucky to have kept all major organs, including his head.

Though his little realm received some light from a newly risen slice of moon and the nearby water glistened faintly, the rest of the world was invisible and, since the splashing fish, silent, existing only in theory. He writhingly crawled under the simulated roof and rolled onto his better side. This was not kind to his hipbone: the sand at the depth to which he had dug was too firm for comfort. He had much to learn. He was too exhausted to crawl out, get the cup, and scoop out depressions here and there to conform to bodily protuberances. He turned onto his back. He had neglected to provide a pillow. He reached up and pulled down the nearest of the T-shirts that made his ceiling. The branch that held it came along, too, its grasping needles in his face. He put the balled shirt under his head and, tasting the flavor of pine, spat out the needles that had penetrated his mouth.

He was realizing a version of the experience he had been denied as a small boy: sleeping all night under the Christmas tree. His aim had been to see Santa Claus for himself, the real one, if such existed, for he could not remember a time, however tender his age, when he believed all those Santas in shops, on street corners, at parties, and on TV were one and the same being in different phases. There had been a Christmas Eve when he was ten or eleven, long past any interest in the matter of Santa Claus, on which his father had sent them a Santa impersonator, driving a big black Lincoln with a trunk full of expensive gifts elaborately packaged. His father had had to stay in Florida, where he was preparing the defense for Tommy Bianchi in the case the government was bringing against the "reputed mob boss," a term Bobby Crews did not yet understand but associated with "putrid," the word being much in vogue among the boys at school. Looking back, years later, he suspected—and got some ugly amusement from so doing—that the Santa Claus who came in the Lincoln was probably some thug from Bianchi's "family" and used the same car trunk for taking bodies to dump, weighted, into suburban marshes.

When Crews woke up, he had no idea of how long he had slept, but it was still night. In fact, he was not at all sure that he *had* awakened, for a bear's head, silhouetted against the slim moon, could be seen through the hole in what was left of the crude roof. As a test, he closed his eyes briefly. Sure enough, the bear was gone when he reopened them. What he had seen was some configuration of the overarching pine branches and/or the nearest garment thereupon in the remainder of his ceiling. Of course, the whole sequence, the test included, could have been, and continued to be, including this reflection upon it, a dream. But the trembling was real. Yet even that took him a moment to understand. It was not a reaction to the mirage in which the bear had figured. He was in the grip of a savage chill. The several layers of cotton were as nothing against the cold. Never before now had he been aware that teeth actually can chatter involuntarily. He tore away the rest of the roof and wrapped it around his upper body, under the thin jacket. He continued all night to shiver violently, and his teeth chattered whenever he unclenched them.

That he did nevertheless sleep, he understood only on being awakened by the morning light, and not the first light that had woken him the previous day but rather a sun that was already lifting itself above the treetops to the east. The woods were especially dense there. For all he knew, a town might not be very far beyond, but the continuous wall of greenery tended to discourage speculation. Better stranded near open water than wandering in circles through an inland thicket without boundaries.

He writhed out of his now roofless trench. It would take a while before he tried to stand erect. His knee had stopped hurting during the night, or anyway he had been distracted from it by the cold, but he had to prepare himself for the possibility it would prove worse when used. He crawled, favoring his right hand, some distance from all that he could currently call home, and rising to his feet at last, urinated.

The place he had chosen to pee was near the edge of the forest. Only when he had finished and was ready to start back did he notice the enormous tracks that led from the woods across the sand to the wretched excuse for a shelter in which he had spent the night.

3

■

CREWS FORGOT HIS KNEE AND RAN TO THE
campsite. From the tracks he could see that the bear had in
fact paused to stare down at him, but decided to attack not his
person but rather what was left of the food, tearing the hamper apart and devouring the remaining sandwiches.

He shared the area with a wild beast far more powerful
than he, armed with deadly natural weapons, and omnivo-
rously voracious by instinct. News reports told of bears that
were sometimes hungry enough to bite chunks out of sleeping
campers: legs, shoulders, or even, he remembered hearing,
heads. At first he could not even imagine what form of defense
to mount against the bear's return. Some sort of pathetic bow
and arrow? He had nothing with which to sharpen either arrow or spear, and any missile too feeble to bring such a creature down would only infuriate it.

He had been thrust into the situation of the first primitive
man to face an animal adversary. No doubt it had been the
beasts who won the earliest encounters, until the man could
effectively bring his mind into play, he who after all was the
wiliest of the apes. You could comfort yourself with such reflections, but realizing a natural potential long buried under
softer concerns was another matter.

Fire was the answer. He could not remain another day in

this place without fire. There was no animal on earth that was not terrified by fire. Fire would also warm him and cook the food he had to find now, for his larder was empty. With fire you could signal to searchers: smoke by day, flame by night. But how to make fire? He had constantly to face the truth that he was helpless when in the wild. There was not a moment in which he could afford to ignore his vulnerability to the menaces of the world in which he was stranded. Added to them now was a lack of food, and of course, for the first time in many years, he had woken up hungry.

The bear was the most frightening of his problems, but Crews had a feeling it would not return immediately. He had no authority for that feeling: he was simply basing it on his own disinclination to hang around some place that had run out of what he wanted from it. Any creature would go elsewhere under those conditions. He was pleased to be thinking like an animal, if indeed such was what he was doing; it had no precedent. The bear aside, then, there remained the matter of: a source of food; better means to keep warm; an improved method of signaling to aircraft . . .

He broke off here to gather the boughs used ineffectively to roof the trench and quickly reconstructed the HELP sign—while suspecting that a pilot who flew low enough to see letters of this size would be able to spot his person as easily, all the more so if he waved vigorously. But at the time of the flyover he might be underwater or back in the woods, and something was better than nothing. He did need a more conspicuous signal. . . . A *mirror!*

His disloyal knee chose this moment to remind him that its sudden recovery had been a hoax. It began to hurt more than ever. He hopped on the good leg to the duffel bag and took from it the little padded box in which his electric razor traveled. A hand-sized mirror was affixed to the interior of its upper lid. Because it seemed to be cemented firmly in place, instead of trying to pry the mirror off and perhaps cracking

42

the glass, he neatly ripped the entire lid away from the small hinges attaching it to the lower half of the case.

He caught the sunshine in the mirror, flashing light at the wall of forest. The facade of trees was itself in the sun now, and the reflection could be better imagined than seen, but the principle was sound. For the device to be effective, he would have to manipulate it, focusing the beam at a flying aircraft. It was not the sort of signal that would necessarily work if the glass was static. Nevertheless, remembering movies in which hostile Indians would, at great distances, notice the glitter of a cavalryman's brass buttons, he broke off a forked piece of branch from the HELP sign, planted its straight end in the sand, and mounted in its fork, angled toward the sky, the half of the box that framed the little mirror. If he was otherwise occupied at the time an airplane flew over, it was at least possible the pilot might see enough of a glint to circle back, and then detect the sign. Again, it was the something that was surely better than nothing, a principle he had consistently disdained in his life before the crash.

Now something must be done about food. There were fish in this lake. He had heard more than one splash when he was not so distracted as to be deaf to such. He was learning that one alone in the natural world did well to register as many sensory impressions as he could, bringing every practical faculty into play. Moralizing was not only a waste of attention; it could result in a failure of mortal consequence. What he had been in civilization had no useful bearing on what he must do here. He had to continue to think of himself as the man who could put a shaving mirror to emergency use. He was not helpless, even though he could hardly walk, even though added to the light-headedness as a consequence of such a sudden abstention from alcohol was a sense of his fragility with respect to the bear.

He opened the leather-covered cylinder he had retrieved from the plane and saw sufficient segments to make one of the lengthy rods used for fly casting, a sport of which he knew little beyond being vaguely aware that it was practiced while standing in a rubberized, waist-high, booted garment, half-immersed in a stream.

The accompanying tackle box offered a profusion of plastic receptacles full of little artificial flies, most of them showing colors and configurations of no insects Crews had ever seen. Also in the box was a reel. He had no difficulty in figuring out how to fit it to the buttpiece of the assembled rod, and pulled the line, which was thick and heavy and coated with some varnishlike substance, through the ringed guides along the considerable length of the rod, which when planted vertically in the sand was taller than he.

One artificial fly was as good as another to him. Obviously, each had its use according to the type of fish sought and perhaps the sort of water at hand, the weather, and the season, but he had no means of acquiring knowledge of this complexity in the absence of experience. He therefore chose the fly that looked least bizarre by his standards, which meant that which was least brightly colored. But the line was too thick to go through the eye of the hook. By now he was too impatient to pursue a better resolution to the problem, and he simply battered the end between two rocks until it had been frayed to a usable diameter, threaded it through the eye, with difficulty made a disorderly-looking knot that would probably not hold for long, and tried to cast the tiny, weightless object into the lake. As he had feared, not being unaware of the physical laws that apply to all forms of motion, the fly was too light to travel far or indeed at all.

He considered tying a heavier object to the end of the line, along with the fly, so that the latter would be hurled out when the rod was whipped—for he eventually developed a technique of wrist that would seem right—yet if the added weight did not float, it might drag the fly under water and ruin the illusion by which the fish was supposed to be attracted. But once again he noticed the weight of the line. Of course: the lure might weigh nothing, but the cast could be made using the inertia (or whatever it was) of the heavy line. Pull out a generous length and whip it. He put his theory into action and was thrilled to find that it worked. After many efforts he was finally able to cast the light fly some distance from shore.

Pleasure in this initial achievement was to be the only reward he received from fishing all morning. The pity was that he had no gauge by which to determine what he was doing wrong. Perhaps he had chosen the wrong fly. He tried a series of others. Maybe he was doing a bad job at casting. He tried variations on it, whipping the line out farther, then not quite so far, then in between, retracting it at various rates of speed, sometimes allowing the counterfeit insect to float as if casually, sometimes causing it to jerk and jump along the surface of the water. Could it be that no lake fish was ever attracted by such a lure, that the use of artificial flies must be limited to running streams? Were fish *that* discriminating? But maybe the trouble was that the area of the lake at which he had started—a hundred yards or so along the beach, so that he was as far from the submerged airplane as he found it convenient to hobble, with his bad knee—was simply not one frequented by fish, who might well have favorite neighborhoods, even as did land animals including man. Therefore he laboriously dragged himself elsewhere, casting out the line at each of a series of places, finally finding himself almost at the point, which as he grew nearer he saw was of more topographical substance than he had supposed from his earlier perspectives. The beach there was terminated by a height the sides of which were sheer stone. On top grew the familiar forest of Christmas trees.

Not only did he fail to get even a preliminary bite, he neither saw nor heard any evidence of piscine life; no fish slapped the water today. It occurred to him that for their own reasons the creatures might simply not be feeding in any place or on anything at the moment, or had their own subaqueous sources of nourishment. He had taxed his knee by all the stumbling up and down the beach. He sat down on the sand. At least the day was a warm one, with a hearty and generous sun overhead, though some clouds seemed to be forming in the farthest reaches of the western sky. He really could not understand why no airplanes had appeared. The other men all had families who were surely bringing frantic pressure on the appropriate agencies. Had Spurgeon been so far off course that he could not easily be traced? And again he wondered about the radio: would Dick not have been in touch with whatever had been the nearest airfield, some version of which however modest should be within electronic reach anywhere on the continent? Even if the radio had eventually failed, it was working when they took off. Would not the subsequent silence have alerted those whose business it was to listen?

But perhaps he was being too sentimental about how other people were supposed to perform, he who never had a profession. It was in any event useless to sit there asking questions that could not be answered until he was rescued. Not only useless but morally degrading. He had work to do, for the first time in his life. Half of another day was gone, and he still had no food, no fire, no shelter, and no weapon with which to defend himself against the bear.

. . . At first the sound was too faint to be identified. It could have been an insect or even the humming of his own blood in his ears. In two days here he had got himself under such management that he could allow for the delusions of hope; he refused to admit he heard an airplane until he finally saw it.

But it was high, far too high! If the plane was to him a winged speck, what must he be to it? He ran, knee throbbing with pain, back to the mirror, tore it from its forked mount, and flashed it at the sky. Now that he put it into play, the glass seemed much smaller than before. He had no way of knowing whether he was catching the sun, let alone projecting a signal in the proper direction. If this pilot was looking for him, the man was doing a bad job. For an instant, Crews yearned for a gun, not for signaling but for firing at the aircraft, bringing it down in flames with a lucky shot.

He continued to gesticulate with the mirror until he could no longer hear a sound and the speck had first lost its wings and then its reality in the blue vastness. His anger was succeeded by a profound depression of spirit that left him momentarily too weak to make any further effort to preserve himself. He dropped the mirror on the sand and sank down beside it, convinced, on no better evidence than this single failure, that he would never be found while alive. He had been able to control his hope, but self-pity overwhelmed him. If he had not been able to cope with civilization, what could be expected of him now?

He felt a warmth on his forearm, through the shirt that, with his trousers, he had pulled on when emerging from the water after the latest dives—he could scarcely afford to sunburn his spring-pale skin. In another moment his arm was painfully hot. Had he been stung or bitten by a venomous creature? He rolled up the sleeve and examined the skin, finding nothing untoward. Was it a withdrawal effect of the two days' abstention from alcohol? Would he suffer imaginary pains at various places on his body? Drinking had surely got him into, or anyway exacerbated his part in, many scrapes, but he had not previously been afflicted with hallucinatory phenomena that could be associated with either the presence or the absence of drink. He knew the DTs only by way of vintage movies. Perhaps they came from the contaminated liquor of yore. But he had suffered a scare at one point when an apartment, hitherto innocent of mice and roaches, was abruptly invaded by both: or *seemed* to be, for examples of both were visible for such brief instants that, to senses corrupted by alcohol, they might well have been illusions. When, having fled to the nearest bar, he saw a mouse run under his stool, it took all his courage, and four drinks, to confess as much to the bartender, from whom, thank God, he heard reassurance. "Been all over the neighborhood since they tore down that building next door."

He returned his arm to its former position. Soon afterward he felt the warmth again. He noticed that the shaver-case top that held the mirror had fallen to embed itself in the sand at an angle from which the mirror reflected the sun as a focused beam on his forearm. He picked the thing up and noticed for the first time, never having used it for shaving, that the glass was not the standard straightforward reflector but rather a magnifying mirror. If it could be accidentally focused to warm his skin to a point of discomfort, maybe it could be intentionally used to make fire.

He went into the trees to fetch firewood, disregarding the pain in his knee, which seemed to belong to someone else, perhaps himself in a dream.

He brought back an armload of dead branches. Some were of brown-needled pine, but he had also foraged beyond the evergreens to find other, huskier trees, among them one of the few he could identify, namely the birch, from which he was able without implements to pull some filaments of bark so thin as to be almost transparent, from places where peeling had begun to occur for natural causes.

To contain the tinder against a random breeze, he scooped out a little depression in the sand. It took a few moments of adjustment in the distance between the mirror and the inflammable matter before the focus could be refined to reduce the point of light to its minimum diameter. But even when he had done this, it seemed far too blunt, too pale, to coax out flame from inert matter at the temperature of cool air. . . . He told himself as much even as he watched the miracle in which the paleness of the tinder slowly turned dark, from tan to brown, then went quickly to a blackening at the heart of which was soon a pinhead of red glow. He blew on it too soon, eliciting a wisp of gray smoke, but returning the mirror to play and, breathing more gently on the new embers, produced a small yellow flame, the most glorious achievement of his life.

He piled on the dry pine needles and shreds or threads of birch bark, and finally the pieces of fallen branches, graduated as to thickness.

In a few moments the fire burned so lustily that he feared his supply of fuel would soon be exhausted. He went to get more from the woods, but now had to range farther. Already the excitement of making flame had been diminished by the fact of its having been made, and once again he remembered his sore knee. But he reflected that now he could heat water with which, with strips of T-shirt, a warm compress could be fashioned— that is, if he could find something in which to heat water. The cups from the thermos were made of plastic, but they were sufficiently heat-resistant to accept the hottest liquids. Primitive peoples, of whom he was now a fellow, were ingenious within the conditions of their ignorance. Before arriving at a sophistication that would enable them to slice off a cross section of a log and call it a wheel, they had used the whole thing on which to roll heavy objects. Before crafting vessels that could endure direct fire, they had heated and dropped rocks into holes in the ground filled with water.

He located some small stones, pebbles, and with care situated them in the fire at a place where they could be retrieved with tonged sticks. With the addition of a third application of wood, the flames were now rising to a formidable height, smoking, sparking, and he was gratified to be almost singed as he dropped pebbles into the embers. If you had fire, you had one of the essential elements of survival anywhere. Except in drenching rain, fire could in itself be the better part of shelter: with a hot enough blaze, you could do without a roof or walls. Also fire could serve as a deterrent against animal enemies. He was no longer defenseless against the bear.

He filled both plastic cups with water from the lake. When the stones seemed to have been heated sufficiently, he rolled them out of the coals with a long stick he had broken from a pine branch that was still green and thus resistant to flame. With another stick of the same sort, which served as the other member of the tongs, he managed after a few unsuccessful attempts to get the hot stones into the cups. This project too worked as intended. He poured the warm water onto the T-shirt and applied the compress to his knee. He felt better than at any time since the crash, but he knew he must resist hubris. He was still lost and still hungry.

The compress did so much for his knee and his general well-being that he decided to renew it when it had grown tepid. This time, however, with an intent to get hotter water more quickly, he found and dropped into the fire a larger stone, and kept it in the coals so long that had it been iron it would have turned white. He had prepared his tongs for the new and heavier burden, pounding the ends of the sticks between two rocks so as to fashion them into paddles. He was also ready to move quickly in bringing the hot stone to the water in the cup lest it burn through the now thin paddle ends, even though the wood was so green as to exude sap when he struck it.

The effort concluded in a damaging failure. The incendiary stone immediately burned itself free of the sticks, but not so soon as to fall harmlessly to the sand. Instead it fell within the cup, but off-center, and where it struck the inner wall of plastic, it burned through. Meanwhile its effect on the liquid was violent. Had Crews not instantly emptied the steaming contents onto the ground, the water would probably have boiled away within seconds, leaving the stone still hot enough to melt the bottom of the then dry cup.

After a momentary dismay, however, he determined to remain positive. The vessel was only half ruined. It was capable of holding about five-eighths of its original capacity and also could still serve as a scoop for digging. And he had learned a valuable lesson. Even in his situation, fire could not be seen as unconditionally friendly. There was no element in his current existence that could not become inimical, in fact lethal, without warning. It was in vogue nowadays to say the same about daily existence in any city, and Crews himself had said as much, sometimes to justify his drinking. Was it better to be mugged when sober? (That, in spite of all, he never had been the victim of such a crime was beside the point.) But this was quite another universe, one in which any advantage could be nullified without warning and without moral significance.

By now more than half of another day had passed, and the clouds that had been visible in the far western sky were moving closer. He could not think of a way to protect a fire from rain—any roof over it would burn—but suspected that a blaze that was hot enough might survive a mild downpour. At least it was a theory worth putting to the test. He must replenish the supply of wood and if possible find some means by which to keep it dry. He remembered the birches, but he possessed no knife or other cutting implement. Next time he was lost in the wilderness he would at least bring a straight-edged razor and not a useless piece of electric-powered junk.

He wasted time in searching for a rock with a sharp edge until it occurred to him that he could sooner make one. In the woods he located a couple of hand-sized chunks of stone and struck them together until one cracked and separated into two pieces each of which was serviceably keen around most of its circumference. They were tools of not the most efficient form, but they could, when used with purposeful repetition, eventually pound an incision in a birch trunk sufficient to permit the peeling away of a strip of bark.

In this crude fashion—much of his effort consisted in slamming the rocks against a tree reluctant to part with its integument until battered into submission—he eventually girdled several birches and collected what looked like enough half-cylinders of bark to roof a woodpile when flattened and placed in a shingled arrangement.

Next he put the rocks to service as axes. When held at an angle, the sharp edges could chop thicker lengths of dead wood than he had been previously able to attack, though the crude implements would be ineffective against the stouter branches needed to build a shelter sturdy enough to stand against the bear or possible other menaces. But of course he expected to be rescued long before permanent fortification was required.

By the time he had accumulated a waist-high pile of fire-wood that was of respectable quality and shingled its topmost layer with the birch bark, the afternoon had seemingly become evening, so dark was the sky when seen from the woods where he had decided his fuel supply would be less exposed to the elements than on the beach. The same could be said for himself, except for the possible greater danger of the bear when among the trees, which was presumably where the animal lived.

With the rising of the wind, he began to doubt the validity of his prior theory that flames could resist foul weather if burning fiercely enough. His morale had been strengthened by the successes with the magnifying mirror and the make-shift axheads, but it fell now as he returned to the beach and saw the whitecaps on the lake and felt the unobstructed force of the gusts that swept in from the water.

All at once the rain appeared without an introductory drop, great angry sheets of it, instantly transforming the fire into cold charcoal, soaking him and his miserable possessions, which he frantically gathered up for the dash into the woods, but, swept by the great broom of wind, he did not know what he had and what he left behind. That protection could be found in the trees was an illusion: the branches served only to channel more water onto him while others, tormented by the wind, whipped his face. How did bears and other wild beasts cope with rough weather? Probably in cozy caves. But the nearby terrain was flat, and he did not dare explore farther afield at this moment, lest he lose the lake and supply of fresh water as well as a situation more easily seen from the air.

He found rocks to secure the birch-bark tiles with which he had covered the woodpile, but before he could get them in place all the bark had been blown away and the stacked wood was drenched. In searching for a place of refuge in the gathering darkness he lost the rest of his goods, but the clothes had been soaked and the picnic hamper was empty and torn and the fishing-rod case was useless.

At last he stumbled and sprawled, but in so doing he found himself in a place of shelter inadvertently created by natural forces: an old tree trunk, fallen at an angle, against which other dead materials had collected, branches and leaves, on the leeward side of which accumulation a desperate man could burrow. He cowered therein throughout a long night in which the wind grew ever more furious in voice and act, bellowing, detonating, felling timber, increasing the volume of rain until the earth had become storm-tossed ocean.

He dug as deeply as he could under the log, heaping himself with forest litter. It was far from being dry but warmer than his bed of the previous night, and he had no fear of the bear in such weather. After a while he was even able to sleep.

4

■

CREWS AWOKE AT FIRST LIGHT, BUT HE HAD
been often briefly conscious throughout the hours of darkness.
The storm had exhausted its rage and the winds had blown
away, leaving the air still full of water, some dripping from
the trees, more falling as a steady soaking rain which felt
benevolent with the memory of the tumult of the night before.
The naturally created lean-to had provided some small protection or anyway the illusion thereof: there was a distinction,
but not one that mattered under prevailing circumstances.

Without the sun there was no means by which to tell time,
and no way of drying the wet clothing that was being further
soaked by the falling rain. He could not make fire for any
purpose whatever till the sky cleared. No aircraft would be
flying in this weather, so there was no point in going back to
the beach, where he no longer maintained a campsite. He had
no home at the moment but the dead leaves and brush that
had collected on the side of the fallen log away from the wind.
But his knee seemed somewhat better as he tried to retrace
his route in seeking refuge from the storm and find the possessions he had dropped. Eventually he collected everything
but the damaged picnic hamper, which had probably been
hurled away in one of the cyclonic blasts that had also felled
several of the trees within his range of vision. He had

heard some of the commotion during the night but had apparently slept through even more, knowledge of which he found reassuring: he had by combined instinct and accident taken the most effective hiding place that the forest offered against the assault of nature.

There had been only two choices the day before, and they had not been changed by the storm: wait for rescue on the shore of the lake, where he could be best seen from the air, or choose a direction and hike out of the wilderness. If he stayed near the lake he should fashion better means by which to make his presence conspicuous. He had to think of some way to keep a fire going in inclement weather. He needed better shelter if he was to spend another night in the outdoors. If he chose to walk, he required some kind of footgear, and his route should be determined according to some scheme. In terrain such as that which presumably lay before him whichever the direction, it would be easy to travel in circles. In any case, he needed food. He had not eaten for two days, and while he was not yet in the condition called, in civilization, hungry (as when one who has missed dinner lurches into an all-night diner), his new rationality told him he would soon require nourishment. He could not survive forever on only the persistent metallic taste in his mouth.

In lieu of making a decision, he decided to reconnoiter the adjacent area of the forest. He had penetrated the trees only fifty yards or so from the beach. Exploring a bit farther would not be imprudent.

He went only another hundred yards before emerging from the woods into a clearing in which stood the bare, broken, dead stumps of many trees, some with fallen trunks beside them, others standing alone. The devastation, which under other conditions might have been seen as ugly disorder, could only mean that human beings had been there. The stumps were pointed like sharpened pencils, not broken off jaggedly as if by winds. Why they were not of uniform height, if the chopping had been to gain lumber, and why so many of the fallen trees had not been hauled away, was of no substantive concern. He was not in a position to be offended by vandalism when the vandals were fellow men. Even if they were no longer on the scene, their trail in reaching this place could surely be traced back to where they had come from.

Civilization must be reasonably close by, even if, as was probable, the visitors had used vehicles. In such a region, distances were gauged by another measure than that of city taxicabs. He might be in for a long hike. But he would be thrilled to make the effort. The worst thing about being lost in this way was seldom knowing what to do beyond the emergency requirement, which was invariably of a negative nature: finding protection against drowning, freezing, starving, or an attack by a wild animal. At last he had an altogether positive task. Once he reached a main road, he would probably be picked up by a car or truck long before he had walked as far as a town.

He decided to keep going now, abandoning the few possessions parked back by the fallen log. Hiking would make him warm enough not to need the other articles of damp clothing. His knee was without pain today, and his bare feet were not uncomfortable, especially now that the ground was wet . . . and growing wetter, much more so than could have been caused by the recent rain, which anyway had almost stopped. In fact he was ankle-deep in a swamp, which soon gave way to an outright pond. He stopped to get his bearings. Now his knee *had* begun to hurt, and he was nowhere near anything that could be a trail or path, let alone a road. He backed out of the water onto the soaked earth and leaned against one of the pencil-ended stumps. It was almost waist-high and had been neatly carved to a ragged point by someone using what must have been a rather small ax or hatchet, judging by the size of the chop marks.

Across the pond, perhaps forty yards away, was a floating field of lily pads, and while he watched, an enormous horse-like creature emerged from the woods, waded into the water, and began to feed on the aquatic plants. It had a small rack of velvety horns, obviously not full-grown. Crews needed a moment to identify the animal as, probably, a moose.

He remained motionless against the stump. He was not likely to see a living moose, as opposed to a cartoon version, soon again. He had no plans to return to the wilderness once having escaped from it, but he would treasure the memories he had accumulated here: the bear and now the moose . . . and next the two beavers he saw swimming to shore. One of them, sleekly fat but agile, was leaving the water when he suddenly understood who it was that had gnawed the trees down and stripped away the bark.

There would be no human path or trail to find, at least not one associated with the naked tree trunks at hand. The beavers—perhaps, given the devastation, a whole tribe of them—had done this work. He made a motion of chagrin, which was followed quickly by a report so loud that for a heart-lifting instant he took it for a gunshot but then recognized that the leading beaver had leaped back into the pond, smartly slapping the water with his big flat tail. The two glistening heads disappeared beneath the surface. The moose too, for all its size and ungainliness, could move rapidly. It hurled itself from the pond and penetrated the woods with a crash of branches. Before he could sigh, Crews was alone again.

In a moment he looked for compensation for the disappointment. He now knew of the pond's existence. Maybe fish would be easier to catch there than in the lake. Also, where did ponds get their water? If in this case the source was a stream, perhaps it led in a direction taking which, on a makeshift raft, one could eventually find fishermen or campers.

But the rain had started up again and soon was falling in volume, discouraging further exploration. He turned and headed back to the log that was his new home. . . . Such was his intended destination, but he had no landmarks by which to be guided. The cone-gnawed stumps were indistinguishable from one to the next, nor were the living trees of the forest behind them any more helpful. Sometimes he had walked in shallow water, which retained no tracks. For every fallen tree trunk that looked familiar, there was another nearby that seemed even more so until he took another perspective on it. Crews had a poor sense of direction even when driving a car on paved country roads marked regularly with route signs.

It was all he could do to restrain himself from panicking and running so far into the woods as to make his problem even worse. Better to keep the pond in sight than to lose even it by a disorienting plunge into a forest that to him was featureless and from which it might be difficult to see the sun when it finally came out. He could reestablish directions once the weather cleared up.

He decided to build a lean-to on the drier ground at the edge of the swampy area. It would give him a task in which to put to work that anxious energy that might otherwise be wasted or put to a destructive use. And though he admitted that the feeling might be sheer sentimentality, this neighborhood, because of the beavers and the moose (who, unlike the bear, were afraid of him), seemed friendlier than any he had yet encountered.

The lengths of tree felled by the beavers but not hauled away after the bark was stripped and apparently (since it was gone) eaten were stout material for building. When he sought to lift some of them he suspected they had been simply too heavy for the animals, as they were for him as well, but he found enough of those he could move to build a sturdy frame by employing as uprights two rooted stumps seven or eight feet apart and gnawed to roughly a common yard in height, and managing to heft a log to stretch between them. But not before making a crude depression at either end to accommodate the jagged tips of the stumps, which resembled sharpened pencil points only from a distance: close up, they were not all that keen. His tools again were rocks: an intact one he used as hammer; another, split, provided chisel-like edges. But with these implements he could not gouge holes sufficiently deep to offer sound connections that would serve for long unassisted. He needed some kind of binding.

He waded in the pond to the nearest stand of reeds, flushing out several small fish that had been feeding or lurking at the base of the plants, as seen through the water— so he had been right: there was potential food here!—and brought back an armload of long green fronds. They proved tough enough to lash the cross member at each end to its supporting stump, though it took him a while to develop a means by which the reeds could get a purchase on the smooth-peeled vertical shafts. More pounding with his crude tools, the hammer-rock sometimes slipping and bruising the hand with which he held the make-believe chisel, produced circumferential grooves to hold the twisted lashings.

Once the frame was up, the arranging of the lengths of wood—in some cases trimmed branches, in others real logs— that made up the slanted roof/wall required no effort of design, but the job was physically taxing, for not only were some of the logs at the limit of what he could tote, but he was obliged to work rapidly before the coming of another night. He arranged the lengths side by side, ends on the earth, irregular tops sky- ward, at roughly an angle of forty-five degrees. When he was done he had a structure that might be called half a wooden tent.

At the moment he had gone as far as he practically could. He had built a roof that was as sound as possible without its elements (except the upright frame) being tied one to the other, which was to say that if there was another such violent storm as the one of the night before, most of it would probably be blown apart and away. But the sky had cleared and was darkening now by reason only of the hour. The rain had ceased to fall some time since. Nevertheless, he carried back from the nearest evergreens sufficient shaggily foliaged boughs to lay over the bare poles, with their many interstices, of his roof, arriving at a result that surely was not waterproof but at least would repel some drizzle if it came. The structure was open to the south, so as to catch the sun when it next appeared, but a storm like the recent one would have soaked the interior of any lean-to no matter which direction it faced.

Not until he was ready to retire inside the structure did he remember that his extra clothing remained back at the fallen log, wherever that might be. The air, though dry enough now, had cooled considerably with the coming of evening. Furthermore, though he had built his shelter on solid ground beyond the deliquescence of the marsh, the earth was soaked from the heavy rains and there would be no material anywhere from which he could make a dry bed. He tried to dig a shallow trench of the kind that had been of some service on the beach, but the ground here was not sand and though wet had stayed too hard to penetrate easily with a sharpened stick. He was too exhausted to chop much with the stone ax.

The fact was that he faced his worst night yet. But while just enough light remained so that he would not lose his way, he remembered seeing a patch of mud near the route he had taken to fetch the reeds from the marshland. He made his way there now and, having stripped naked, scooped up handfuls of the stuff and coated every part of his body he could reach except for the head and the privates. To protect his back, which got coldest when he slept, he smeared a thick coating inside the T-shirt he would wear against his skin. The mud happily turned out to be rather a kind of clay, a stiffer ointment to apply but no doubt preferable as insulation and with less of a connotation of dirt, though he was getting beyond such concerns. At the moment of application the wet stuff felt cold, but only a few moments later he had at least the illusion of being encapsulated in a deliciously warm investment, a sort of armor, and he began to feel as if protected against the bear as well as the cold. Before returning to the lean-to, he even capped most of his head in clay, including the backs of his ears, leaving only his face uncovered.

Under the roof of poles, he had a mattress of more shaggy pine branches, which when shaken vigorously were not as wet as the ground. When he lay down upon its springiness he felt warm enough by reason of the clay coating underneath his damp clothes to recognize that, given the conditions, he had actually attained, wondrously, a state of comfort. He went to sleep immediately.

When he woke, as usual now, at first light, the clay had dried here and there on his body and for a moment it might have seemed as though he were imprisoned in pottery. But when he vigorously flexed his limbs, chunks of the armor loosened and, as he rose, fell down the legs of his pants. The chest plating too detached itself easily and collected in fragments at his belt, bulging there until, leaving the lean-to, he freed the tail of the T-shirt and let most of the rest of his clay underwear fall to the ground. It had done the job in an emergency, as had he.

The air was still cool at that hour but seemed to grow warmer by the moment, for the sky was beautifully clear except for the intense striated colors of the rising sun, which was just at the point of his horizon that was farthest from where he would have placed the east. Therefore his lean-to faced north, not south. How right he had been the day before to stay here by the pond and not attempt to return lakeward. Caution was the way to survive. The moose, big as it was, was not ashamed to run from a harmless midget like himself. When in doubt, choose the prudent alternative. That was nature's way.

His hair was still full of dried clay, and a good deal remained stuck inside the T-shirt, making him itch. He stripped, ran to the pond, plunged in, and almost fainted from the heart-stopping, suffocating cold of the water, which felt as if at a much lower temperature than that of the lake. This enterprise had scarcely been prudent. For a few instants he could not move his gelid arms, and his immobile legs were inanimate weights that pulled him down. . . . He was standing on the bottom, in water that was waist-deep. Prudently, he had belly-flopped. But very soon his personal temperature had altered, and suddenly finding the air colder than the water, he crouched to cover his trunk while he rinsed the clay from his head.

By the time he had finished his ablutions the sun was all the way up and though still not at quite the angle to provide maximum warmth, it was a glorious sight for the cheering of spirits—which, however, fell with his worry as to whether he could locate the fallen log near which could be found the top of the electric-razor case with its magnifying mirror.

He toweled himself on his T-shirt, which he wrung out after having washed it free of clay in the pond. He left it to dry on the roof of the lean-to and, dressed in the trousers and polo shirt, barefoot, set off through the trees. He had apparently not strayed that far the day before: he soon arrived at the shore of the lake, though seemingly not near the place where he had camped the first two days. In any event, he could not find the trench nor what remained of the HELP sign, and finally had to believe they had been obliterated by reason of the storm. He had established no landmarks on the opposite shore, an unbroken wall of green. He would not have understood, at any earlier time, how easy it was to become disoriented in a state of nature from which all other men were absent.

By now he had gone without food for several days, which days had furthermore been characterized by strenuous physical labor. Therefore when he returned to the pond he decided to focus his immediate energy on the acquisition of food. The fish seen swimming in the water around the reeds were an obvious choice. After several attempts with various dead branches and one that he had chopped off a living tree—some of the dry ones were too brittle, whereas the fresh limb was too tough, too wiry, to sharpen with his tools—Crews fashioned a pointed spear that looked and felt as though it would do the job.

He waded into the water. He was barefoot but he kept his pants on, not even rolling them up. He entrusted his naked feet to the pond, the bottom of which he could feel as an ooze, not unpleasant, but he was leery of exposing his naked legs to carnivorous eels, snapping turtles, or God knew what.

But the problem with the pond turned out to be not the presence of hostile creatures but rather the absence of any animate thing. Today he failed to see a single fish in or near the reeds. When at last he emerged, spear trailing, he almost stepped on a small green frog sitting in no more than a quarter inch of water. By the time he brought up the weapon, the miniature creature had long since leaped to invisibility among aquatic weeds. It had anyway been too little to provide much food. He remembered from schoolboy biology that the plump midsection was all guts and such meat as there was could be found only in the legs, which on this tiny fellow had been lean indeed.

The sun had already climbed high in today's clear skies. More important than food—such food as he would be able to provide even when his efforts were efficacious—was the matter of an effective means of signaling to aircraft, and he had come up with a good idea. The submerged airplane surely still held some gasoline. If he dived down and opened the cap of the fuel tank, the gas, being lighter than water, would soon rise to the surface of the lake, where it could be ignited at the first sound of an engine overhead. He also remembered that the others' baggage, no doubt packed with warm clothes, had been stowed in the wing compartments.

But first he had to locate the fallen log at which the magnifying mirror, along with the rest of his possessions, was cached. He made exploratory trips into the woods in various directions, but after several of these in which he recognized nothing in the terrain, he was once again threatened with demoralization. It was ridiculous and degrading to get lost within a few hundred yards of trees, and all the more so when you were already lost in the larger sense. In chagrin he sat down on another huge fallen tree, which was somewhat similar to the one he sought, in fact very similar though different in a subtle way, tapering at the wrong end, which meant it had fallen to point south, not north like his. . . . But the fact was that when he had last seen "his" log, rain was falling, the sun was not in evidence, and he had had no idea of where either north or south was.

At last he stood up, walked around to look at the other side of the log, and saw the den he had dug out of the dead branches and leaves to take refuge in two nights before, and therein lay the goods he had cached. He cried out in triumph, the first sound he had produced vocally since the crash. He knelt and touched his precious possessions, each in turn. Never before had he been a materialist. In the early years of his drinking, when he still had things that other people coveted, he was quite capable of presenting costly gifts to near-strangers, such as the Patek Philippe he slid from his wrist and presented to a bartender who had been exceptionally patient with him at a time when he had been ejected elsewhere.

He carried everything to his new headquarters beside the pond and stowed it in the lean-to, the sight of which filled him with pride and that emotion one is supposed to have when contemplating one's home but which for him had been rare indeed, time out of mind. It was with reluctance that he left it to go to the lakeshore.

As the days had gone by, he found it ever less endurable to think of the dead men in the airplane. He was stronger now than he had been when he tried, without success, the morning after the crash, to free Comstock's body from the seat belt. He could, and no doubt should, before looking for the gas tank or the luggage in the wing compartments, try again to retrieve his late companions from the lake. A general respect for life, as well as his particular connections, demanded as much, yet whenever he considered making a dive for that purpose, he was claimed by a debilitation both physical and moral. And knowing that it took its source in the conflict between a human sense of guilt and a savage instinct for self-preservation made it no easier to overcome. They had been men, and their remains deserved better. But he was alive and lost and hungry. And now, brooding on the matter, he felt the return of the pain in his knee. He quickly stripped to his underwear and plunged into the water. He swam to the area of the lake over the wreck, some forty yards from shore, and taking the maximal breath, dived.

He kept no count, but he made so many dives that when he finally had to give up the quest, at least for the morning, he was so exhausted he had hardly enough strength to gain the beach, at last crawling on hands and knees up onto the dry sand and collapsing. The plane was no longer where he had last seen it.

In fact, it had vanished altogether. And what was worse, he could conceive of no explanation for the disappearance beyond that which simply attributed it to more of the divine malice that had brought the craft down in the first place.

He rolled onto his back, exposed to the heavens. The sun was too bright even for closed eyelids. He threw a forearm across his face. Where could an entire airplane have gone? Where it had gone down, the lake was no more than fifteen or twenty feet deep, and except when a strong wind made the surface of the water opaque, the top of the wreck anyway should have been visible from the air. Yet it had not been seen by the plane that came looking for it—unless it had not been there at all. Or maybe the aircraft in the sky had not been looking for the one that had crashed. He was confused and demoralized. He had been coping very well with disaster, but had no defenses against altered reality. Could the storm have brought winds so powerful that something as large as an airplane would be moved *under water*?

He was rushing toward terror. Lose one vital line to the real and all connections begin to unravel, and what part of existence can then be identified?

He threw the arm off his face, to stare into the merciless blaze of the sun and thereby either see truth or be blinded . . . but he found himself in shade. The massive head of the bear was between him and the sky.

His reason was intact. That the bear was not a hallucination (should there be any doubt) was confirmed by the coarse sounds of its breathing and, even more forcefully, by the feral stench it exuded, which was all but asphyxiating. It sniffed at him with distended nostrils, its little eyes having virtually disappeared in the furry head.

Crews's blood had converged behind the pulse in his neck and closed his throat. His limbs were too cold, too brittle, to be moved, lest toes, or a whole foot or hand, break off. Yet he was a man, with a rational mind and a coherent voice. Having no other weapon, he tried to speak to the animal. At first he could make no sound at all. Next he emitted a stream of almost noiseless air. This inchoate whistle intrigued the beast, which now brought its face near enough to take a prodigious bite of his if it so decided.

At last he managed an inner scream, but what emerged was the thinnest of whimpers. Something in it gave pause to the bear, which arrested the movement of its head, then withdrew slightly. Crews was encouraged. Using all his strength, he whimpered again, persisting until he was able to develop an outright whine. Repeated, the whine became a moan, descending from nose to diaphragm.

The bear slowly backed away, giving him reason to believe its purpose had been more investigatory than hostile. But it no longer looked curious. Perhaps he had annoyed the creature, and it was preparing for a brutal charge. He continued to produce vocal noise, converting the moan into a hum that in turn became a melodious chant, a recitative with bogus words, sheer gibberish, and eventually, by a progression that was almost natural in the sense that he did not think consciously about it, he was singing at almost full volume the lyrics of a song he had not heard since childhood: the theme of a television cartoon series of which the hero was a multicolored parrot that not only spoke comic Brooklynese but solved crimes. In truth, the rendition was far from adequate. Having a tin ear, he was aware he butchered the tune, nor did he remember the words with any clarity. The bird was named Gus, and it made a fuss when something, something, got in a muss, or went bust, or went out of line and was a crime . . .

The bear continued to back away, though its expression seemed to grow more unfriendly. But Crews's morale rose with every receding step the animal took. Soon it had withdrawn so far that it could not conveniently be seen from his supine position. He sat up and stopped singing. The bear ceased to move. Crews hastily resumed his song, but stayed in the seated position. The bear gave him a lengthy stare with its little glittering eyes, then quickly swung its snout around, taking its bulky black body along, and left the beach in a kind of lope that for all its ponderousness also looked carefree.

Crews continued to sing the nonsense song for some moments after the animal had ambled out of sight among the trees. He sang in relief and triumph, and also as insurance against the bear's return. The experience had flushed from his mind all previous doubts as to his sanity, and some of his earlier fear of the bear, though he had even more respect for the power of the big beast now that he had been close enough to smell it, and suspecting that his musical weapon might not have been so efficacious had the bear been really hungry, he was far from being blasé. Were he to remain in this region for long, he would have to take more substantial defensive measures, though what kind of barriers could be built, with makeshift tools and vulnerable wooden materials, could not be said. In zoos, dangerous animals were separated from the public by smooth walls of concrete and perhaps a moat as well. In summer, they floated cakes of ice in the latter, and the polar bears plunged in and swam with obvious pleasure. . . .

This was no time for nostalgia. The matter of feeding himself was paramount. He could only assume he had lost the wrecked plane because of a mental confusion due to physical weakness, which in turn owed to the lack of nourishment in his system. He had applied reason to the problem of the bear, when the animal was face to face with him. He must do as well with the problem of acquiring food. What did bears eat to become so large and burly? He believed they were omnivorous, stealing pawfuls of honeycomb as bees swarmed furiously about them, stings impotent against the thick and long-haired hide. And were they not famous fishermen, wading in rapids and scooping up and tossing huge salmon onto the shore? But as with berries and nuts, he had seen no bees nor salmon locally.

The beavers had gotten so fat and sleek on a diet of bark. He put on the clothes he had removed for swimming and went into the woods along the route he had blazed. Fortunately, it was some distance from that used by the bear. He was leery of evergreens. He could not distinguish among them as to type, and was not hemlock a legendary source of poison? The birch would seem preferable. Its pale skin had the sympathetic connotations associated with Indian canoes, and while not edible in itself, on being peeled away it disclosed subcutaneous layers of juvenile bark-to-be and living greenish tree flesh. The stuff had a fresh smell but no discernible taste. Nor was it, however relatively tender when considered as wood, easily chewed. To answer his need for nourishment, he would have to girdle even more trees than the beavers had ruined, and in his case, for questionable nourishment.

One of the few other trees he could identify (because of the Canadian flag) was the maple. He found several bearing the characteristically shaped leaves, but their bark was even less inviting than that of the birch. If the sap of the maple could be boiled into syrup, surely it must be edible, or drinkable, as it came from the tree. No sooner did the idea come to him than he remembered the pictures one saw of buckets hanging from the trunks: the background was often snowy. Nevertheless he banged at the nearby trees with his sharp rocks. He got no sap. It was the wrong season. Molly, the wife from whom he had lately been divorced, professed to be a conservationist: he could imagine her scorn. Pointing to the beavers as fellow depredators could not legitimately be done, for at least they survived by what they ruined.

The only second course he could find to follow the bark appetizers comprised samplings of a succession of weeds and grasses. He chose these preeminently by appearance, the smoother-surfaced and the paler-green in color the better, avoiding the spiky- or hairy-leafed or harsh-looking. What he ate was quite pallid in flavor, but presumably, being fresh, was full of the vitamins and minerals required to keep at least its own life going.

From the course of the sun, he could identify the general points of the compass. If he walked south, he must eventually, inevitably, reach some form of civilization. It was, of course, possible that what he was looking for was much closer in any or all of the other three directions, including the north. But he felt obliged to go by probabilities. He had lost most of his conviction that he would soon be found by rescuers. The one plane that had flown over was far too high to have been looking for Spurgeon's party. He would be well advised to go on the assumption that Dick had been so far off course that no one could have the vaguest idea where the craft had gone down.

If he was in for a long hike, he needed footgear. He returned to the birches that had provided the first course of his pitiful lunch and hacked off some more bark. This time he wanted the full thicknesses of all strata, for what he had in mind was a walking shoe or slipper that began with one sock inside another (he had enough to add a third, but found that combination too tight at the instep and decided to pocket the spares, to be exchanged at will with the inner ones in use). To the outer sock he would stitch a birch-bark sole, using fishing line as thread. To be sure, the line was thick and stiff, but those properties would make it easier to steer an end through the weave of the socks and then into the perforations he would pierce around the margins of the bark soles. Anyway, he had no needle. In tales of castaways such implements were commonly made of fishbones, he remembered wryly. Had he abundant access to fish, he would likely stay where he was for a while longer and not feel obliged immediately to hike out to no defined destination on crude homemade shoes, with no better prospects for food, and perhaps less for water, than he had here, where furthermore he had built a stout new structure to call home.

He went ahead and started on the shoes, trying, with only conditional success, to flatten the bark to the point that it would provide a comfortable surface on which to put a man's weight. But he continued to think about the fish that surely thronged the depths of the bodies of water surrounding him. It was ridiculous to starve in such a place. He needed to be as resourceful as he had been in making fire and constructing the lean-to.

A new idea made him put aside the unfinished footgear. He had disassembled the fly-fishing rod and returned it to its container. Now he found that case at the end of the lean-to where his possessions were arranged much more neatly than anything he had ever owned in civilization and removed from it only enough segments of rod which when joined made a thin pole slightly shorter than himself.

He pulled off ten or twelve feet of line from the reel and chopped it free with the stone ax. He tied the length of line to the guide ring nearest the end of the partial rod he had put together. With the fingernail clipper he cut free from its tiny hook all the colored hair, feathers, etc. that had made the artificial fly. To a nonsportsman like himself, the naked hook looked much too small to catch any trout worthy of the name, but obviously it had been fashioned by experts who knew better.

Then he went looking for live bait. He had not noticed an earthworm since childhood, and he could not locate one now in this terrain. He did encounter a leaping insect, a sort of grasshopper, but lost it momentarily in a patch of weeds and before trying to flush it out, saw a flat rock on the ground nearby, on instinct overturned it, and found several pale squirming wrigglers, not long pink earthworms but shorter, gray grubs or maggots or larvae (or were they one and the same?). The first that he tried to impale on the hook turned to paste in his hand. He chose another, working with all possible delicacy and succeeding. He went to the pond and dropped the bait-bearing line into the water near the growth of reeds.

The first nibbling vibrations that reached his fingers, not long afterward, so thrilled him that he could not restrain his impatience, and with precipitate action of the pole he lost whatever had stolen the bait. He threaded on a new grub and tried again. This time it took a while. The fish may have been alarmed by the violence with which he had tried to set the hook in the previous encounter. The spasmodic style was unsuited to survival in the wilderness. What was needed was fluidity: to be strong, sure, consistent, and careful in the sense of both caution and taking care of particulars.

Though the bank of the pond, not much higher than the surface of the water, was still damp from the rain, he sat down on it and composed himself, holding the rod with but two fingers, its butt on the earth between his crossed legs. The day was quite nice, with its balmy air and warm sun.

He felt a bite! This time he did not jerk the line abruptly but rather let the fish proceed for a moment as if unnoticed. Then he pulled hard and felt the barb take hold. He was disappointed when for an instant the fish did not resist at all, but immediately thereafter the creature did what it could to fight against capture: not much. Swinging it from the water with one yank, Crews could see why. The little silver thing was scarcely larger than a sardine. Yet it was food.

After he had caught two more minnows, exhausting his supply of grubs, Crews came up with something better. He chopped a live branch from one of the pines and, having trimmed it of foliage, formed a hoop with the thinner, more flexible end, lashing the tip to the shaft with fishing line, leaving enough of the thicker butt end for a handle. Inside the hoop he hung an upside-down T-shirt, neck and arm holes tied off. The line was stiff enough to stitch the hem to the rim of the hoop without a needle. The result, though crude, looked like a workable net.

In practice the T-shirt was not as porous as he thought it should be, performing more as scoop than seine, retaining too much water for too long, but when he was finally able to put it into action—having found it necessary to wade into the pond thigh-deep and then wait for the school of minnows to recover from their initial alarm and return—he collected a number of the little fish with one swipe, and though many escaped before the water had oleaginously drained very far below the net's rim, he held on to three.

He stuck at the job till the accumulated catch exceeded a dozen. He intended to use the heated-stone technique to cook them, but since this time the water must be made, and kept, hot enough to boil the fish, the plastic thermos cup would not do. The primitive hole in the ground would seem to be called for.

All three of his wives had had obsessions concerning food. Ardis had been the one fanatically concerned about the freshness of anything that had its origin in water. Molly, an animal lover, would not touch lobster, which was never cooked except when alive. Michelle's peculiarity was an aversion to eating much of anything lest it affect her figure.

A dim memory having nothing to do with his marriages came within reach. In his day he had watched a lot of informational TV, sometimes even when fully conscious: British ornithologists crawling about on the barren rocks of Tierra del Fuego; stout-bellied fishermen in baseball caps, casting lures from shallow-draft boats on Southern lakes; hooded climbers toiling up Everest and K-2. On one such program, a woodsman made the claim that water could be boiled in a container made of birch bark and was about to demonstrate when Crews fell asleep. By no means would he have remembered this had he not been in his current need, so strange were the workings of the mind. Not that he believed the assertion, which defied the physical laws as known to him.

But he anyway went into the trees and again girdled a birch, obtaining a foot-square roll of bark, which, after warming it over the newly made fire, he spread and pounded flat. Next he folded it to make an open box. The crimping and doubling over at the corners would not stay as fashioned until effective fasteners were found: the hooks of artificial flies.

He had earlier found the long, thick conglomeration of sticks and mud that formed the dam by which the beavers had made the pond: at a quick glance it might have been taken for a random mess of dead vegetation that had been washed downstream, but closer inspection established its effectiveness for the intended job. On the downstream side of the dam, the brook reconstituted itself by means of the constant overflow in this season of rain, and probably a certain leakage. Though he would eat the little fish from the pond, because at the moment they were all he could catch, Crews was not keen on drinking its water, which was not all that clear to begin with and was made murkier whenever he waded across the oozy bottom, occasionally snagging his toes on slimy submerged branches that when brought up for examination showed beaver tooth-marks.

He drank from the presumably skimmed and filtered stream beyond the dam. He now went there to fill the birch-bark box with water. Back at the fire, he mounted the container on a grate made of stones, over a modest edge of the fire, where the flames were lowest.

The meal could have been prepared more quickly had he put the minnows into the water at the outset, bringing them to boil with the liquid, but since he could not really believe the unreasonable method would work, he did not dare risk ruining his supply of food: he left the fish where they were and, against tradition, watched the pot. This vigil served only to stop time and ensure that nothing whatever happened, which might be called miraculous in the case of the noninflammatory bark, but after a series of finger testings, the water stubbornly remained cooler than the air.

He was hungry enough by now to swallow the little fish raw, but forced himself into distractions. He examined his hand. The wound had continued to heal, making so much progress, despite all the dirty labor, that it was all but gone. . . . Because his attention had been elsewhere, he had worn the same pair of pants for many days, and they were a disgrace. He exchanged them now for the jeans from the duffel bag (which already were loose at the waist), and while he was at it, he changed his drawers. He wore socks as little as possible, to save wear and tear on his supply of four pairs. He checked the birch-bark pot once again. It might have been only his imagination, but the water no longer felt positively cool to the fingertip.

He gathered together his dirty laundry and went to the

stream. He had no soap, so the clothes would not get really clean, but on the positive side was the fact that washing them would not befoul the brook, for all the dirt on the garments had come from this quarter mile of wilderness.

When he had returned from that chore and spread the clothes to dry on the roof of the lean-to, he found that the water in the birch-bark vessel had, when not watched, reached the proper temperature and was simmering with conviction. So it was true that the miraculous sometimes happened in nature. Why the bark failed to burn was not his business. He got his minnows and put them to boil.

Probably he cooked the little fish too long: they were falling apart when he took them from the pan. But the fact was that they proved to be the most delicious food he had ever put into his mouth. Even most of the bones were edible. The trouble was that the supply proved woefully meager. He devoured the entire catch in hardly more time than it took to empty the steaming contents of the bark kettle onto a bed of clean leaves.

He put another potful of water on the fire and went to seine up more minnows. By the time the bark vessel boiled again and seconds had been caught, cooked, and eaten, much of another afternoon was gone.

It was a luxury now to sprawl next to the pond, with a full belly, in benevolent light and warmth, stout lean-to nearby, laundry drying on its roof, breeze stirring the rushes, sun shimmering on the water. It could be that he was less alien here than in society, were the truth known, and, thoroughly sober for the first time in years, he could reflect on what he had been with another and less limiting emotion than self-pity.

He felt so good that he had the courage to lean over and catch a glimpse of himself on the looking-glass surface of the pond. He was shocked. He knew he had not shaved or combed his hair (which in fact had needed a trim for some weeks before the trip), and though he had bathed his person, willy-nilly, by sporadic immersions, he had not often washed his face nor brushed his teeth, but he was not prepared to see the swarthy derelict who stared back at him. He could have looked at himself at any time since recovering the shaving mirror from the airplane, but he had not considered so doing. The mirror was a tool by which he sought to survive. To see his face in magnification had never been a pleasure.

At that moment—and suddenly, because the wind was blowing in the wrong direction—he heard a plane hardly sooner than he saw it fly overhead, at an altitude much lower than that of the one that had come the day after the crash.

He scrambled to his feet and waved. He shouted uselessly. He ran to fetch the mirror and signal with it. He ripped at the nearest greenery and threw it on the fire, which by now, the cooking long since completed, had been allowed to go to embers. Wisps came soon, but a good mass of smoke, enough to be visible from above, was excruciatingly slow to gather, and did not really do so until the craft, after a wide and momentarily promising circle, picked up speed and shot beyond the horizon of treetops. Had he stayed on the shore of the lake, he would have been much more visible, for it seemed likely that the larger body of water was what the plane had circled. Had the pilot seen the wreck through the transparent water? And now gone back to report as much?

Yet he had not himself been able, that morning, to locate the submerged aircraft by repeated dives to where it had last been visited. Had the searching plane really circled the lake or was he making his own self-serving interpretation of what had been another maneuver altogether? From the ground it was difficult to say with any authority what an airplane was doing thousands of feet in the sky above. The only clear truth was that he still had not devised a means of attracting those who might rescue him.

All his successes—with food and shelter—supported staying here, not leaving. He was agitated again and had to do something to relieve the tension. He began to collect poles with which to add sides to the lean-to.

5

■

CREWS HAD NOT WORKED LONG BEFORE HE
had to quit and go into the woods and vomit most of what he
had eaten. He had no way of knowing for sure, but he was
convinced that the trouble was not with the quality of the
minnows but rather with the quantity he had eaten. He had
gorged on too many, too fast, swallowing whole more than he
had masticated thoroughly. So finally, after all his efforts,
there would be no nourishment in his body.

The experience so dispirited him that he went to bed even
before twilight came, but not before providing himself with a
fresh mattress of fragrant, springy pine boughs. This looked
better than it felt, but he had to raise himself above the damp
ground and at the moment could not come up with an alternative. He eventually squirmed into a position in which no
sharp end of branch probed any sensitive place on his person
if he remained motionless in sleep. Getting warm, however,
was another matter and without reference to the actual temperature. The sun had shone all day and the air was probably
warmer now than it had been at noon. The heat he craved was
that of an enveloping cover, a blanket, a great big thick wool
blanket in which to mummify the entire body from toe to
crown, and even keep all one's exhalations until it was so
deliciously, suffocatingly hot inside that, at the instant before

asphyxiation, you saved your life only by a quick thrust of the index finger up into the outer world.

The second night in his sturdy new abode was a disaster. For the first time he was conscious of the nighttime sounds of the wild, which until now—because he had previously slept through the hours of darkness—he had ignorantly believed silent. Whereas this night was all but clamorous, with murmurs, siftings, crashes in the woods; splashes from the pond and drippings and sighs; and from overhead and at a distance and nearby and at hand and almost out of earshot what could be called sobs, groans, moans, yells, shouts of rage, screams of joy. Reason told you they were not really such. There was a range of human emotions of which nature surely did not partake. But the sounds of pain could not be mistaken. Living creatures did not go unprotestingly between the jaws of others even though God had constructed them for that purpose. There were squeals and screeches and violent agitations of limbs, tails, wings. There was insane laughter (the legendary loon?), what could have been a roar, what was undoubtedly a sequence of howls, and from something that was probably dying came ever fainter bleatings.

To which din Crews was soon to add his own contribution. Until now he had taken little more note of insects (except in the case of the larvae tried as bait) than he did when at home, but suddenly they asserted their claim for his attention. He felt crawled on by tiny things with multitudinous limbs, which often, when he went to arrest their progress, turned out to be inanimate fragments of evergreen bough, manifestly incapable of independent movement, yet which began again to move vigorously as soon as he probed elsewhere. There were squirming beings in the thick of his scalp, in his facial and body hair, and in the farthest toes of his socks, none of which he could find when he went there. Little creatures strolled across his forehead and nose with the same impunity. They were gone before his hand reached them. He slapped himself violently, and whenever he did so, the other sounds of the night were instantly stilled. Could the entire world around him know, by this noise alone, that he alone was alien?

Then the aggressors went too far. He was finally stung by a mosquito so voracious that it stayed at his blood till it was smashed dead there, and no sooner had it died than an entire flock, a cloud, of others descended on him. In a moment he was driven from the lean-to to look for the patch of clay, but though the night was dry enough, the moon was obscured and very little illumination was available. He had put out the fire with water, lest a spark ignite his nearby home while he slept. In the darkness he did not dare go far. He dipped some water from the pond and made ordinary mud from earth and smeared it on his exposed parts. He stuck his trouser ends in the socks and made sure the other garments were buttoned at throat and wrists.

He returned to the lean-to and lay down again on the boughs, but as it dried the mud itched him and kept him from sleeping except in fits and starts, and when his stomach had recovered from the heaves he was hungrier than ever, though not for boiled minnows. He would have sold himself into slavery for a piece of bread—a loaf, a warm loaf, to be torn apart in great chunks, pushed into the mouth, and chewed. A character in a movie did that, but after only a gulp or two forgot about having starved for days, dropped the bread, and went about his business. This was not a French film or, like all the other characters, he would have taken food seriously. With French movies seen in America the subtitles permitted Crews to pretend he understood the dialogue, and everywhere in Paris he and his first wife stayed or ate or bought things, those who served them insisted on replying to Ardis in English, which was not charity but malice. His first wife was too proud to indicate as much to these tourist-spoiled functionaries, she being the sort who got satisfaction from reflecting that they surely did worse to others not fluent in the language, which in fact she was. As Crews was certainly not. But his own pride, though much feebler than hers, was such that he could not come clean on the matter, or in fact on much else. He was capable of admitting to himself that she was brighter than he, but could hardly do so to her, for she would use it against him. The real trouble was that she also had more money than he. They lived in Europe for a while. In the Tyrol, Ardis skied beautifully and he immediately broke his leg and spent the rest of the season at a tavern where expatriates spoke about the other foreign places they had tried and compared Davos with Cortina, St. Moritz with Kitzbühel, Rapallo with Dubrovnik, and Sardinia as opposed to certain little-known isles of Greece. Crews thought he might earn her approbation by mastering German, but of course he did not keep up with his lessons, and anyway Ardis said he spoke like he was chewing excrement. Her foul mouth was incongruous in such a precisely made person, physically incapable of grace-lessness. She was a superb horsewoman and as a teenager could have been an Olympian in dressage, but as soon as she was seriously threatened by the possibility of an actual accomplishment, she fled elsewhere, as if in embarrassment with her near failure of taste. They had married young, so young for Crews that he still believed he might eventually do something with himself, like sell wine or high-performance cars. In those days he was relatively sober until nightfall and would even from time to time put in a few teetotaling days to clean out the liver. At just which point Ardis took her first lover he could not have said, but he bore her no ill will for doing so, and in fact he rarely encountered a guy of hers he did not immediately hit it off with.

His own choice of female intimates at that time favored those with jobs but not professions. He was attracted by a young woman who worked at the counter of a bakery until he discovered that with her husband she owned the business, whereas the daughter of an owner might have been okay. He assumed that for a female to be attracted to him, she would have to be a subordinate in her current situation and unfulfilled. He still had some of his own money in those days, but he also still had enough pride not to reflect on such allure as it might be expected to give him. In this he was, uncharacteristically, justified: none of his women ever tried to put the bite on him until the divorce, and then not they but their lawyers were the sharks.

What he saw as his principal appeal was good humor. He embarrassed many a woman, but he tried to avoid quarreling with any. Crews reserved his combative feelings for his fellow man. With women he was agreeable even under adverse conditions. He would rather be abused by a woman than admired by a man, perhaps because men dismissively took him as he was, while women expected something more. At least at first, they believed there was a possibility he would prove capable.

Here in the wilderness he must finally have gone to sleep, for he woke up in daylight, but had no sense of having rested. He drank a lot of water and washed the mud off his face and the backs of his hands. Once again he needed to find food. He had not yet looked for the upstream continuation of the brook that the beavers had dammed to make the pond. He decided to do so now. It was possible he could catch some fish there.

From the tackle case he took some of the little compartmented clear-plastic boxes of artificial flies. He had never yet delved into the depths of the case. He did so now and belatedly discovered, below the plastic boxes, spools of different sorts of line; a scissorslike thing that proved to be tiny forceps; little bottles identified by label as containing dry-fly spray and fly dressing, whatever they might be; a small folder lined with fleece; a miniature reel of measuring tape; and other clips and tabs and gadgets and oddments the purposes of which he could not have known but which seemed infuriatingly useless to a man in his situation . . . but then a most precious treasure, an extraordinary tool that would answer every need. In his elation he went too far. He had been sick, weak, starving, lost, but with this instrument could prevail over any challenge of the wilderness. It was, in one small unit of stainless steel, a little saw, a knife, and a pair of pliers, to name only the features of obvious value to him. He might have no bottles to open or screws to drive, but simply recognizing the potential for such civilized services was morale-lifting.

He enjoyed a burst of emotion for a few moments and then returned to the level of practicality at which he must live or perish. The tool was six inches long. The saw blade itself, when extended, less than five; the knife, even shorter. It was a happy discovery and would enable him to do more effectively and neatly that which he had done with makeshifts, but the multipurpose gadget was not an ax or a full-sized saw, nor was it a gun.

He returned everything to the tackle case and hung its strap on one shoulder. On the other he slung the tube that contained the segmented rod. He set off on the expedition.

On circling a growth of rushes, he saw what previously he had not: a dome of sticks and mud rising from the water, looking almost man-made. This was surely the beavers' lodge, a nice piece of construction for a creature without opposable thumbs and no cutting tools but its front teeth. The roof looked impervious to natural enemies, and the entrance apparently was underwater. The animals probably remained there while he was in residence.

He found the stream that fed the pond. It was no more than four feet wide, and, obstructed, it was scarcely swift-running. Owing to the trees that overarched it from both banks, he could not have fished there with a long rod. It was difficult to walk along the right bank, which between the trees was thick with undergrowth, but he persisted, stopping now and again to pluck himself or his gear from the clutch of importunate branches. The other bank looked less overgrown but only slightly so, and he was reluctant to wade across, if only because he was completely dry for the first time in days.

Though the changes of direction were indiscernible as they were happening, the brook obviously bent or even twisted here and there, for the sun was frequently in another part of the sky than where it had been the last time he looked—and then of course the sun itself was in incessant though slow motion. Only now did it occur to him that the sun unassisted could not serve as a reliable directional guide. That it rose in the east and traveled to set in the west was true only in the most general sense. Without better orientation than that, in the absence of any fixed coordinate, you could have no real sense of where you were. He had the courage to make that recognition now, because however crookedly the stream flowed it continued to be the same brook, and so long as he followed its course, he could never be lost—that is, within his immediate area, whatever his situation relative to the greater world. And as long as he knew where he was in this limited way, he was not helpless.

Eventually the line of trees on his side receded from the bank of the stream. The ground was rising. He climbed for a while and reached a sheer rock face, at the foot of which the water ran with such force as to throw up a spray that misted his face as he paused to rest. If this current was not rapid enough for the legendary trout, then there was none such in the universe. He assembled the eight-foot rod. He opened the tackle case. When fishing the lake, he had chosen flies that to him looked realistic, namely the drabbest of the lot, and had not gotten a bite. Now he plucked up the gaudiest he could find in the plastic boxes. Remembering the trouble he had had at the lake in attaching the fly to the thick line, with the knife on his new tool he sliced off a length from a coil of transparent, synthetic twine or thread that for all he knew might well have been designed for the purpose, and knotted one end to the proper line and tied the eye of the fly's hook onto the other.

He went to the stream at a point at which, having undergone the worst of the turbulence, the water, though still flowing swiftly, was not frenetic. He knew no more of these matters than he ever had, but it simply seemed to him as a fellow creation of God that when swimming full tilt you would not be searching for food, but you might well be in the market for a snack once the going got easier.

82

He cast the fly as deftly as he could. He had learned something of what seemed the correct technique from his experience at the lake. The fly came down to the water with less force than the line, and the light length of clear plastic made little impact and was almost invisible. The bogus insect with the red midsection, orange mane, and long striped tail floated high in the fast-moving water, but not far. Within six feet of where it had reached the surface, it vanished into the snapping mouth of a sleek fish hitherto unseen in water that though in swirling movement was pellucid.

Crews was unprepared for the speed of this event. He payed out line much too slowly. He had tied the knots to the plastic line not tightly enough: the one attached to the fly instantly unraveled at the onslaught, and the trout, if such it was, disappeared with the imitation insect from which it would get as little nourishment as it would furnish Crews.

At least he had learned that the fanciest of the artificial flies had been good enough to dupe one fish. Now if he could only find its like. He sorted through the segmented boxes and in fact soon found several examples of what seemed to be the same though with slight variations from each to each that owed, presumably, to their being handmade. In addition to those for whom it was a hobby, there were people in the world who tied flies as a profession, as there were those who carved duck decoys and goose calls, and did other things that until only four days earlier he would have thought foolish if he considered them at all.

Since his utter failure in recovering the bodies, he avoided thinking of his late companions with particularity, especially of Dick Spurgeon, the best friend a human being could ever have, for whom in return he himself had been the unworthiest. The tackle case and rod had belonged to somebody now lost at the bottom of the lake, perhaps Comstock, whose daughter wanted to study art, or Beckman, of whom Crews inexcusably knew next to nothing. Maybe there would be some point to his miserable existence if he survived for no better reason than assuring the families left behind that their men had died as heroes. Dick now had a different wife from the one with whom Crews had had the short-lived liaison that was so loveless for either. It was hardest of all to think of Spurgeon's two children. In three marriages of his own, Crews had come closest to being a father only with Michelle's abortion, and surely the world was better for that negative fact, though no doubt he was worse.

He was in no position to surrender to shame. He attached the new fly, with what he meant to be a nonslipping knot, and cast it upon the water. This time, and for a number of repetitions, he had no taker for his bait. Maybe there had been but one trout extant today, and it had painfully learned its lesson. After countless casts, the fly was getting bedraggled, its fuzzier parts soaked, and soon was more in than on the stream. At last he pulled it out and substituted another of the same general type but not quite so colorful.

It was taken immediately. He had no reason to make a sport of it, and quickly jerked the line to set the hook, then with brutal speed, using both hands on the line, yanked the fish from the water with such force that it flew over his head and landed on the boulders behind. The impact was such that the fish was killed. That had not been Crews's intention, but that it happened was convenient. He brought in the next catch more carefully, which meant he had to kill it or let it pantingly drown in air. The minnows had not bothered him much, simply because they were so small. There was a morality for you, one founded on inches and ounces. But you had to admit it was only human to stride nonchalantly over a colony of ants while deploring the vivisection of mammals. Spraying fur coats with red paint while they were being worn: though she had not yet done it herself, his third wife approved of the practice. They never quarreled about such things, though he had not shared her zeal and when not in her company heedlessly ate meat. Molly stuck to her principles. She turned down more than one job on discovering that the prospective clients wore mink, and then there were the woman who asked her to upholster a chair in unborn calf and the man who wanted the walls of his study covered with zebra skin.

Crews kept fishing until he had a half-dozen of the lovely speckled fish that were presumably trout, though of another breed than he could remember eating in restaurants. His immediate hunger could no longer be denied. He had tucked the magnifying mirror into the tackle case before starting out. He removed it now and, having collected tinder and heartier fuel among the desiccated driftwood flung up onto the rocks by bygone floods, quickly made a fire during the brief period the sun moved between two high, feather-pillowy clouds. He was getting good at the trick.

The variegated, iridescent beauty of the trout as they had come from the water was fading in death. With his new knife he slit one from gills to tail and cleaned out the innards. Then he strung it lengthwise on a long green stick. He slowly turned it over the flames. The stick quickly dried and caught fire from time to time, and despite his care in turning the spit, the fish was charred in one place and almost raw in others, for the flames were too high and he was impatient. But when eaten the trout was no less than glorious. He burned his fingers and tongue during the meal but checked his impulse to gulp without chewing.

He was able to limit himself to only two fish. These examples were six or seven inches long and, smoked, would have served only as appetizers back in civilization. But however ravenous, he could not afford again to abuse his system as he had by bolting down the minnows. Smoking would seem the best means to deal with the remaining fish. There was a generous choice of stones along the banks of the stream. He was able to find just what he needed for a frame around the fire, now reduced to embers much hotter than the preceding flames on which he had impatiently burned his meal.

He went downstream to a point at which the cliff declined to a grade which he could conveniently climb to reach green foliage. He brought back an armload of fresh pine boughs. These went onto the hot coals within the circle of rocks, across which he placed the four cleaned fish, spitted on green twigs. Soon they were bathed in dense smoke. He hoped that while preserving the trout he was also sending into the sky an unmistakable signal that a human being was in the forest below. But the brisk currents of air that flowed down the stone face of the cliff dissipated his hopes along with the smoke.

Leaving the trout in their fragrant fumes, Crews explored upstream, proceeding gingerly because only rocks were underfoot here, some with sharp edges against his unprotected soles. He came to a place at which the cliff had been divided as if with a giant wedge. Between the halves was a notch, stony but with enough vegetation to make a climb possible, and he undertook the ascent, which once underway proved much more demanding than it had looked from below. When he finally toiled onto the summit he found himself within the grove of tall pines that had been visible all the while but which he had failed to evaluate. To see beyond, he would have to climb one of them. He had not been in a tree as an adult. The task was not only physically taxing but so scary in the upper reaches of the ascent that subsequently coming down would be unthinkable. Therefore he did not think, and so managed to reach the topmost branch thick enough to bear his weight, and from which he saw a universe of unbroken green, except for the visible portion of the blue lake, from where he was to the horizon on a circuit of 360 degrees.

He successfully came down from the tree, a task not so forbidding as the anticipation of it had been, and then descended the cliff, of which the reverse was true, and finally returned downstream to the fire, which was no longer smoking. The trout had turned to brittle leather—but in fact when tasted were exquisitely tender inside the crackling carapace. Not only was it tastier than the fish he had cooked so badly at lunch, but with their smoke the boughs had supplied additional flavor, in which even the welcome illusion of salt was included.

He placed the three remaining smoked fish in plastic bags from which he had emptied the previous contents and stowed them in the tackle case, slinging it across his chest on the strap. Crossing that was the strap of the cylinder that carried the disassembled rod. All was neatly packaged on his person, and he was refreshed by the meal, though hardly stuffed. He looked forward to getting home, eating the rest of his food, and working either on a pair of shoes in which to hike out of the wilderness or on the improvement of the lean-to.

Now he knew where fish could be caught. Next time he would arrive earlier and stay longer, catching enough trout for the smoking of a portable supply of nourishment that could sustain him on a long walk to civilization. He had already learned how difficult it was to live off the land. He would pack enough smoked fish to live on even if he found nothing else to eat en route. Any fresh food he did find he would use immediately, reserving what he carried for emergencies.

He hiked back home through the failing light, and while once again the distance traveled seemed greater than the route out, it was a breezily clear evening, and having his neat shelter to look forward to, with the remaining smoked trout as either bedtime snack or a breakfast to anticipate, he felt, of all things, an impulse to whistle. For an instant he was shocked by this urge, which seemed almost rude. He was an intruder here. He who had made a social career of being offensive now worried about behaving improperly in a milieu of plants and animals. That was good for a laugh, but not having laughed in so long a time, he found an example hard to produce. What emerged was rather a croak, appropriate enough on nearing the pond, where the night before the sounds of the resident frogs had contributed to the din that, with the mosquito attacks, had kept him awake. In answer now he heard a couple of *plops*, the first evidence of the beavers since he had moved onto their turf. The animals had been lying low throughout his lean-to building, minnow seining, and other activities, but felt free to get back to normal when he was gone all day.

It was great to get home. Simply to see and touch the few of his possessions he had not worn or carried on the fishing trip was reassuring. He unslung the rod and tackle cases and stowed them in their places at one end of the structure. At the other end, as pillow, he put the duffel bag that contained such clothes as he was not wearing.

He was not quite ready to retire, but neither had he sufficient remaining energy to deal with the bed of boughs that had been so uncomfortable the night before. He sat down on one of the nearby stumps and ate a smoked trout, slowly, savoring every morsel, including the now brittle brush of tail, and when he was done, he proceeded to eat the other two fish as well, though not with unalloyed satisfaction: thinking of the bear, he believed he was safest when he kept no food on hand to attract the animal. This consideration added a problem to the matter of accumulating enough smoked trout to sustain him on the projected hike out of the wilderness. He was too tired to think further on that subject or any other. He put on an extra shirt against the expected chill of the night and lay down in the lean-to, on the boughs, and immediately went to sleep, disregarding the possibility of a renewed attack by mosquitoes.

Whether or not any marauder visited him during the night, four-footed or winged, he woke in the morning without evidence of having been molested. No doubt the breeze had kept the mosquitoes away. It had chilled him somewhat, as he could remember as if from a dream, but not so painfully as to have brought him to full consciousness. He had nothing on which to breakfast, but he was learning to accept an animal-like way of life in which you ate when you could and kept going until you found the next meal.

Yet he must resist a similar state of mind regarding his predicament in general. There could be no further postponement in drawing up a comprehensive plan of action that would take account of his needs and his aims, along with the possibilities of successfully addressing both. The needs took precedence, but he had made a good start with food and shelter. No doubt he could better his previous performances in both areas, especially if he decided to stay in place until he was found. He had not been effective in signaling to aircraft, but not for want of trying. It was hard to say what else could be done. Keeping a fire burning at all times, so that at the first sound of an engine damp wood could be hurled onto the flames, would be impracticable. Touching off a forest fire would presumably bring attention but with a sudden change of wind the fire might eliminate the need for rescue by burning him alive.

He had to be frank with himself: he did not believe he would ever be rescued if he remained where he was. At the same time, and despite the discouraging panorama of unrelieved forest from the top of the pine, he was convinced that, with protection for his feet—or even, if they continued to toughen up, without—he could walk back to human society.

He was therefore startled when he asked himself which he really wanted to do, stay or go, and could not for an instant give a hearty or even an honest answer. But the moment was soon gone, and he began seriously to plan for the hike.

For the smoking of a supply of fish, he found a number of robust stones and from them built a larger and sturdier version of the simple arrangement he had used alongside the trout stream, and gathered the dry makings for the fire to come. He cut green twigs for the spits and fresh boughs from which to make smoke. He traveled upstream to the place where he had caught the trout the day before and, after having no success now with several of the gaudier flies, tried the drabbest, and caught one fish after another.

He had a good day, returning with ten trout. He had taken care to clean them on the spot and not back at the pond, where the offal might attract unwelcome visitors. After the preliminaries, he put the fish on to smoke and attended to the business of making sandals. The knife on the newly discovered tool made an easy job of cutting the birch bark to size, and the little auger head on another of the blades effectively pierced holes around the margins of the soles, for the thread that would lash them to the socks. As thread he had a choice of those spools of synthetic line from the tackle case. He took the finest, which still was stiff enough not to require a needle.

He had weighted down the bark under heavy stones for more than a day, but since it nevertheless retained a stubborn tendency to curl, he heated water again in a container made of the same material and straightened the soles-to-be in the steam therefrom. He sewed them onto a pair of socks. The result was close to what he had projected. He could walk in or on what he made, and even more comfortably if wearing them over a second pair of socks. How long the bark would stand up to the wear and tear of a long hike was another matter. Therefore he cut out and perforated two pairs of replacements that could quickly be stitched on if needed, without stopping at the nearest birch.

To sustain him in his labors, he ate two of the trout after they were cooked through but not yet fully smoked. This food tasted even more delicious than it had the day before, and he was again warmed with that rarest of feelings for him: a well-being not simply physical but moral as well. Food, when he could get it, was now his sole indulgence. It did for his spirit what, way back before alcohol became a way of life, the first drink of the evening had done. At first, the latter had been beer, usually taken at the college-town tavern with the scarred tables and fellow students who waited on them with more apparent care and less efficiency than the professionals of cities.

He was suddenly too hungry to restrain himself from eating another of the trout and another after that, which left only six on which to make the hike. On the other hand, he might reach civilization much sooner than it would seem from the pine-top view. How far could one see from such a height, anyway? Even if as much as twenty miles, he could surely walk that in less than a day. He dismissed the consideration that twenty miles would not necessarily bring him to civilization, and he ate still another of the fish, reducing his supply by half: he was well aware of that fact, but he was hungrier now than when he had eaten the third. He made a heroic effort to stop at that point, more than he had done with the drinking. The fact was that he had always been at a loss with women when cold sober. He had noticed this girl, a waitress, before Spurgeon had. It was he who had brought her to Spurgeon's attention: that's what hurt.

"You don't mean the little redhead? I hope you know she's married to a campus cop."

Crews grimaced. "Of course I don't mean Evvie. This one's new. She's kinda short and round. I don't mean fat. I should have said a round, sweet face, long dark hair, round eyes."

"Doesn't everybody but Orientals have round eyes?"

"No. For example, Evvie doesn't. Hers are flattened ovals."

"I don't look at her that much," said Spurgeon. "I don't like real pale skin with freckles, or old women, or ones married to local guys."

Spurgeon's way was always to resist whatever he was told, even when it was totally banal—*Rainy? What does "rainy" mean exactly: raining? About to rain? Just got done?* How much more tiresome he was then, if the subject at hand was the opposite sex.

"Evvie's no more than twenty-five or -six, for God's sake, your sister's age."

"You want my sister," Spurgeon said gleefully, extending a hand and rubbing two fingertips together, "you got to go through me, and it won't be cheap."

Crews shrugged but was actually offended by that sort of joking. Spurgeon's sister, Dee, was a motherly sort of young woman who had seemed older than she was until, paradoxically, she became pregnant. She was married to a man with a small office-supply business that Dick predicted would go nowhere. Already, as a college sophomore, he considered himself an authority on commerce, and in fact time had not long afterward proved him right. It was no doubt due to the same sort of ego that he was fearless with girls.

"Has she got a name?"

"Look," Crews told him, "don't make too much of it. I just noticed she was new. I just wondered if you had seen her."

Spurgeon tossed his head, his signal for an assertion of moral superiority. "I can't afford to hang out that much at the Hole." He was at college on a scholarship from some fraternal organization to which his father, a municipal employee in a middle-sized city, belonged, and Dick worked at full-time jobs every summer. He was not exactly poor, though it was true he did not have Crews's allowance. Nevertheless it was snide of him never to miss an opportunity to remind the latter of the financial difference between them.

. . . Crews could see no advantage in this reminiscence. He was beset by practical problems, and reliving old experiences that would only make him feel more inadequate could serve no purpose. As it happened, he had eaten more of the smoked fish while so distracted. Now his supply had dwindled to three: obviously he could not travel far on those. Also he was beginning to worry that he had overeaten again. He was so worried, indeed, that to calm himself he ate one of the remaining trout.

Dick Spurgeon could not afford to hang out at Cal Cutter's, immemorially known as the Black Hole, yet he went there immediately on hearing of his roommate's interest in the new waitress and not only struck up a conversation with her, but proceeded to date her "incessantly," he claimed, for a week. He even professed to have fallen in love, piously assuring Crews, "And you know, I don't say that lightly."

"For Christ's sake," said Crews. "Why do I have to listen to this?"

"Because," Spurgeon said, with a smile he believed "debonair"—another of his favorite terms at that time was "lugubrious," and he really misused both—"you brought us together."

"How lugubrious of me."

"Come on," said Spurgeon. "I'm serious. You know there *is* such a thing as love. It's not all just sex."

"And you're in love with this Nina?"

"You don't have to say 'this,' like you never heard of her."

"Well, I never did till just the other day."

"Well, you do now." Spurgeon's indignation was tongue-in-cheek. He could not possibly have any deep emotion about Nina. He was incapable of genuine feeling with regard to anything but his intention to become a millionaire by the age of twenty-five. Since he would not get his B.S. until he was almost twenty-two, he decided not to waste still another year on an M.B.A. In fact, as a sophomore he had begun to doubt whether even completing the undergraduate program was the best he could do with that time. His favorite mode of operation, at least in theory, was the bold move. No doubt he had put it into practice with Nina.

Crews thought her common, had no further interest in her, hated to hear her name on Spurgeon's lips. "I wish you every happiness together," he said.

"You're jealous," said Spurgeon, grinning into his face. "You saw her first, and could have made your play. But you didn't. She can't even remember seeing you."

Crews had met Nina once in Spurgeon's company, but as briefly as possible. For that matter, he was pleased she had not noticed him earlier. "You're having delusions of grandeur. I made some slight mention of this new girl at the Hole. I didn't have any reason to speak to her. You're with her now, that's great by me. I've got nothing against her. She's okay-looking and, you say, very nice. Congratulations."

Crews got drunk for the first time, alone at home, except for a maid in a distant room, when he was twelve, trying to determine for himself what was so great about the wine given his father that Christmas by a client. Having neatly slit and withdrawn the lead-foil cap, he removed the cork without deforming it much with the screw. With the first few sips the wine was wretchedly sour, another of the unpleasant things adults ingested, but improved somewhat when he persisted, though it never got what could be called good. He drank about a third of the bottle, then brought its contents up to the original level by the introduction of tap water, pounded the cork home with the heel of a shoe, and reapplied the lead cap. He returned the bottle to its horizontal diamond-shaped bin in the wine cellar, taking care to lift as many of the other bottles as was necessary to fit his in bottommost, where, if what his father said was true, it would acquire many years of precious aging before being tasted by anyone else. Maybe by the time it was finally opened, the water he had added would have turned to wine. In any event, he was under the influence, legs wobbly and brain and face overheated, and while he did not get legendarily sick to the stomach, he did not care for the feeling he had, went to sleep as if anesthetized, and woke up with a taste in the mouth that reminded him of how mildew smelled.

He had got used to the feeling in the years since, though only sporadically, in company, and usually on beer, the taste of which he genuinely came to like in those days, as opposed to that of most wines. The feeling he could take or leave. With such moderate examples of it, he was well aware that the heightened powers furnished thereby were illusory. One could not do more push-ups when drunk than when sober, nor better understand texts in philosophy or French. You might seem wittier when drunk, but perhaps only to those themselves full of alcohol—judging from the drunks encountered when you yourself were sober.

It was at the Hole that he first drank so much as to alter his behavior in a basic way. He had thought he was sincere in assuring Spurgeon of his indifference in the matter regarding Nina, but he had lied to himself, as he discovered with enough vodka in him, which he had switched to because the amount of beer needed would have made him bilious. Though there could be no sane reason to resent her having failed to notice him while running burgers to a clamorous roomful of people, when his table was not even among those she served, she could not be forgiven for her interest in Spurgeon, which would have been inexplicable to Crews even if he had never previously laid eyes on her, unless of course she was simply a prostitute.

It would not have been so bad if Spurgeon had just gone for tail. But no, he always had to be in love with whomever he went out with at the moment. Crews despised that kind of falsity, that vulgarity, but then his roommate (for the second year) was just a cheap little bastard (though physically larger than Crews): what else was new? It could also be said that Spurgeon's basic trashiness was what made him a more respectable roommate than a finer sort of person would have been, if one even knew what a finer sort would consist of.

On the evening in question, Spurgeon having been called home for what well might be his father's last few days of life following a massive heart attack, Crews stayed at the Hole, drinking, until Nina finished her shift at nine, when the kitchen closed. Once again she had not noticed him, and again reasonably enough, for he sat at the remotest end of the bar, on a stool that tried to trip him up when he finally left it, hurriedly, so as to get outside and pretend to be strolling by the rear door at the moment she made her exit.

The first embarrassment was when the bartender yelled at his back, in loud and brutal tones. He had not paid his tab. By the time he had done so and returned outside, Nina's neat figure was halfway down the block on the side street, walking with a rapid, staunch stride that was not easy to overtake on legs such as his. Not to mention that when not directly under a streetlamp, she was invisible to him and also unheard, on soundless shoes. The whole thing seemed like a dream. He had never been so drunk before.

"I didn't mean to scare you," he said when he at last caught up, in one of the circles of light, which embraced a street corner, the curb, and below it the grating of a storm drain.

"You didn't," said she, with a quizzical forehead: he could see that through his personal mist.

"Guess we're going the same way." In case his pronunciation showed the effects of his drinking, he said, "I had a few. But I'm okay."

Nina peered at him. "Should we go somewhere for coffee?"

What was important here was her offering to associate herself with him. She could simply have suggested he get the coffee by himself. He had had no such expectation. He was touched and became somewhat soberer. "I'll sleep it off," he said. "Coffee would just keep me awake." They started to walk. He tried to keep from lurching against her.

He mumbled something about Spurgeon's father, though whether clearly enough for her to understand was questionable. He had shaken the man's hand once during the two years he and Dick had been roommates. Spurgeon had never met Crews's own father. Nor did the roommates entertain each other at their respective homes on vacations. Undoubtedly Spurgeon believed his own was too humble.

Despite the care he was taking, Crews's equilibrium slipped away for a moment and, seeking it, he bumped against the side of Nina's body. She was very firm, and the slight collision did not seem to affect her, so he checked his impulse to apologize and thus call attention to an inadequacy. Instead he thought of something to say.

"Dick intends to do better than his father, a lot better."

"That's nice," said Nina in a tone that told Crews that because he had bumped her she believed he was drunk and would henceforth address him only disingenuously. Nevertheless, he went on. "It's my ambition to do worse than mine."

"That's dumb," she said, but genially.

He lied, "I'm just kidding." They were already at another corner, and he had to take care that he was ready for the step down from the curb. He was too deliberate about it and once again only called her attention to his state.

"Do you really know where you're headed?" Nina asked. "If it's home, you can't get there in this direction."

"Where are you going?"

"I live right up there." She pointed along the street. This

was a murky block of big old houses, most of which were now dark. He had never been in the area before and was totally disoriented now, with no sense whatever of its relation to where he lived.

"You're not in a dorm?"

"I get a better deal here," Nina said. "It's just the room rent. I eat free at Cutter's: that's a big part of the pay."

"You get paid in food?" He felt so sorry for her that he could have wept, or so it seemed.

"Wait a minute," said she. "Plus minimum. That's not bad, considering what the lousy dorm food costs per year. Then there are tips. Not all the kids understand that and don't leave much, if any, but others do."

Crews felt guilty. Such places seemed quite different from bars and restaurants that did not cater to college students, and he himself was probably not as generous with tips as he would be elsewhere. Furthermore, he had never before understood that a student waitress might seriously need the money and not be working as a kind of hobby. Crews had a checking account into which ample funds were regularly deposited by his father's secretary. Beginning this year, he and Spurgeon shared a two-bedroom apartment in town, to the rent of which Dick contributed only what he would have paid in a university dormitory, and Crews picked up the remainder.

"Listen," Nina said, touching his arm at the crook of the elbow, "why don't I walk *you* home? You probably have to cross Broad Street. They really race along there."

She was concerned for his welfare! They had stopped before a large gloomy old house with a veranda. "Is this where you live?" He was aware that he had not responded to her offer, and he did so now. "I'll be all right, thanks." He pointed at the veranda. "Maybe if I sit down for a minute."

"Okay," said Nina. "But only a minute, please. I've still got reading to do and an early class tomorrow. And please keep your voice down. I don't want to wake anybody up." She leaned close to him to say this quietly, and her breath was warm and sweet. No artifice had gone into her making. Her hair was long and sleek and parted in the middle; she tied it behind when waiting on tables, but now it hung free. Her face was round, almost broad, yet fine in its particulars, with soft eyebrows and lacy lashes.

They sat down on a white wicker couch, the cushions of which were covered in flowered vinyl. Visibility was good, owing to the presence of a streetlamp at the curb. He understood that Nina was speaking in an undertone because she did not want to disturb the people in the house, not because she had an intimate interest in him. He understood that, but the alcohol gave him the power to alter reality and transform situations and persons into what he wanted them to be. He stayed where he was, in the corner of the wicker couch, and spoke in a whisper, forcing her to lean toward him.

"You should know this," he said. "I was the one who noticed you first at Cutter's, not Dick. He looked you up only because I mentioned you. He wanted to score some points off me."

What he could see of her expression was inscrutable. "Why are you telling me this?"

"I'm crazy about you," he said, with an exaggeration that did not seem such in his state, for his voice was dispassionate insofar as he could judge. She remained inscrutable. He added, "I think about you all the time. It's not right."

"What's not right?"

"It's not right that you don't, didn't, know about it." He altered his position so that his shoulder was not as close to hers.

"I just wish I knew what it meant, though," she said solemnly, as if to herself. "You mean you want to go to bed with me? Is that it?"

He was both offended and eroticized by this question. Aroused for obvious reasons, but offended because he had no better idea of what he meant than she. Actually, until now he had never thought of her in a physical way. Pawing her breasts, getting her underwear off, and the rest: the subject was embarrassing. Such sex as Crews had had thus far in life had been just for pleasure, with prostitutes or fun-loving amateurs, not tainted by emotion. However, he was now on an exalted plane of existence. He could do as he wished without restraint. He was willing to participate in some sex, if that's what she was suggesting, and afterward consider what effect it had, if any, on his attachment to her.

"Look," he said. "It would be all right with me, if that's what you are saying."

"No, I wasn't saying that. I was just trying to figure out what you mean, because it just seems crazy. You drink too much, then run into me, and we don't even know each other, and yet you're all of a sudden crazy about me? Does that make any sense at all?"

It was not that you didn't know what you were doing when drunk: you did, and never more than when acting as you would not have done if sober. The difference was that when drunk you expected either to triumph or not be held accountable for failure.

"You probably aren't aware," he said now, "that I could do a lot more for you than Dick can. You wouldn't have to work at that damned job. Money's no problem."

Nina stared at him for a long moment, but not in apparent hostility, for she seemed to be smiling, though her face was at an angle to the light from the streetlamp and the resulting shadow of nose and elongation of nose might have misrepresented the expression. In the early years of drinking, Crews could sometimes be an overprecise observer of minutiae that yielded little on analysis, as here. It mattered not at all whether she displayed amiability. She despised him.

"You want to *buy* me?"

Perhaps he should have denied the implication vociferously, but instead he defended the offer. "Why should you run your legs off serving beer? My father makes all kinds of money representing mobsters. Why not give some of it to a good cause?"

Nina said gently, "Excuse me, I don't know your name."

"Bob Crews. I'm Dick's roommate."

"Dick who?"

Crews was indignant. "Dick Spurgeon, of course. Your boyfriend."

"I don't know anybody of that name."

"I saw you two together in the library."

Nina was shaking her head. "Maybe it was somebody who asked me some directions."

Crews was in no condition to react swiftly. Instead, he said reasonably, "I guess that's where I saw you two."

Nina said, "I've *seen* you once or twice at Cutter's, haven't I? So many people come in there." She stood up and smiled down at him, assuming much the same attitude that she displayed as waitress. "So you were trying to cut out your friend? Was it some kind of bet or something?"

Crews realized that to make his point he too should leave the couch, but the fact was that his legs refused to move on command. "The hell with that," he cried, abandoning the undertone. "None of that stuff matters. You belong to me!"

"Now you're getting out of order," she said, extending her hand. "And shut up before you wake somebody." She was very strong. When he clasped her fingers, she pulled him to his feet without evident effort. "Go home and sober up."

Crews took his hand back when he had found his balance, and supported himself by a knee against the wicker armrest of the couch. "I apologize," he said. "It was not my intention to insult you."

Perhaps his tone was more plaintive than he knew. She touched his arm. "No harm done. You're not the world's worst."

He was dizzy, but he rallied. "I won't bother you any more: you can count on that." He tried to leave but was so wobbly he paused before undertaking the steep wooden steps.

She was there, restraining him at the elbow. "You can't go home like that." She took him to the door, unlocked it with a key that hung from the chain she took from around her neck, and guided him into the darkened house. The door of her room was at the end of a hall of which he was only dimly aware, but she moved confidently along it, as if it were brightly lighted. In the room, she switched on a lamp, the sudden radiance of which he found too much, and he averted his head. She sat him down on the bed.

"You can sleep there if you take off your shoes." She looked at him for a moment and added, "I don't want it wet, either. The bathroom's right across the hall. I'll leave my door open so you can see the way there."

In the bathroom, having no faith in his ability to shoot straight from that far away, Crews sat down on the toilet to pee, facing the raised seat. Back in Nina's room, he saw she had replaced her clothing with a long robe of white terry cloth.

"I'll curl up in this chair," said she, patting its shabby upholstery, and told him again to remove his shoes.

"I should take the chair."

"Don't worry about it," she told him. "I'm turning the light off now. Good night."

Next day he woke up and saw by the black-faced alarm clock on the bedside table that the time was within five minutes of noon. When he bent over to put on his shoes he found a note in one of them.

Lock the door from inside when you are ready to leave and just pull it shut. Don't do this though if you just go to the bathroom and want to come back, or it will lock.

N.

After his performance there was no reason to expect she would express any endearment even of the ritualistic, insignificant kind. He was cold sober again, but remembered every moment of the evening before. Spurgeon had duped him completely, and he had all but disgraced himself. Obviously he could not endure the idea that Nina would ever see him again even at a distance. The Hole was off limits forever. But he could not let it go at that.

Spurgeon was home when he returned. "Jesus, I was about ready to call the police. I got back at ten last night. Dad was out of danger, so I came back for the econ test this morning. What happened to you? You look like shit."

"I spent the night with your fiancée," Crews said, pushing a jaw at him. "Got some objection to that?"

"Yeah, sure."

"You phony. Nina doesn't have any idea who you are."

Spurgeon grinned in his face. "What's that supposed to mean?"

"What it says."

Still grinning, Spurgeon asked, "Don't you think I could do better than *that*?" He was gloating, his victory having been much more sweeping than he had obviously expected.

Crews thought of punching him, but being out of shape and also in a debilitating moral confusion—whom would he be defending, Nina or himself?—he went to take a shower.

As if in a diabolical hurry to consolidate his defeat, he was often drunk after that. He could not keep his vow never to visit the Hole again, until, after one of his many quarrels with the bartender, the police enforced it for him. He came to the verge of flunking out in the same semester and so alienated his adviser that he was urged to leave college, which, typically, was the only advice he ever took, but not before making one more effort to avenge himself on Spurgeon, by offering to pay the apartment rent for the rest of the term.

"How could I let you do that?" Dick asked, as if in genuine indignation. "If you're not going to be here?" Within a few days he had arranged a proctorship for the semester soon to begin, which came with a free room, in fact a suite, in one of the better dorms.

The truth was that Crews was liable for the entire semester's rent anyway, unless he found a tenant to replace him. He thought about prepaying the rent in a lump sum, which would take no more trouble than giving his father's secretary a call, and then turning the apartment over to Nina, in some remote way, never seeing her again. But even sincere generosity had now begun to seem false to him, at least in his conception of it, and he left the college town without doing anything at all, counting on the confiscating of the two months' security deposit to satisfy the landlord. It did not, but his father took care of the matter.

To Nina he had been nobody at all. Yet he had loved her all these years, and was wont to believe, in his weakest moments, that she could have straightened him out. Not until now, truly on his own for the first time in a life in which his excuse had ever been that he was always alone even in a crowd, did he understand that he had been no less to Nina than she had been to him. He had never even learned her last name. She had been nothing to him but a pretext. But in so being she was not even unique.

6

■

By the time Crews's reverie came to an end, the entire supply of smoked trout was gone. Given the current context, his addiction was as bad as ever, with food replacing the alcohol of civilization. It was all he could do not to puke again. But he forced himself not to do so, and thus established at least some difference between what he had been and what he was.

Too much of another day had come and gone to undertake a project that would carry him very far from camp, but there should be sufficient time before darkness to trace the route of the continuation of the stream that the beavers had obstructed to create their pond.

With the stream to follow, he could not be lost when returning. But having no knowledge of how long the journey would be or what conditions he would meet en route, he put on his jacket and slipped into its pockets the magnifying mirror (though the sun would soon be beyond the proper angle to make fire, he allowed for the possibility that he would be away till next morning) and lengths of different kinds of fishing line, useful for many purposes, and made sure the multifunctional tool was secure in his pants pocket.

He put on a pair of socks and over them the new sandal-socks with soles of birch bark. This presumably short journey of exploration would serve also as a trial of the footgear, the potential of which, though he had tested it briefly, strolling alongside the pond, remained theoretical. His bare feet had become habituated to the forest floor by now, so long as the sharper sticks and pine cones were sidestepped, and the grassy shores of the pond had never been a problem. The sandals not only felt awkward; the more or less rigid soles were uncomfortable to walk on. Nor were they altogether flat despite the steaming and weighting.

But going downstream took less effort than climbing to where he had found the trout, and the terrain was gentler, grassier, with fewer stones. When he got within sight of the lake, the right bank of the stream had broadened into a meadow, where wildflowers bloomed, amid the general greens and tans, in patches of gold and red and vibrant purple. In its farthest reaches, perhaps a quarter mile from him, where the forest began again, a trio of deer continued to graze for a moment after he had come in sight, but soon, probably when his scent reached them on a fitful breeze—they were downwind—the animals had gone, without his seeing, at that distance, quite how or where.

On his left flank the ground had risen to an acute height: surely this was, on its other side, the headland he had seen from the shore on which he had first been stranded. Within another hundred yards of stream he had reached the greater water into which it flowed, which at first sight seemed so vast as to be oceanic. For a breathless instant he could see no land beyond it. Entranced, he had stared in but one direction. In another moment he decided he had been looking at the length of the lake, and not its breadth, for elsewhere the far shore was visible, in fact closer than it had been from his original camp on the beach. The lake must be long and relatively narrow. It would be within his power to swim across it at this point, less than half a mile by eye, but the unbroken forest over there offered no incentive. The urge to make a longitudinal exploration was, however, irresistible, though maybe

105

unadvisable. He had by now been cold sober long enough to call false hopes worse than none. Furthermore, he could find food and had fabricated shelter and shoes. Prudence would have kept him where he was until rescue arrived, but it was only human to dream of more than that which merely kept body and soul in business.

To explore the lake would require a means of buoyant transport. He had the ability to build a raft, the materials for which were readily available and the design self-evident. Ready-cut logs were to be had from the beavers' leavings in the devastated area near the pond, but not being of uniform length, they must be trimmed to size, then bound all together with reeds and rushes of sufficient tensile strength. A pole must be found or an oar made. The former would serve if he hugged the shore, staying in shallow depths, but given the idiosyncrasies of bodies of water, such a route could be overlong. A crow's-flight voyage, straight up the lake, would get farthest most quickly, but would probably be over a deeper bottom than a manageable pole could reach. But making a paddle or oar would surely be a lengthy and fatiguing job with the undersized blade of the all-purpose tool and the crude chopping stones.

Before beginning any work, however, he would do well to explore the middle distance by foot: that is, the meadow, which would be easy going, and even pleasant, to traverse. At its farthest lakeside extremity, the grass gave way to a barren point from which it might be possible to see more of the reaches of the water than from where he stood at present.

He removed the sock-shoes and the extra socks inside them and proceeded on bare feet. The footgear had not passed its test. The longer he walked, the more the bark remembered its cylindrical origins and tried, curling on either margin, to return to that form. In some places the soles had gone brittle as well and cracked, not to mention the peeling caused by the abrasive contact with the ground. He had done better as architect-builder and fisherman than as cobbler.

With unprotected feet, the field was not as comfortable as the carpet of vegetation had suggested when seen from afar. What had looked to be soft grass proved rather tough weeds, some of which were edged or spiked and few of which were yielding, and the flowers were fewer and farther between than when arranged by eye from a remote perspective. Those he did get near he gave wide berth to, for they were thronged with stout-backed black-and-yellow bees, humming like motors. He had no taste for walking shoeless on overgrown terrain where you might not see a snake before stepping on it. He was half-way through his hike, too far to make it practicable to go back and cut a walking stick, something between a cane and a cudgel, when he realized that was what he needed.

But the sun, though low in the sky, was brighter here in the open than when conditioned by the cliff and trees, and encouraged in him a sense of expanse and possibility. The lake was gleamingly calm, with the authoritative serenity available only to bodies of water, for nothing else is so experienced in turbulence. Only endless trees occupied its visible far shore, but who could say what might be offered when he reached the point and could see farther?

Yet it would be foolish to expect too much—in fact, anything but more forest and water, extending, without a human implication, to infinity. . . . In which case he could always go back home, thatch his roof watertight, catch and cook more trout, and design better footgear, continuing to survive, not without some satisfactions, until rescued.

Weeds eventually did give way to a thick-leaved version of grass as Crews approached the point, and then the vegetation was replaced not by sand but by solid rock. The stony promontory was higher above the lake than it had looked in the delusion of distance, and jutted above the true shoreline at this point, a beach ten or twelve feet below, too far to jump with impunity. But he needed to get down there, for from the rock he could see no farther than the cove or bay that began just beyond and curved within banks as high as where he stood, so that there was no hope of seeing uplake without descending to the strand and hiking around to still another point.

He found a sloping place of descent, but before using it scanned the available horizon once more and learned nothing new except that evening was coming more quickly than he had estimated. He had to get home before dark. All of this would be there the following day, and he had all the time in the world.

But in fact next day he was delayed by the old need for food. He wondered how long it had been before primitive man became a gardener and a shepherd. Fishing was an uncertain enterprise. Using the same tackle, lures, and technique as in his successful ventures, he suddenly had been unable to get a bite, and not only at the point in the stream where he had previously done so well, but also at every other place he tried. But now that, for two days, he had got used to eating once again, it was much harder to go hungry than it had been when starving seemed natural for a man in his situation. He hacked a living branch off a tree, trimmed it bare, and sharpened the slenderer end into a point, but when he hefted the finished spear, he had little faith in it, and after he hurled it at various arbitrary targets, all stationary, none animate, he had even less.

He stuck the sharp end of the spear into the ground and bent the shaft into the shape of a bow. The resilient length, cut from a living tree, did not break and, when released, powerfully sprang back to its natural form. He dulled the point, circumscribed each end with a notch, and stretched in place a bowstring made of fishing line. He made arrows of various sizes from the smaller branches of various trees. It was gratifying to put the first of these against the bowstring, pull back, and let go. But when, after at least fifty tries, the projectile failed to get anywhere near the target, a curling square of birch bark that had lately been a sandal sole, he was disheartened. He could hit the mark only when almost on top of it, and not always even then. He came to believe that his energy might be better employed in developing a technique for close stalking than working endlessly on the refinement of his aim.

As if to tantalize him while he was engaged in this frustrating effort, a pair of ducks—mallards, the only kind he could identify—appeared on the pond. The idea of roast duck was too unbearable to entertain in his current state of impotence: any attempt at a shot with one of his wretched missiles would only drive them away, perhaps permanently. In a moment *any* movement on his part would have done so, for the birds had paddled near enough to where he sat on the bank, whittling a keener point on an arrow, to come within the ten-foot range he had set as the limit of reasonable effort—only to put even that in doubt with prolonged practice.

He tried to resist the foolish hope that one or the other would helpfully waddle out of the water to thrust its neck into his clenched fingers. He had yet to kill any living creature but the fish, and they did not quite count in the squeamish sophistry concerning what could decently be slaughtered for food. Not even Ardis, whose favorite meal was roast duck and who was capable of passion with regard to its preparation, liked to think that a living creature had been violently deprived of life (the only way death comes to the healthy). But whenever their disagreements extended to the table, Crews had been happy to remind her of that truth. (Know how geese are stuffed to produce morbid livers? What happened to the pig en route to becoming *porc au pruneaux*, the duck prefatory to its being eviscerated, plucked, roasted, and squeezed in the silver press?)

The mallards began to wrestle, duck-fashion. The drake, with much flapping of wings, leaped onto the hen's dun back, forcing her under the surface of the pond. Hey, was that fair? The male was no larger in size, but his iridescent blue-green head and aggressive manner made him seem the bully, especially insofar as the female accepted the brutalization, her head going submissively under the water as her back accepted his weight. It took him a while to recognize that the ducks were not fighting but copulating. He was a fool to sit there and starve when they were within range of his bow and in a vulnerable state.

Man lives only by killing something regularly, be it a plant. He would probably miss both ducks, given his equipment and technique. If he hit the more conspicuous, the hen would only be a widow but he would have a much-needed meal, the first since the day before, and he was a unique human being, whereas a mallard was just a bird, easily replicated: in fact, that was what they were doing as he watched, reproducing their own kind, something he had managed to avoid throughout three successive marriages.

But by the time he had surreptitiously begun to fit an arrow to the string, keeping the bow flat against the ground till he was ready to raise it, the ducks had finished their coupling, the drake being no Crews, who in his heyday, even with all that drinking, could withhold his climax until his partner had more than one: his sole talent as husband, which when gone left him resourceless. As the mallards had not cuddled before, they did not do so after the encounter, but paddled about separately, the hen modest as ever, the male with what might be seen, anthropomorphically, as a new smugness, handsome sleek head at an arrogant angle, yellow beak cocked—but in a moment this attitude proved rather preparation for a new encounter than gloating on a past triumph.

Another male mallard had come out of the air to set down on the water, halfway across the pond. It was he for whom the first drake now headed, unknowingly saving himself from being a target for an arrow, which might not have struck its mark but was finally ready to be launched from the raised bow.

Just as Crews had not immediately recognized that the grappling between the male and the female was sexual, he was now slow to see that the two drakes were about the meet in combat. He was also distracted by the moral dilemma of which bird to shoot at first. The hen was an obvious target, being much nearer him and at the moment static in the water. But though ravenous he still had scruples with respect to the sex that produces offspring. In this case she could be presumed pregnant. In another moment, her mate, swimming rapidly toward the newcomer, was out of the effective range of Crews's poor weapon even if accurately launched. Regretfully, he sighted on the hen and pulled the bowstring back. . . .

The first drake leaped onto the back of the other, much as when servicing the hen, but this victim was not so serviceable. It struggled, fluttered, and writhed, but its head was restrained by the attacker's beak, clamped into its blue-green throat, and then forced under the surface and kept there by the upper bird, kicking furiously with spatulate orange feet, to increase the downward pressure.

Crews was arrested by the spectacle, he who had himself been in so many fights but none of them over a female—at least never on his part, though it was possible that some of his opponents had been avenging an insult to wife or girlfriend. With *him* what had always been at stake was "honor," not the genuine article, which of course could hardly be defended dishonorably. Wild animals were innocent of such abstractions. One drake attacked another for a motive at once deeper in the blood while more superficial in mind, if indeed ducks had minds. They ate whenever they could find food and mated only when their hormones told them to, and drove off rivals, probably in some instinctive obedience to a law of natural selection. He did not believe the loser in this conflict would die. Was it not a fact that only human beings and rats killed their own kind? No, that was applicable only to war, between armies.

The fact here was that the underduck was killed by the upper after a very short battle, in which all the savagery was exclusive to him who had lately mated, and who, having discharged another of the functions assigned him by the inscrutable God that made and maintained him, swam robustly back to the vicinity of the hen, emitting quacks that were voluble but not loud, but whether or not in triumph Crews could not judge. The longer he tried to cope with nature the more he necessarily learned, but the less he understood in human terms, which might even be an encumbrance.

In any event, he received a windfall. The dead mallard's body was floating in the middle of the pond. Crews had gotten his dinner without firing the arrow, which would probably have missed. He dropped the bow and raised himself from his long-held crouch. At this threat the living ducks lunged into the air and desperately winged away. Having so often endured wet clothing since coming to the wilderness, he went to the lean-to and stripped to his drawers, hanging the garments nicely on one of the projecting roof members. When he returned to the pond, a large black crow, in mortician's swallowtail, was riding the body of the floating dead duck, dissecting its belly with a beak that served first as scalpel, then as hinged utensil with which to pull out and gobble up spaghetti strings of wet red guts.

"The hell you do!" Crews shouted in fury, his voice in this use sounding even to himself like a deafening feral roar, and plunged into the water. At this moment he would have charged an eagle. The noise alone routed the crow, which did not wait for the arrival of the naked ape but lifted itself effortlessly to a branch of the nearest tree on the far side of the pond, from which it complained raucously at the theft of its meal—impotently, for Crews, bigger and stronger and smarter, and therefore more deserving, claimed the now gory prize and swam back with it.

He started a fire, burned off such feathers as he could and skinned the duck where he could not, spitted the blackened and somewhat mangled bird on a green stick, and roasted it over flames that leaped and flared when fed by the abundant dripping fat. The result was partially charred and elsewhere raw, like most of his open-fire cookery thus far, but generally glorious, and he ate everything but the bones and cartilage,

112

which he flung to the crow, who had stayed around all this while, cawing sometimes and often changing perches, finally coming to a tree on Crews's side of the water, from which it peered down at him, anxiously shifting its claws.

Michelle on occasion brought home frozen dinners from the menu served in first class. There were some passengers who ate nothing even on overseas flights, as Crews himself could testify, being of their company, and nobody seemed to care what disposition was made of the surplus meals. The wines, however, were policed, being of quite a higher order than the food, despite the grand claims made for the latter, supposedly the creation of the celebrity chef whose face was exploited in the ads. The duck, for example, seemed to have been basted with an ammonia-flavored marmalade. It was garnished with potato puffs too often taken from heat to cold and back again, slimy infant green beans, and inedible "roses" coiled from tomato peelings.

But never that concerned with food, they had fun anyway. Michelle was Crews's favorite among his wives, and not just for her remarkable body, which never showed a hint of her remarkable abuse of it. One of his great pleasures was simply to lie in bed and watch her wander around the apartment in the nude, often aimlessly, seldom with any immediate awareness of her state. This was true even at those rare times when she had lately smoked or sniffed something. She was also the most generous human being he had ever known. At first he had, in admitted bias, associated this attribute with stupidity, but Michelle did not lack in intelligence: it was rather a matter of attention. Hers was often elsewhere than where the moment would seem to demand. But where? Sometimes brooding on the question made him furious, but as much with himself as with her, and one thing that could not be done with Michelle was to quarrel. She began by granting the validity of all differences of opinion and was by nature incapable of an Ardis-style of opposition. *If you want to believe that, go ahead.* It was simply never the sort of thing she took seriously. What then was worthwhile? Holidays, public and private, some made up on the spot, such as the first day of sun in an otherwise wet week. She needed no champagne to make the occasion effervescent. Gifts, for which she had a genius. The expensive ones, of precious metals or rare skins, were inconspicuous; but the cheap ones, the jokes, were loud and gaudy: blow-up dolls, goofy paper animal masks, carnival hats from far-flung places. And sometimes she brought back a one-of-a-kind present that enchanted Crews, e.g., the belt from Istanbul which when you pulled the buckle from the leather sheath revealed the flexible blade of a steel so thin and elastic that it became a sword when not encircling a waistline. Judging from what, later on when he was in need, he got for it from an antiques dealer as notoriously mean when buying as greedy when selling, she must have spent several months' salary on this alone, and with what went for drugs, Michelle could rightly never spare a dime.

Crews, who always stuck to alcohol with the to him compelling argument that it was properly a food, of which he might be temporarily a glutton but from which he could at any time return to moderation, was drunkenly late in recognizing that she had a problem, but even when he did so he believed her addiction, by exceeding, excused his own.

The crow had carried quite a large hunk of duck carcass to a high branch, where, one foot clamped on its meal, it plucked and devoured such minuscule morsels of meat as were left. It continued from time to time to caw, though perhaps in satisfaction now. Most nonhuman animals had but a narrow range of voice in which to make their barbaric yawps. Crews could call himself only semiarticulate when it came to women: another way in which he was no chip off the old block. His father had been overweight and bald, yet could with a few words seemingly enchant any female in whose presence his son had ever observed him, despite losing no time in betraying any to whom he became close and letting them *know*: that was essential to his satisfaction.

Crews had begun to notice that his reminiscences, which necessarily tended toward the lamentable, invariably came to mind only at those times when his current existence became more rewarding—if gnawing the half-burned, half-raw corpse of a wild duck could be so called, but of course it could, according to the law of prevailing conditions, a clause in the general rule of survival, which made standard the practice of eating that which did not eat you. So long as you kept living, you were damned right to feel satisfaction. Crews cawed back at the crow, who was sufficiently startled to stop pecking bones and to gawk.

He got back to work, the moral value of which he could at last appreciate, for nothing else so keeps one from fleeing the moment at hand, the only one that can ever be used. The sandals had not been successful, but the theory thereof had by no means been repudiated. Better materials must be found. And now that the possibility that the farther reaches of the lake might be explored with profit had suggested the construction of a raft, he had a lot to do.

But heavy rain all the next day not only postponed work on the raft but also reminded him, huddling therein, that the lean-to left much to be desired as shelter from wind-driven water, which came in from any of the three open sides it willfully chose, and even through the spaces between the logs of the roof-wall. A reliable raft would take a while to build, and meanwhile there was always the matter of food. He would need his house for some time; it should be improved.

The next day was dry. He gathered enough of the smaller fallen trees, the beavers' leftovers, to form the other half of the roof, making the former lean-to into a tent-shaped hut, or a pup tent constructed of wood, for it was only three and a half feet high at the ridgepole and had to be entered on hands and knees. He closed in one of its ends, and for the other lashed together a panel that, when hung on hinges made from the thick, rubber-insulated wire from his otherwise useless electric razor, formed a door. The many interstices of the door would admit some rain and much wind, but had a function as peep-holes from which to take the lie of the land before emerging.

He plastered all the chinks in the other three surfaces of his home with clay from the invaluable deposit near the pond, doing this while the logs were still damp from the rains, so that when the clay dried it would not shrink too much as the wood thirstily absorbed its moisture. Memories that had practical value to him were now returning from childhood, when, as an only child at the country house, he was wont to frequent the workingmen who came to do repairs, such as the stone-mason who assured him it was advisable to wet well all materials that came in contact with fresh concrete.

What with the hut and a fishing expedition so successful that he prolonged it, bringing back enough trout to sustain him for a while, several days passed before Crews could deal with the matter of the raft. When he did get to it, the problem was soon evident. A platform sufficiently substantial to remain buoyant under his weight would be too wide to be floated down the narrow stream. But if the assembled product would likely be too large for the stream, you could send the logs down, one or more at a time, and when enough had been transferred, build the raft on the very shore of the lake, or even in the shallow water, where the heaviness of the members would not be a hindrance.

He set to work, rolling to the brook such ready-cut logs as remained and then sending them afloat downstream. He accompanied every consignment, a job that took hours, for the lake was at least half a mile from the pond, and despite his shepherding, the logs tended at places to get turned crosswise and hang up on projecting rocks or roots along the narrow waterway, and then for the earliest trips he had to plow a path for himself through virgin terrain, trampling down some vegetation but being forced to evade that too dense or bristling with thorns.

Before reaching the lake, the stream degenerated into a

swampy delta, in which the water was shallow and clogged with a profusion of aquatic grasses. This was where Crews collected his logs. When they had all been moved down the brook, he lashed them together, using fishline and twisted reeds and braids of long marsh grasses, a labor which took several days and was now and again interrupted by the need to find food. He was too busy to undertake the lengthy journey to the good trout-catching place. The lake was right at hand and must be teeming with fish. He had had no luck when he first wet a line there, but that was many days before and at a different spot, predating his becoming a homebuilder and naval architect. He now set about the matter in a new way. He cut the feathers, hair, etc., off one of the artificial flies with the largest hooks. He went to drier land and dug here and there with sticks until he had accumulated a mess of earthworms. He cut and trimmed smooth a thin young sapling. With this pole, a length of fishline, and a hook on which a worm was impaled, he made a rig that began to repay his effort as soon as he waded into waist-deep water and dangled the bait eight feet beyond. Almost immediately he felt, through line and pole, the gentle nibbling of something live beneath the surface. He yanked out a fish a bit smaller than the average trout and not as smartly colored, being white with a faint yellowish cast, but presumably as edible. He caught another as soon as the hook was rebaited. Apparently he had encountered a pack or school reminiscent of the minnows, though he doubted whether another makeshift seine would work with fish this large. Yet surely some better method could be found than the inefficient one-at-a-time. He collected more worms and made three more poles. While he was at it, he improved the rigs, tying on a pebble to weight each hook and finding a piece of dead porous wood that furnished buoyant bobbers. Thus he could plant the poles erect in the shallows and work on the raft while fish caught themselves, signaling as much through the dance of the porous chunks floating on the surface above them.

He caught fish on all poles, some of them new breeds to him, rounder in form, some all silvery, others with blue-tinged scales. All were delicious when spitted over a fire of hot coals. He had begun, as an anticonstipation measure, to try a more varied diet, eating small test samples of such marsh plants as looked harmless. The grasses that seemed safest were usually uninteresting on the palate, but in one place, at the land edge of the marsh, he found a low bed of what would seem from its spiciness to be a form of watercress, though it was of a slightly different shape from the familiar and therefore sufficiently suspect, to a man in his situation, to be tasted in very small amounts until proved nontoxic.

He abandoned the idea of making a paddle—any kind he could imagine would require more craftsmanship than he yet had at his disposal—and furnished himself with a long, sturdy pole, which would serve on the shore-hugging route he had decided to take. For all his care, the raft could be no better than the quality of the lashings that held it together, and they would not really be tested until the voyage began: it would make sense to avoid deep water.

As to what to take with him on the expedition, he had to weigh alternatives. Some possessions, such as the fire-making mirror and the all-purpose tool, should go wherever he went, along with coils of fishing line and a selection of flies and hooks from which he had stripped the decorations, but nothing that could not fit in the pockets of his seersucker jacket, a garment now much the worse for wear and too dirty ever to get clean without soap, so he had not tried to wash it. The extra clothing would not be needed and might if carried only wash overboard. If he found nothing but more forest at the other end of the lake, he could return to a comfortable home and a little collection of useful equipment. If on the other hand he encountered any form of civilization, his miserable hovel and lode of wretched goods would instantly become trash that had served its purpose.

He began the voyage and almost immediately was beset by

a problem that had not arisen in the several short trial runs of the completed raft, probably because the purpose of those was only to ascertain whether the structure would carry his weight and whether the crude lashings would maintain their integrity. No attention had been given to the matter of steering a roughly rectangular collection of logs joined together by primitive fastenings that might loosen at any moment. If he put his back into pushing on the pole—and a great deal of effort was needed to move the sluggish thing at all—he was likely to run the raft aground near the shore, and so dangerously send a shock throughout its parts, with another to come on the relaunching. But too gentle a push was useless. Nor did he dare go out into deeper water.

He had peeled the bark off the pole, to make it less abrasive to handle, but his palms quickly developed areas of sore discoloration, visible despite the dirt. These were en route to becoming blisters. Another unanticipated problem. Had he known, he could have made pads.

Favoring his more tender left hand, his next push was disproportionate. Reluctant to start from a dead stop, the raft once in motion was as slow to halt, especially when an opportunity to ground itself was offered. Its starboard bow went against the sandy bottom near shore. Having no success with the pole, he stepped off into the mid-calf water, waded to the recalcitrant corner log, and agitated it. The lashing thereby came undone. It had to be rewrapped and retied, with sore hands. This was more comfortably done when sitting. He towed the raft to a place below a high rock, where some large flat stones, perhaps fragments fallen from the granite outcropping, projected from the water. Seated on the outermost, he could keep the raft afloat as he worked.

When he had finished the job, Crews propped the newly refastened corner of the raft on the stone that had been his seat, waded to land, and climbed up a kind of natural stairs at the side of the rock and continued on to the edge of the field behind, which was the one where the wildflowers grew. He was looking for something with which to pad the pole, but a quick survey of the area, with its wiry grasses, failed to furnish what he required. He got a better idea, and started back down the three or four natural steps to the beach, not part of the rock but eroded naturally in the slope alongside and sometimes sustained by tufts of grass. One was really a little ledge, sufficiently wide and deep for the planting of both feet, though on the ascent he had used only one, without examination. Coming down now, he found it natural to look more carefully.

In the loose dust, added to which were the grains of sand he had brought up from the beach on damp soles, was the fresh print of his bare left foot. Farther over, almost at the edge of the shelf, was the print of someone else's right shoe, slightly blurred or smudged, but not so much as to obscure the elaborate pattern of a man-made sole, a complex of waves and wafflings and graph marks. This print was significantly smaller than his own.

His first emotion, which only a moment later seemed nonsensical, was fright. He fearfully examined the landscape, including even that on the far side of the lake. He went back to the top of the bluff and scanned the meadow, and then descended to search the beach. He found neither another footprint nor any other evidence humankind had ever visited the area. He went again and again to the pattern left on the surface of the little ledge. It could not be mistaken for an accidental arrangement of dust made by some natural force or the track of any nonhuman creature however fancy its paws or claws.

But why had he been afraid? Perhaps because he had been taken unaware, and he had now been in the wilderness long enough to believe by instinct, not reason, that any surprise was more likely to be bad news than good. He must become a person again, at least insofar as he dealt with the fact that somebody, not something, had left the impression of a shoe. Someone who wore a much smaller size than his had been when he wore shoes. Perhaps a smaller man, or anyway one with smaller feet, or a woman, or a child.

The truth was, he could read almost nothing from the spoor, including any sense at all of when it might have been made. He had visited the rock a week or so earlier. Had the print been there then? Was the smudging due to wind and rain, or had other feet, human or animal, trod on the footprint without leaving a trace of another? It was a fact from which he could make nothing, but it was impossible to disregard. Where did X go on reaching the ground above? Most of the terrain was heavily overgrown. A path through the grasses and wildflowers, such as his own from the earlier visit, would have been invisible only a few hours after it was made. Beyond the meadow on all three sides was thick forest.

He had to get on with his business, which was to explore the lake. Pushing the raft ahead of him, he waded away from shore until the water was deep enough to sustain it with weight on board and then climbed on. For some reason, the poling went better than it had gone earlier. He gradually learned how better to direct the awkward craft, and to get more forward progress by using less force: it was a matter of subtlety in the placement of the pole and the adjustment of balances. His hands seemed not as sore as earlier on, now that he did not fight that with which he worked, and he still had not moved to implement the idea that had come to him at the field: to fashion some sort of sail.

He was poling along a shoreline that at the moment was so consistently linear that it could have been drawn against a great ruler, with as regular a strip of beach, backed by uniform pines so dense as seemingly to be inanimate. The one touch of humanity offered by the footprint revived in him an irony that had presumably been drowned with the submerged airplane: was it that of a child on a family outing? Scrambled up there for fun, then hopped back down, jumped in the speedboat, and they all roaringly returned to their comfortable vacation home, equipped with microwave oven, fax machine, and TV set on which the news broadcasts had long since reported the loss of a private airplane carrying tycoon Richard

Spurgeon, two business associates, and a worthless drunk nobody missed.

He was hungry again. Except for a few hours after he had gorged on enough to fill him, he was always ravenous. You just did not get enough to eat if you had to track down and kill for every mouthful. Ask the bear about that, and it was even omnivorous. If you build a civilization, start with groceries and restaurants or you won't go far.

He sent the raft carefully against a sand beach, went into the forest and cut a fishing pole, then dug for earthworms, but not quickly finding any, overturned rocks and collected the creatures underneath them. Back on board and underway, he affixed the pole in one of the interstices between the logs so that its line and baited hook would troll behind the moving raft. But after an hour or so, he had caught nothing on it.

It was midafternoon. His progress was hard to measure against the featureless shore he had been following since leaving the projecting rock. Since finding the shoeprint he had seen no living thing aside from the squirming grubs used as bait. No fish broke the water, no birds flew overhead. This was often true, and to see mammals was rare enough in the best of seasons. Under ordinary circumstances he would not have been disturbed, but now he felt as though adrift in a void. He had no food and he was en route toward no destination. He had wasted time on making a raft that served only to take him away from a comfortable shelter and sources of food that were at least sometimes reliable, and when one source failed he had been in a position to find another. Had he put as much work into making an effective bow and arrows as he had wasted on the raft, he might be eating an excellent dinner now of at least trout and watercress, or if he had applied himself to the matter of footgear, it would not be out of the question that by now he could have hiked out to someplace with showers, mattresses, and room service.

He heard two gunshots.

It was by reflex action that he swung the raft into the shore and hopped off. He had no reliable sense of where the shots had come from. The beach was vacant, which had to mean that the shooter was somewhere in the woods, but the nearer Crews came to the trees, the more he was aware of the problem he might have in locating anyone within them if he simply penetrated the wall of close-grown pines that faced him: he would soon be disoriented and might well get shot for his pains.

He began to yell. After multiple repetitions of *Hey*! he announced he was a person, on the beach, and lost. From time to time he stopped shouting so as to listen for evidence he had been heard. None came. He cried out his name, should the shots have come from a party searching for survivors of the downed aircraft. There was no response. He began to doubt his earlier conviction that the gunfire had come from close by. He had no experience in gauging distance by sound, but it seemed possible that noises of a reverberatory kind might come from any choice of places across a great expanse and produce echoes from far away.

But this was not another of the necessarily short-lived opportunities afforded by the two planes that early on had come and gone so rapidly. Whoever had fired these shots would be on foot in wild terrain (unless there was a superhighway, or even a dirt road, behind the trees) and would stay in the area for a while, even if departing.

Nowadays he took self-preserving notice of natural conditions. The wind was coming off the lake, which meant that the forest animals would have his scent long before he reached the pines, and also that human beings in the near distance could smell the smoke of a fire built on the beach. So he took the mirror from his pocket and made one, feeding it first with the bone-dry driftwood of which there was a random supply along the shore.

When more smoke was needed, he added brushy green branches and fanned the flames with others. He continued sporadically to shout. His voice had gone unused for so long that this strenuous employment of it made him hoarse after a while. He restrained himself from running into the forest; he continued to work by reason and not emotion. How far would he have to go to exceed the reach of his yells and the odor of the fire? And the farther one went in a wrong direction, the greater the angle of error. In a territory so vast he might find neither what he looked for nor the route back to the lake.

He stayed where he was. Spending the night there seemed to make sense. He gathered enough wood to keep the fire replenished till he went to sleep. He also dug for earthworms, but not finding any, caught an insect found under a rock, not a slug this time but a small adult beetle. Primitive though he had become, he yet felt a twinge of regret as he impaled the live creature on a hook. But perhaps it was that very movement of life that did the trick: he got a bite almost as soon as the insect disappeared beneath the water. The fish when hauled in was not quite so large as it had seemed when fiercely resisting its capture, but it was a handsome plump specimen, the biggest thus far.

He gutted his catch and spitted it over white embers. He ate everything but bones and tail, which he carefully returned to the water so as not to attract scavengers: meaning, for him, the bear.

It was a delicious meal, but he was too preoccupied to enjoy it as much as he might have. He continued to shout from time to time between mouthfuls. The presence of others, though as yet unseen, unidentified, and apparently not aware of him, changed the basic conditions of his existence. He was no longer alone in a nonhuman void, yet neither was he thus far in company. He had additional responsibilities without additional rewards.

Before going to sleep, he moved his fire to a pit dug in the sand, so that while the light would be visible at a distance in the darkness and the odor of the smoke would continue to be broadcast, there was a diminished danger that sparks driven by a fitful wind would set the forest aflame.

Next morning Crews awoke with a decision if not a solution. The shots must have come from hunters too far away to hear his shouts and by the time he produced the smoke not in a position to smell it, having moved in the opposite direction. Looking for them in the thick woods made even less sense now than it would have the afternoon before. The best thing was to resume the exploratory voyage, hard as it might be to leave the only place where he had encountered evidence of human life since the crash.

The wind was up this morning, raising foam-crested wavelets on the surface of the lake. By now he was used to passing up breakfast. He was preparing to shove into the lake the corner of the raft that was held by the sand when he was struck by the fact that the breeze was blowing in the direction he wanted to go.

He went into the woods, where with the miniature saw blade he worked until he had felled a slender six-foot sapling that could serve as mast. The problem came in fastening the mast to the raft. He dug out a niche between the two central logs, but even when the upright was planted in it, butt going down almost to the water, there was no support horizontally. He had to fashion and force-fit lengths of wood as braces.

The labor took time, but all of it was regained when at last his jacket, pinned with fishhooks to a frame of stout twigs, was attached flexibly to the mast and the craft was launched. The makeshift sail took much handling. The wind-filled jacket was hard to control, and more than once ripped away from its fishhook fastenings, growing more tattered. Only at the top was it secure: an extra-long stick extended through both arms, scarecrow-style. Then too, the mast was wont to threaten to come down, especially when the sail caught a hearty gust. Crews had frequently to tend to the crude braces, holding the downwind one in place with his foot. And along with everything else, he had to keep the craft on course with the pole, pushing off when in danger of going aground, yet being careful not to let the wind take him out to deeper water.

The raft was slow to get into motion, and the square yard of the old seersucker jacket had only a limited capacity to convert the power of the air to another use. Nevertheless, the heavy, crude platform began to run, or anyway lumber, with the wind, and little muscle was required, except at such times when, having gusted with unusual force, the wind briefly abated, catching, so to say, its breath before resuming normal aspiration. Then Crews would plunge the pole to the lake bottom and push. But he kept the other hand at the mast, alert to the return of the breeze.

Such attention as he had left he applied to scanning the shoreline for evidence of human activity. Since he heard the sound of the shots, the basic conditions of his immediate reality had changed: looking for people was no longer a hopeless exercise in wish-fulfillment. He was still by himself but no longer alone at manning the universe, which is how it had once seemed, but that was what had kept him going: a sense of his uniqueness in surviving on his own in the wild. He might now have to make other moral arrangements.

The terrain on shore had begun to change as the raft continued sluggishly but surely to sail toward what must eventually be the end of the lake. The pines gave way to an inlet made by the debouchment of another stream like that down which he had come from the beaver dam, though this one was much faster-running and probably not so obstructed in its upper reaches. Its farther bank was treeless and floored with big chunks of stone that had likely fallen, over the course of eons, from a cliff perhaps a quarter mile distant from the lake. From where Crews was kneeling on the raft, the height seemed to have a face of sheer granite.

He might have seen something of note at its top, a flicker, a glimpse of something that would have caused him to peer longer, but at that moment the sail caught a sudden burst of wind that would have knocked the mast over had he not braced himself against it with all his strength, which in turn meant he had briefly to relinquish a controlling grip on the pole. The raft went heavily against the shore, here more rocky than sandy, with projections of those bulky stones that dotted the ground behind, and on the impact, several of the cruder fastenings between the logs burst apart.

The craft was not quite wrecked, but he considered it too disabled to continue without repairs. Wading, he pushed it to a less demanding part of the shore, and worked most of it up onto a gravel beach. He had to get replacements for the lashings that had given way. Too much fishline would have been needed, and his supply was dwindling. There was a strip of greenery along the bottom of the cliff. Perhaps he could find some material there, vines or grasses, that would serve. He set out for it, keeping his eyes on the summit when the terrain underfoot presented no hazards, looking down when big rocks had to be avoided. His bare soles were now toughened to a condition in which walking on hard surfaces heated by the sun was no longer painful. He probably no longer needed shoes in which to hike out of the wilderness: his feet were durable enough. The leg he had hurt in escaping from the plane had been perfectly okay since a few days after the crash. The only excuse left was that without an accurate means of determining precise directions he could not be absolutely certain which way to go.

Avoiding boulders, he had kept his eyes down. When he next glanced up at the cliff, a figure was standing on its level summit. He waved and shouted. The figure vanished without having responded. He was still too far away to know more than that it was of human conformation. He could not be sure that it had seen him. Its movement in retreat had been quick but, assessed at such a distance, not necessarily significant. Nor had he any scale by which to judge its size.

He picked up the pace through the rocks and finally arrived at the grove of deciduous trees at the base of the cliff. They lined both sides of the stream that flowed there, the same that bent later to come out and empty into the lake. Within the trees, his line of sight at an acute angle, he had a limited view of the summit above, but he was closer now. He cupped his hands at his mouth and shouted up. Few sounds are so dispiriting as a cry unanswered when one is lost in the wild, and as he found now, all the worse when you know another human being is extant nearby.

He waded across the stream, which fortunately was no deeper than his waist, and he could hold up and keep dry the laden pockets of his jacket, which he had reclaimed from the mast before leaving the raft. He went through the trees and looked for a route up the granite rampart, so sheer at this point it could not have been attacked except by an experienced and well-equipped rock climber. He traveled farther along the base, shouting up from time to time. At one point he flushed a rabbit from some undergrowth. The animal slowly hopped a hundred feet distant, then stayed in position till he got within fifty. Crews paused at this point, and the creature loped off into the bushes that fringed the trees. Hungry as he was, he had to fight off the urge to pursue it.

He came to the end of the sheer wall and found a slope on which greenery alternated with rocky outcroppings. Even so, the angle of ascent was only a little less than perpendicular, and when pausing he clung to whatever grew or jutted at hand lest he slide back down that height he had so laboriously gained. The last few yards, the terrain proved such that it was more easily negotiated on hands and knees. When he reached the edge of the summit, it was as if he were stealing furtively upon it, had anyone been there to see him. But the plateau was empty. It was also much smaller than when estimated from below, falling quickly in back to a forest of large, tall trees widely spaced but so thickly leaved as to keep the floor in shade on a sunny day. Unless someone was concealed behind a thick trunk, the woods too were uninhabited to at least the middle distance.

He shouted some more. He searched unsuccessfully for tracks or broken foliage. He went to the edge of the cliff and looked down to where he had beached the raft, which was not

only visible but fairly conspicuous, even at the distance, because it was markedly inconsistent with all else there—and
surely had been even more so when afloat. The person could
not have failed to see him, and therefore the subsequent flight
had been intentional. Whoever it was wanted not only not to
find him but positively to avoid any contact at all. The real-
ization that the first human being he had encountered since
the crash considered him someone to avoid was at first morally debilitating, and then Crews became angry. But having
no clear object for his anger—what he had seen was essen-
tially a silhouette—he put it aside and descended to the trees.

He found a dead but solid branch from which to fashion a
club. He lay in wait along the area of undergrowth where he
had last seen the rabbit. He stayed there, motionless, perhaps
for hours. For this purpose, like an animal he had a diminished sense of the duration of time. The moment was eternal.
There was no alternative reality.

When the rabbit finally appeared, it was allowed, for another eternity, to go about its business unmolested, hopping
here and there, sniffing, nibbling, until it came within range
at which one deadly blow could be accurately delivered: he
assumed that if the first did not do the job, he would not get a
second.

Having never before taken warm-blooded life, Crews was
unaware of how resistant it could be to expiring. He had to hit
the defenseless creature many more times than he could have
anticipated, and yet the long legs would not stop kicking, nor
the furry nose cease to quiver, until he did what he should
have done sooner. He got out the tool, as the rabbit thrashed
under the club that held it down, and cut its throat with the
knife blade.

Just as the animal had fought harder for life than he expected, its blood was more abundant. Not yet entirely rapto-
rial, he was revolted by the episode . . . until the rabbit had
been skinned, spitted, turned over a fire, and devoured while
still so hot the flesh singed his mouth. It was the most deli-

cious meal he had ever eaten. He would kill in good conscience anything he could eat: there could be no regret in that.

It was late afternoon as he sucked clean the last bone and dropped it into the swift-moving stream. He had disposed of the skin in the same fashion, not knowing how to preserve it for subsequent use. The lake wind on which he had traveled all day had turned to blow against the land. The temperature was falling as the sun sank. He would need protection from the breezes of the night. He quickly constructed a small lean-to.

Next morning he headed for the beach. He was not prepared to discover that the raft was gone. The wind had been brisk, but hardly strong enough to move such a substantial object. Nevertheless, he pretended that it might have happened, and he searched the shore for a considerable distance should the raft have first been blown out on the water and later back to land, though he knew all the while that it had been taken by the other human being in the area, who thereby proved to be not simply no friend but a declared enemy.

7

■

CREWS COULD HAVE NO IDEA AS TO WHICH
direction the thief had taken with the raft. Toiling up the cliff
again would be purposeless. He could scan more of the water
from up there, but if he did see his enemy, the man would be
too far away by now to pursue with any hope of success. The
only choice he had was to continue to explore the lake, by foot
along the shore, or hike back to his old camp at the pond.
What distances must be traveled to do the former could not be
estimated, but to go back by land to where he had come from
by water would be a defeat of a kind that he could not accept.

He began to walk and before long was beyond the area of
stones and once again on the sand beach. He took the route
firmest underfoot, at the edge of the forest, and at a regular
pace probably covered as much distance per hour as he had
even with the crude sail, given its constant need for manhan-
dling, and certainly more than when merely poling the raft.
As he hiked he thought about what he would do if he did
encounter the man who had stolen the raft that he had built
by hand with so much labor, and though at the outset he
amused himself with fantasies of violence, after a while he
imagined only asking the other what possible justification
there could be for doing such a rotten thing.

The question was a familiar one to Crews, who had been

asked its like many times by intimates in his previous life. But never by his father. Never by his mother, either, but that was different: she usually did not know. His father certainly did, for it was a lawyer from his father's firm who always sprang him from whichever immediate predicament that had legal consequences: the car crashes, the fights when property was destroyed, the disturbances of the peace. In the city, where everybody in an official capacity had a price, these crises became minor inconveniences, and his name was even kept out of the papers. But it could be different in the country. One magistrate refused to set bail when after doing 140 in the Testa Rossa he was roadblocked by a hick cop, and Crews spent the night in jail despite the lawyer's best efforts for a client who had a high blood-alcohol reading and had furthermore rejected arrest until being knocked out.

The legal services ended once his father was dead: the firm was one of the places from which he was permanently barred. Not only had his father never punished him; he had never even been criticized by the man. They had not known each other that well.

All this self-pity came from the theft of the raft. He hated his enemy for causing him to remember his own failings, which he had begun to forget in his struggle to live off the land.

Lateral visibility was good, but after a bright dawn the sky had gradually become overcast. Unable to see the sun, he could not have said how long he had been walking. With the usual unvarying topography of beach and forest, he had little by which to mark the gaining of ground until he saw coming into view on the opposite side of the lake a sheer cliff similar to the one he had climbed the day before (and in so doing given somebody an opportunity to steal his raft). The shoreline before it was very like the other as well, and the entire section of terrain, if it had been directly across from the first, might have been taken as a reflection of it, perhaps a mirage, due to some peculiar condition of atmosphere. That is, if the eye was playing tricks. Actually, there were any number of differences: the cliff behind the far shore was not so high as the one he had scaled, and the grove of trees at its base was denser than that in which he had killed and eaten the rabbit and spent the night. Of the nearby stream he could see nothing but its mouth, which emptied into the lake.

The fact undoubtedly was that granite cliffs pretty much all looked like one another, with trees along their bases and probably streams as well.

But to see something that reminded him of the raft was unpleasant. He decided to keep going until it was out of sight before halting to look for food, and also attend to a related matter: namely, to pierce another hole in the belt which throughout this time in the wild he had repeatedly tightened lest his pants fall down, and he had begun as a slender man, with a normal waist appropriate to one-sixty on a five-eleven frame. He must be down fifteen or twenty pounds after so much physical labor on a diet much less hearty than that imposed sporadically on herself by Molly, who was capable of regimens of chemical liquid on which she lost a fourth of her flesh, only to gain back more with a return to solid food, as he never tired of pointing out. Pitifully, it had been his only weapon against her. Molly was an exemplary self-made woman, with her own interior-design business, and at the outset she had made the grievous mistake of loving him. At the end he assured her the fault had been hers: she should have known better than to have trafficked with the likes of him. What could she have expected? And she was supposed to be the smart one! If you ever sobered up, she told him, you would understand that all your cynicism is fake. Molly was the one he felt guiltiest about, because though by any standard she was the most admirable of his wives, she was also the one who had attracted him least.

In the absence of the sun he could not make fire and thus could not cook anything he killed. There was no good reason to stop unless he could eat. While walking he was able to make the new hole in his belt if he held the belt end and the waist of his pants with his left hand.

When he had closed the all-purpose tool and returned it to his pocket, resuming a normal stride, he glanced across the lake and saw, against the far shore, what was presumably his raft, or anyway a sizable fragment of it. He had pulled it up for repairs just before it was stolen. Apparently it had since partially disintegrated under the strain of further use and been abandoned by the thief, near what seemed to be the mouth of a stream that came down from the forest behind. Farther along, the shoreline rose to a headland.

The thief had apparently not stayed in the neighborhood. In any event, Crews was too prudent to expend his energy on a swim of that distance. He continued to walk doggedly on. The overcast had begun to be breached by the sun, which seemed to be in the wrong place in the sky, that is, in his face rather than at the back of his head, but without a compass directions would always be imprecise, and natural things were never regular. The lake might well not be the oval he assumed it was; its shore was probably not as straight as it had seemed when walked. It might slant gradually, to a degree that could not be determined on the ground.

When the sun next appeared, it was on his right side. This made so little sense that it was simply not worth bothering about, and the clouds quickly closed in again, for all practical purposes removing the problem.

He did permit himself to reflect that, aside from the area of the cliff, he had seen no striking landmarks on the far shore. When the sun next returned, it came at last from the proper direction, behind him, proving he was right not to have worried about its previous shenanigans. But his failure as yet to reach the lake's end had begun to discourage him. How long could it be?

That he had in fact encircled the body of water entirely did not occur to him even as suspicion until he had unknowingly passed the beach where he first landed—offshore of which the airplane, with his companions' remains, presumably still rested somewhere on the bottom—skirted the base of the promontory beyond, and come to the mouth of the stream that flowed down from the beaver dam and the attendant marshland, which looked sufficiently similar to the place where he had built the raft for him to pause and consider the matter and then find fragments of fishline and chips of log.

So when after hours of hiking he had seen the familiar-looking cliff that morning, he was looking at the very same he had climbed the day before, and when later on he spotted the broken raft across the lake, it had been he who was on the far shore!

He was back where he had begun, having lost several days of arduous labor and several more of travel, but he had accomplished, willy-nilly, what he had set out to do, namely, explore the length and breadth of the lake. It had proved rather smaller than he expected, and though at any point there might have been, only a mile or so beyond the facade of pines, a village or ranger's station or even a couple of campers under a tent, he had seen along his shore route no suggestion of a trail leading to such or any other evidence of man save the figure atop the cliff and, earlier on, the gunshots.

There was now no reason to retrieve the busted raft. He had nowhere to float on it. He headed upstream. There was no place like home.

He approached the pond so quietly that he saw a beaver on the bank before it saw him and leaped into the water, slapped its tail loudly, and disappeared under the surface. The exterior of his shelter showed no evidence of molestation, but inside, the duffel bag containing his extra clothing had been roughly torn open and the contents pulled out and left so, though they were undamaged. Nothing had been bitten or chewed, but the box of fishing tackle was gone, as was the leather rod case. It was not possible to believe this the work of the bear.

He had been careless in assuming the man who stole the

raft had gone in another direction. While in some ways this wilderness could be seen as vast and undifferentiated, it was marked with obvious routes that any animal, including the human, would take by nature. These followed the banks of bodies or courses of water and skirted the bases of high points. Few living things, except in an emergency, would try to penetrate thick growths in preference to open ground. His enemy had arrived here by a combination of instinct and chance.

With the ransacking of the hut, added to the theft and wrecking of the raft, Crews knew the feeling of outraged helplessness peculiar to the victim of crime by stealth. That such an offense could take place in the wild, where he and this man should make common cause and not prey on each other, was inexcusable. He could think only of tracking the guy down and punishing him. He would choose the optimum time and place to jump him from ambush. He would not only reclaim his own possessions, but by right of conquest appropriate any of the man's goods he wished, foremost among them the gun. With a firearm he would not be lost for much longer. He would have a means of making his presence known to searchers on land or in the sky. Meanwhile he could kill all the food he needed, and more humanely than with club and knife.

It took a moment for him to arrive at what should have taken precedence: there was no reason to believe that his enemy was lost. Once he had taken away the gun, he could force the man to lead him out of the woods. The problem now was to find him.

The ground near the hut was clear but not soft, and such faint footprints as had presumably been left by the other were obscured by his own, which, made by bare feet, were distinct and distracting.

It was too late in the day to cast the search in wider circles. Further tracking should be left for the clear light of morning. Crews returned the clothes to the duffel bag and put it in place as pillow on a bed of freshly gathered pine boughs. Inside the hut he felt snug for the first time since setting out on the raft, though he was aware that the sense of security he took from being there was mostly an illusion. He went to sleep asking himself why the other man was here at all, and why he had twice stolen his property while taking great pains to avoid personal contact. Why had he been roaming the forest and lake for at least two days, on more or less the same route as Crews, if he knew how to get out?

Next morning a steady rain was falling, which ordinarily would have been regrettable, for he had never been successful when trying to fish in bad weather and he could not have built a fire. He had been careless in the chinking of his roof, and some water had found him inside. Yet he surely would have stayed indoors had he not had the new mission, to find the man who had done him dirty, and for that purpose the rain was a godsend. Tracks could easily be seen on wet ground . . . unless the other had found shelter in which to wait for clearer skies. But pessimistic reflections, while palliative amid the ironies of cities, could be deleterious here, where failure was the rule.

The choice of directions in which to go would have seemed infinite only to the tenderfoot. As a woodsman now of some experience, Crews could assume that the other would not plow through the bristly underbrush or dense forest when clearer ways were at hand. The obvious one was along the stream that fed the pond. Its bank on the near side was invitingly passable, by contrast with the other nearby ground.

Crews went upstream, proceeding cautiously so as not to alert his enemy. The rain helped him, dampening the sounds of his footfalls and, in its bursts of sudden energy, making noise to mask his. What he looked for were not yesterday's tracks, which would be washed away, but any made since.

He reached the part of the upper stream where he had caught the trout. He had seen nothing useful en route, and now the rain had picked up in volume and force of fall. Nobody would come out of cover until the cloudburst ended. Though he was by now as wet as if he had been swimming fully clothed, the pelting of water had become so oppressive that he looked for a place of refuge of his own. After having been interrupted by one of the minor stone cliffs characteristic of the region, the forest began again upstream. He headed there, the driving rain blurring his vision sporadically.

At the base of the cliff was a bush that looked out of place. Crews noticed this though his vision was distorted. No other vegetation grew nearby. Despite the rain, the foliage of the bush was wilting. Had it been altogether dead, it might have broken away from its lifeless roots and blown here. But this one, in this situation, was a contrivance.

He approached it warily and from the side, hugging the cliff, until he got close enough to see that the purpose of the bush was to conceal a fissure in the rock face. In better weather, that the makeshift door was in place at the mouth of the cave would not necessarily have indicated that anyone was inside, but in such rain as this the occupant was certain to be at home. With a gun. In the dark, with a would-be intruder silhouetted against the light.

Espaliered against the granite, still being pounded with rain, Crews decided he had no choice but to wait for nighttime, if the man did not emerge before. He could anticipate a miserable vigil, being redundantly soaked, going without food even longer, and suffering from some doubts as to his ability to deal with an armed man when he did flush him out, or even, in the most grandiose projection of all, when crawling into the cave after dark to take him while he slept. But there was no reason to wait against the cliff so long as the rain did not abate. A less uncomfortable place of surveillance was available in the woods farther on. He could move closer when the weather improved. He must be in position to exploit his only weapon, surprise.

When night came it was uncompromisingly dark. From his place within the trees Crews could not see the bush that obscured the mouth of the cave, but its foliage was not so thick as to block all light from within, had there been any. He saw nothing, no flickers or radiance of fire, flashlight, candle. Which meant either that the occupant had no means of illumination or that nobody was inside the cave.

He now had to decide whether to wait for morning, and thus lose the advantage of darkness, or, himself without any kind of light, to go crawling, probing, confined within stone walls with an armed adversary.

But the rain continued to fall, and not much of a shelter could be constructed in the dark. What a fool he would be if he stayed out in the wet while the cave was unoccupied. Not only was it uncomfortable to crouch in falling water; it was morally degrading.

He went across the open ground and found the bush easily enough, by touch. The rainfall was even heavier against the base of the cliff. Despite the thickness of the now overgrown hair on his scalp, he felt as though he were being incessantly battered. He hurled the bush aside. He felt for the contours of the fissure in the wall of rock. The aperture felt too narrow to admit a human body. There might not even be much of a cavity beyond, but just a shallow crack, leading nowhere.

But even as he had these defeatist thoughts, he knelt and felt farther. The opening widened toward the bottom. He could slide in on his back, feet forward, if he did not raise his head more than a few inches from the horizontal. Added to the disadvantage of not being able to see anything in the darkness outside and in, he would be helplessly supine. Nor did he know how thick were the walls of the entryway, or indeed whether it was an entrance as such and not simply a shaft that would never broaden throughout its length. Caves were another of the things of which Crews had had no experience, nor was he likely, under normal circumstances, to have sought any, being a selective claustrophobe, liking tight bedclothes and snug-seated high-performance cars, but having a distaste for most other constraints. But after he had slid for no more than half his body length he could no longer touch the sides of the tunnel. He was in fact inside a cave of unknown capacity, but sufficiently spacious to allow him first to sit up, then rise to his knees, and finally to stand and extend his arms overhead without finding a ceiling.

An instant of apprehension returned him to his knees. He turned and crawled against a solid wall. He had lost the entranceway! He frantically beat his hands on the cold stone and might have surrendered to panic had he not quickly imposed order by remembering the several ordeals he had survived by now: the plane crash, the storm, the bear. Then he found the inside aperture of the cave's mouth. It would be easy enough to lose again in the darkness unless he devised a means by which to keep its location fixed while his own was mobile. Working by touch in the darkness, he tied the end of one of his coils of fishline to the all-purpose tool and tossed the latter toward the outside air: presumably its weight would keep it in place while he payed out the coil.

He began to crawl again, following the right-hand wall now, so as to have another reference to his position in space, the darkness being much more disorienting than he had imagined. The surface beneath his knees was not the level floor of tourist caverns but rockily uneven, with sharp points and punishing edges. He stood up again, but this time rose only to some five feet before pressing his head against the ceiling, and as he slowly, gropingly proceeded, the height of the cave gradually diminished, bending him until his back was horizontal with the floor, which felt ever rougher underfoot.

He had reached the end of the fishline without reaching that of the cave, but after his experience in circling the lake, he allowed for the possibility that he had been following a curved rather than a straight wall. What was more important was his failure to encounter evidence that any person was or had been within, and surely by now he had produced enough noise to evoke a reaction from a man with a gun.

He traced the line back to the mouth of the cave, where he could not see the outside world but could hear the rush of the rain still falling there. At least he had found shelter. He scraped away the loose stones from an area large enough to lie on and curled up against the wall, near the entrance tunnel but not blocking it, lest a bear, out for a nighttime forage, came home. The cold, unyielding floor was an uncomfortable alternative to the luxury of his usual bed of boughs, but he soon found the most comfortable contortion of body, and after retrieving the tool and opening the knife blade, he placed it where he could find it in the dark and went to sleep.

Crews did not believe he was dreaming when he was awakened by a blow to his shoulder and heard an unpleasant voice address him abusively. He assumed rather that it was real enough but that time had been reversed, taking him back to his first marriage, for the voice was female and the unpleasantness in it was by intent, not nature.

But when he opened his eyes he was staring at a wall of rock, visible in the flare of light that must be coming by way of the constricted entranceway through which he had crawled the night before. So obviously he *had* been dreaming.

He rolled over to look. A human figure stood near enough to have kicked him. It held a blazing, smoking torch. In its other hand was his tool, with the extended knife blade.

"Who the hell are you?" The tone was harsh, but the voice was that of a woman. She brandished the blade. "I'm not afraid to use this."

"God almighty," Crews croaked, from a throat unaccustomed to speech. He was getting his hands and one knee under him. "You're—"

She pushed him forcefully with a foot, and he fell back. "I asked who *you* were."

"I was in a plane crash," he said angrily. "It went into the lake. I've been trying to keep alive ever since. Why are you threatening me? Why did you steal and wreck my raft? It took me days to make that, without any tools but the one you're holding. Why do you need my knife when you've got a gun?"

The flame was sputtering and getting smokier by the moment. The young woman, for such she was, held the torch as far from her body as she could. She had tousled long dark hair and regular features, so far as could be seen in the light that illuminated only part of her face and threw distorting shadows on the remainder.

"Are you telling the truth?" Her voice had lost some of its edge.

"Look at me," Crews said. "Do I look like things are going my way?"

"All right," she said, gesturing with the knife blade. "Get to your knees and start crawling out of the cave, and be quick about it: this torch is about ready to quit. Remember, I'm right behind you, with the knife. When you get to the outside, keep crawling away from the mouth of the cave, until I tell you to stand up."

He did as ordered, but when he reached the outside, where daylight had come, he immediately sprang erect, bent down as she crawled out, wrested the tool from her hand, and, seizing her denim jacket at the scruff of its neck, pulled her to her feet. She was fairly tall, only a couple of inches shorter than he, and slender but very fit-looking. She tried to struggle with him, but he pushed her away.

"Stop it, goddammit! This is my property." He folded the blade back into the handle and dropped the tool into his side pocket. "Now suppose you tell me what *you* are doing here." He could not resist adding bitterly, "Aside from stealing stuff from people who are fighting for their life."

Her blue eyes continued to show residual fury for a moment or two. In full daylight her features were in fact very fine, but her face was smudged with dirt. She wore filthy jeans. Her denim jacket was torn on its left side. She snarled, "Touch me again, and I'll kill you."

He had forgotten the gun, but if she had been carrying it, she would surely have drawn it by now. And if she had had a firearm, why would she have brandished the knife?

"I'm not impressed by your bluster," he said. "I won't have

any reason to touch you if you aren't carrying any weapons. Empty your pockets. Turn them out."

She hesitated for a moment and then complied. Her front pockets were empty.

"Turn around."

"The hell I will." She was fierce again.

"I just want to see your back pockets. Come on." She had no weapons or anything else. She could do him no serious harm. "I was telling the truth about the crash. I don't want to fight with you. Just tell me how to get out of these woods. I've been traveling in circles."

She blinked briefly, but raised her eyes in some lingering defiance. "Why'd you come into the cave?"

"To get out of the rain," Crews said. "Why are you so pugnacious?" She met his stare, and he broke before she did, because all he wanted now was her help. "All right, forget about the raft and the stuff from my hut—"

"You keep mentioning that. *I don't know what you're talking about.*" She looked away. "If you're lost, so am I. I don't have any idea where I am. I've been running for my life." When she turned back to him, there were tears in her eyes.

"Running for your life? Then you're not the one who has the gun? Who's chasing you?"

She shook her tousled head but stayed silent.

Given the situation, he was annoyed. "I told you about me. If I could submit references, I wouldn't be here, would I? I know I must look awful. I haven't been able to shave, and it's hard to get clean without soap. You just have to think why someone in my shoes would lie." He lifted one of his bare feet.

"No, I don't," she cried bitterly, still weeping.

Her trouble seemed genuine. "Okay," he said, "don't tell me. But can't we work together on getting out of here?"

She grimaced, impatiently, and wiped her eyes with the back of a dirty hand. "I certainly don't have a gun. The man who's after me does have one. He might do harm to you too if we link up."

143

"If he's coming this way," said Crews, "we'd better find some cover. But not in the cave again. Too easy to be trapped there."

"He tried to kill me." She seemed to be telling this primarily to herself and with a certain disbelief.

"He's not superhuman, is he?" Crews asked. "I've held my own out here for weeks. And look, you got away from him, didn't you?"

She stayed grim. "He killed my husband. We were camping, and he just came out of the woods with this gun and shot Michael."

"I heard those shots."

"Then he tied me up." Her voice had lost all identifiable emotion. "I hate camping. I was just trying to be a good guy. That was important to Michael."

"Who was this man?" Crews asked. "A complete stranger?" Suddenly she was too weak to stand erect. He pointed to a nearby boulder. "Why don't you sit there?" She finally did so. The ground, though stony, was still too damp from yesterday's downpour. Crews remained standing. "This criminal, do you have any idea who he might be?"

"He's some kind of woodsman," she said, almost contemplatively, looking at the rocks between her feet. "I think he probably lives around here. A hunter or trapper or something. He's got a beard."

"Like mine?"

She kept her eyes down. "Big and bushy. He's filthy dirty."

"You're sure your husband is dead?"

"I don't see how he could have survived. It was at close range."

"I'm no authority," Crews said, "but I've heard about people who have survived worse."

"That was two days ago."

"Even so, I think we should find the campsite. He might still be hanging on, you can't tell. I've got a general idea of where it might be, because I can remember where I was when I heard the shots, more or less. Who was it I saw on the cliff?

Was that you or him? I yelled and waved my arms. I was sure whoever it was saw me."

"It wasn't me. I didn't see anybody after I got away. He went off somewhere for a while. He left me tied up, but it was easier getting out of the ropes than I thought. I didn't know where I was running. I only know we're a couple of days from anywhere. That was what Michael wanted. To leave it all behind." She put her hands on her face.

Crews was reminded of his failure to retrieve the bodies from the submerged airplane. Perhaps he could earn some extenuation. "If there's any chance your husband might still be living, we ought to try and find him. I'd spare you the ordeal and go myself, but I don't want to leave you alone."

"I'm scared. There's nothing you can do against a gun."

"There are two of us," Crews said. "And we know he's out there. We're not going to be jumped without warning, like you and your husband were. One of us will stay on guard at all times. The gun is not necessarily a deciding factor. There are other weapons available to us." Much of this was bravado, but the need to gain her respect gave him more faith in himself than he otherwise would have known. "But we've got to get organized. Do you have any idea where this gunman might be? If it wasn't you who stole the stuff from my camp, then he did it. But I don't know when. I thought he might have come this way, but if he did, the rain washed away any footprints. The first move we should make is climb up there and see what we can." He nodded at the heights above the cave. "Do you want to go first?"

She seemed not quite to have lost her distrust of him. He took the knife-bearing tool from his pocket. "Hold it, if you want. It's the only thing I own that could be called a weapon."

She waved it off. "Don't mind me." She was shivering.

He took off the seersucker jacket. "Here. I'm sorry it's so dirty."

"I'm not cold that way." She began quietly to weep again.

Crews put his jacket on. "We should get going."

145

She stared at him. "It was completely by surprise. There was nothing I could do."

"I saved myself in the crash," Crews said, "and even brought along some gear. I did nothing for the others. I tried, but then I passed out. Maybe I could have saved some or all of my friends, but I didn't. The difference with you is that you could not have done anything about what happened. But you're alive, and I'm not going to let any more harm come to you. You can count on it! Now let's find a way to get up there."

It was she who located the best route to the top of the cliff above them, a ravine to start to climb which took more initial effort than the one he first chose, but his presented an un-climbable impasse a third of the way up, and he had to come down and follow her lead. She waited for him on the level summit.

This was the highest point from which he had yet surveyed the territory in which he had been lost for—however long it was. One end of the lake could be seen, but the other was hidden by the forest, as were the pond, the area of fallen trees, and his hut, along with the stream except for its immediate length just below them. The killer could be anywhere.

"Did you and your husband have a lot of camping equipment?" She gazed blankly at him. "This guy stole the only stuff from my hut that was worth anything. He's tracking down the only witness to his crime and yet he takes the trouble to steal my fishing stuff. Maybe sooner or later he'll go back to your campsite to get whatever possessions you left there."

She nodded in what might have seemed indifference had her anguish not been known. She could surrender her vigilance, now that he had come forward. It was an expression of trust, perhaps as much as he could expect from her.

"Here's my idea," he went on. "If all we do is keep trying to evade him, we won't have a moment's peace of mind, and we might lose in the end if we think of ourselves as his prey. We don't know where we are, and we are unarmed and amateurs at this. Whereas he's presumably a native of the area and has

146

a gun." She was listening, but her face was so expressionless he could not believe she heard him. He would, however, have said as much to himself. "The conclusion I therefore have arrived at might sound crazy. I say *we* stalk *him*." He gave her a moment to protest, while counting on her to stay remote while he worked out what he really meant. She made no response. "There are two of us, you see. In effect, he'll always have his back to one or the other. That is, we should see that's the case. We can make weapons of our own, spears, clubs, and so on, or just rocks. But our most effective weapon will be surprise. The last thing he'll expect is to become the pursued."

She stared down across the forest and said nothing. He had looked at her for an hour now without seeing that what he had believed a sooty smudge from her left cheekbone to the chin was rather one great area of discoloration, a bruise that occupied more than a quarter of her face.

"Maybe *you* should stay here," Crews said. "If he did try to come up, there's no way but the one we took. You could see him coming from a long way off, and roll those boulders down on him. There's no place in that ravine to maneuver. You'll be okay here. I'll go down and catch some fish and bring them up, and some water too. We'll eat, and then *I'll* go after that bastard."

She shook her head violently, though she continued to avoid meeting his eyes. "No."

He tried not to be exasperated. "If you just want to try to get out of here, remember that we're almost certain to run into him anyway. There's probably just one main trail, and if he can't find you before, he's likely to wait there."

The woman said slowly, in almost a moan, "He shot me." She lifted the torn side of her jacket. She wore nothing under it. There was an ugly purplish wound in the soft tissue between her ribs and the waist, not a hole as such but a kind of slash. It looked as if the bullet had gone across, tearing skin and flesh, but not into her body.

Crews winced. "I've got some antiseptic down at my camp. I

don't think he stole that. Let me go get it. I should be back in an hour or less."

"No, no," she said. "You mustn't." She clutched at her jacket. "You'll get killed."

"No, I won't!" he cried. "He's not going to kill either one of us." Then, so as to make a case even he could find credible, he went on. "You see, I've got a charmed life. There has to be a reason why I of all people was spared from dying in that crash. I was the least worthwhile person on board. I'm being given the opportunity to prove I'm worth a damn." She dropped her hands. He could not tell whether what he said had had any effect on her. "I don't like the way that wound looks. It might be infected. It should be cleaned and treated. I wish you had mentioned it before now. You must be in pain."

"I don't feel anything," she said. "But I don't want to stay here alone."

"All right," said Crews, and turned to lead the way down. It was then, making one last sweep of the land below, that he saw the thin wisp of gray smoke coming up from the dark forest on the other side of the lake. "Look. Over there." He turned back to her. "That's a couple of miles away. We're one up on him at the moment. We know where he is, but he doesn't know where we are. Let's go." He did not wait for her reaction.

They made good time in reaching his camp. He found the little spray can and gave it to her. But when he saw the difficulty she would have in reaching the far end of the elongated wound, he reclaimed it.

"Just keep your shirt lifted. This will feel cold at first, but the local anesthetic in it will take over in a second." The gash, though ugly, did not seem to be infected. Washing off the encrusted blood with water from the pond would have been too painful at this point, in his opinion. She recoiled slightly when the spray first touched her, as he expected. He welcomed the reaction as evidence that she had not fallen into a state of semiconsciousness.

He took the tool from his pocket and squatted in the dirt. He began to scratch out a crude map with the screwdriver blade. "Here's the lake, and here's where we are." This was an oval and an X. "Here's the stream, the pond, my hut. Here's where I was on the raft, on the lake, when I heard the shots." He touched the blade to the earth. "Think your camp might have been about here?" She was still standing. Crews was impatient. "I need your help with this." But when he saw her woeful expression, he rose. "We can do that later. Let me put some stuff together, and we'll get going."

"There was a clearing," she said. "It was less than fifty yards to the beach. He didn't want to be closer to the water, he said, because the tent would be too exposed if a storm came. He knew about things like that."

Crews squatted again and x'd the dirt map. "Does this look about right? . . . " He glanced up at her. "I know this is painful, but can you remember any details at all? Where the sun rose or set? Any landmarks? One of those cliffs, for example?"

"I didn't know about anything," she said. "Mostly, I didn't know about him."

Crews put the tool into his pocket along with the can of disinfectant. From the hut he got the thermos, which, after filling it at the pond, he tethered to his belt with a loop of fishline that would allow it to dispense water without being unhitched. In the duffel bag he found one of his knitted shirts. During his raft-building days he had taken time to do some laundry in the lake, and the shirt was as clean as soapless cold water could make it. He took it out to her.

"Here. Put this on under the jacket. It'll help at night." He considerately turned his back. "I've only got one other pair of pants, and I didn't get around to washing them after the raft was finished, and they're full of mud." When he turned back she had the shirt on. It was even looser on her than he had anticipated. She had trouble getting back into the smaller denim jacket.

He took a last look at the house he had built. He was proud

of what he had done and wished that he could have shown it to her under different circumstances.

"We'll stay back from the lakeshore. We won't make as good time through the woods, but he won't be able to see us as easily, if he's looking. I'll lead the way. Anytime I'm going too fast or you don't feel good and want to stop, just tell me. And please stay close. I can't keep looking back to check."

Nevertheless, he did keep looking back, every few paces, on their way along the bank of the stream, for the route was much more demanding than it had been when he used it alone. There were places where he had simply waded in an undergrowth that then had seemed sparse, but mysteriously had since grown burrs and thorns, too cruel to lead her through. There were fallen trees which, alone, he had easily climbed over but now considered too formidable for her. Because of his detours they made much poorer time than he had anticipated and sometimes encountered even worse terrain than that they were avoiding, which required still further evasive action.

But at last he could say, "Right down there is where the woods end and the marsh begins. That's where I built the raft. It's an exposed position: we *could* be seen from the opposite shore. So we'll turn right here and keep in the trees."

Despite the pains with which he had led her around the worst thickets, a little twig end had caught and broken off in the abundant fall of rich brown hair that swung across her left ear. He thought about removing the twiglet, but doctoring was one thing and grooming another. Also, it was not unattractive, a kind of wilderness jewelry.

He had forgotten that before long the woods gave way to the meadow where the wildflowers grew. He halted at its edge. The alternative was to go the long way around, keeping to the trees a quarter mile behind.

"We'll go on across. He's probably still way back in the woods over there. He may even be farther away." The smoke had never been seen again once they had come down from their observation post on the cliff, but Crews had decided that that

150

was a matter of relative perspectives and not necessarily evidence that the man had put out his campfire and gone back to the hunt.

They started into the field in single file, wading through grasses that were usually no more than knee-deep, from which rose the occasional plant only slightly taller, not enough for cover. The wildflowers, somewhat disappointing on his earlier trip, were more profuse now. At a distance those of the same hue seemed to be massed into floating islands of gold, orange-red, or purple, but when approached separated first into confetti and finally became distinct blossoms, some a foot or more from any other. But there were also kaleidoscopic areas shared by many colors.

At one such place, without breaking his regular stride, Crews broke off a little flower of dusty blue. An irritated bee chased his hand for six or eight inches before turning back to more serious work. The sun was warm on his back. The woman was behind him, walking in his swath. He often glanced back at her, should she forget or neglect to signal him. Her eyes were always down. The twig was gone from her hair now. He would have liked to replace it with the blue flower.

On the other side of the meadow they entered wooded, rising ground. Once they were well within the trees, on the gentle slope, he halted, took the cap from the thermos on his belt, and swinging the container on its loop of fishline, poured some water. He offered the cup to the woman. She gulped greedily at it.

"You must be hungry, too. When we come to a likely spot, I'll do some fishing." He refilled the cup. "I've been thinking. We need a contingency plan. If we run into this guy, I'll keep his attention on me as long as I can. You take off and head for cover. His attention will be diverted. He'll have to deal with me. You should get a few seconds anyway." She did nothing to indicate she had heard what he was saying.

He took the lead again. In silence they gained the crest of the hill, where he paused to look down onto a valley that was familiar to him, as was the cliff behind it.

151

"Down there, over on the lake side, is where he took my raft. I had previously seen him up *there*." He pointed at the cliff, higher than where they were, and on their right. "I yelled and waved, then I climbed up. But he was long gone. He must have come down somewhere else, circled around, and grabbed the raft. It was coming apart, but I guess it held together awhile." He was still in effect speaking to himself. "You were hiding someplace? I only wish I had known it then." He stepped so as to face her. Her eyes fell. "If we don't encounter any rougher going than we've had so far, it should only be a couple more hours. I went by raft, so I don't know the ground between here and there. But you do. Can you remember any obstacles?"

She shook her head.

He took the can from his pocket. "Let's have a look at that wound again." She lifted the jacket and the hem of his shirt, which she wore tails out. It was hard to say whether the scab had claimed more of the raw flesh. He sprayed the area and then lowered the shirttail himself, to determine whether it cleared the wound. "It's knitting up," he told her. "Lucky his aim wasn't better." Her eyes rose, full of anguish. "Forgive me," he said. "Dumb thing to say. I was just trying to make conversation. . . . Let's get going. We've got lots to do before dark, and you can never tell what problems will suddenly come up. I've never yet found one thing in nature that I could have predicted."

A sudden burst of sound came from the trees just ahead of them on the downward slope, and instinctively he recoiled. A small deer, a doe or not fully grown fawn, unantlered, was sprinting uphill, at an angle to them. Each instant less of it could be discerned through the intervening trees, and in a moment it had vanished altogether.

The hike to the end of the lake probably took more than the two hours he anticipated, even though the route was without serious topographical barriers, the terrain being mostly level, not densely forested, and marked by only one narrow stream, shallow enough to wade across. But just where the lake's "end" could be identifiably located was another matter. He had been so disoriented on his previous trip of exploration that he had encircled the shore while believing he was traveling in a straight line.

He tried again to speak with the woman. "This is really important. Can you take your mind back to before your husband was shot?" They were now among the pines just behind the beach. "Do you remember anything we might look for? Any kind of landmark? So much of the shore is the same in one place as it is in another. You did come out to the water?" He squinted at the sun. "I'd say it's late afternoon, and we've been going north, more or less, all day. While the light's still good, maybe we should go out to the lake and have you take a look. Maybe you'll recognize something."

She stared through the trees at the sparkling water. "I took a swim. I was hot and dirty after the hike in from the river, where the current was too strong to safely swim in, or anyway that's what Michael said, I wonder why now, because it didn't look like it. So I hadn't had a bath since leaving Fort Judson. He wasn't that good a swimmer himself to help me, he said, if I got in trouble. I was actually touched by his saying that. He wasn't usually so protective—anything but, in fact. Once—" She stopped herself.

"River?" Crews asked. "You came by the river, on a boat of some kind?"

She was still abstracted. "Godforsaken place. You get there by a little plane. Nothing much is at Fort Judson but this outfitter who rents the canoes."

"Where did you leave the canoe?" Crews asked. "How far away is this Fort Judson? How far from your camp was the river?" That there was a human settlement of any kind that could eventually be reached from this wilderness, which to him had grown to seem infinite, was exhilarating.

"I hated it all," she said. "I don't mean that: it was beautiful. I just hated my being there." Tears came to her eyes, and she turned away.

"If we can get to the river and find the canoe—you must have left it someplace there for the return trip? . . . But it's getting late in the day. I'd better make camp. Otherwise it'll get dark before you know it, which always happens quicker when you're lost, I couldn't say why, except all the normal things have to be looked at in a different way. Everything's new. That's really hard to get accustomed to at first. It's like being a child again, only not so comfortably." He was still addressing her back. "I'm going to build a lean-to. Can you give me some help? Collect a lot of pine boughs?"

He prowled until he found a deciduous tree from which to cut a fishing pole, then gave her the tool. "I'm going to try to catch something. It's time you had a meal. I'll go right over there, where you can see me all the while. If anything unusual happens, anything at all, or you just get lonely, just give me a yell."

She showed some slight spirit. "I want to do my part."

"Fine," Crews said. "Look, if you want: we'll need two forked sticks about this high, and thick enough to hold another stick or pole between them." He made explanatory gestures. "Then pine boughs can be put against the frame to make a tent-shaped structure, you see. Don't worry if it doesn't seem terribly substantial. It's only going to serve as a decoy. If this guy shows up, we won't be sleeping there." He had just got this idea and was proud of it, but if she really understood what he was saying, she displayed nothing that could be called a reaction.

He went to the lake at the place he had indicated, a grassy point that extended only eight or ten feet into the water but broke the uniformity of the shoreline. He attached one of the artificial flies to his line, and extending the pole as far as possible, jerked the fake insect along the surface in a fashion he had never tried before, testing another of his ideas. This one worked. In about half an hour he caught two fish, one of a reasonable size for a meal, the other hardly larger than a minnow.

Remembering the torch with which the woman had discovered him in the cave, he asked for her matches, but she had none left. He had neglected this matter until the sun was too low in the sky to furnish rays strong enough for ignition when reflected from the mirror.

The remaining means of making fire from scratch were flint and steel and the bow and drill, both known to him only as depicted in movies, probably inauthentically at that. He chose the latter as being least incredible.

He cut and bent several lengths of limber branch before finding one that would serve. From the end of a dead log he split off a flattish section of very dry wood. He prepared an ignition-attracting wad of stuff from the pods of dead weeds and fragments of desiccated bark. He went to the woman, who was doing a good job of accumulating materials for the lean-to.

"I need to borrow a shoestring." Without waiting for a response, he knelt and began to unlace the running shoe on her left foot. She wore thickly knit athletic socks that were, at least in the part covered by the shoes, wondrously white for anything to be seen in the woods by someone like himself who had been lost there so long.

He found a sturdy dry stick to use as drill. He put one end of it into the depression he had gouged in the flat piece of wood, and spun it therein by means of the little bow of which her shoelace made the string. There were the usual fits and starts, the miscarriages inevitable with all primitive efforts—he had neglected to provide something to hold against the end of the drill to steady it vertically while pressing down on the horizontal member of the apparatus—and before ignition came, two drill sticks and one bow cracked under the strain, but her shoestring held fast, and finally a blackness appeared in the socket and his nostrils caught the first faint bouquet of burning wood. More grinding produced a wisp of outright smoke, bits of tinder were pressed against the infinitesimal spark, and he not so much blew as breathed heavily on it. . . . The spark went out, as did a succession of them, but at last one was snared and fed and reared to be a genuine flame.

They had been able to see the killer's campfire at a considerable distance, but the criminal had no reason to conceal his presence by keeping his fire to the minimum. Crews's purpose was to attract as little attention as possible. By now he had learned a good deal about the fuels in his patch of the world, and though he could not have identified many woods by name, he knew which gave the most heat with the least smoke. He dug a little pit in which to contain his modest blaze and limit how far its radiance would extend when darkness came. He was still taking a chance, for however sparse the smoke, the odor could surely be detected at a great distance. But it was to counteract that risk that he planned the decoy lean-to.

Making fire had taken so much of his attention that he was not aware the woman had not only assembled all the materials for the structure but had almost completed the construction thereof when he turned to that task.

"You were able to do this just from a description?" He walked admiringly around the little structure. "It beats the first one *I* made, I'll say that." She shrugged in apparent indifference, though his praise was sincere. "It's a fine job. Now come on and eat some dinner. There's only one course, but at least it's fresh."

She came and sat near the fire while he grilled both fish on the same stick. He restrained his usual impatience and took more care with the cooking and thus did not char the larger. Owing to the difference in size, the same could not be said for the smaller, but that was the one he gave to himself. He had found a birch and cut from it a section of bark to serve as plate for her meal.

"Forks are in short supply in this establishment," he said. "But at least let me cut it into pieces that are easier to pick up." He warned her against burned fingers.

She was able to eat very little, and he did not press her on the matter. There would be other meals. What she probably needed most at this point was rest. It was apparent to him that the effects of shock, postponed during the time she ran for her life, had accumulated throughout the day she had been under his protection. Taking the longer view, this could be seen as healthy. Nevertheless he would worry.

He led her into the thick underbrush behind the clearing in which the lean-to stood. "I don't think he's anywhere near here. Where we saw smoke was off in the other direction. I watched the lakeshore all day long. If he was heading this way, he'd have had to come out to the water at one point or another. But we'll play it safe. We'll make a place for you back here. I'll find somewhere to conceal myself nearer the lean-to: if he does come, that will naturally be his focus."

While she was fashioning a kind of burrow within the bushes, Crews cut some pine boughs to keep her off the ground. He took such equipment as he might need before dawn from the pockets of his tattered jacket and presented the garment to her for a cover against the chill of the night.

"No matter what, don't make any noise," he said. "I'll be on guard all night. He won't get past me if he comes, but he won't come. You'll be all right here." He had plumped up some of the boughs to serve as pillows, but the weight of her head had compressed them. What wretched accommodations he had provided. Tomorrow he must heat water so she could wash her face. He timidly took her hand, which was lifeless but at least did not recoil. "Try to get some rest. I won't be far away." He was reluctant to leave her.

She seemed to be weeping quietly, obscurely, her face on its unbruised side, her dark hair across it. He left her, pulling the bushes together as he went out to the clearing. In what was left of the twilight, she could not be seen.

Crews had always been pretty good with his fists, giving as good as he got, even with larger opponents, probably because alcohol removed the inhibitions against violence that restrain the sober. But he was not drunk now, and his adversary was a cold-blooded murderer, not some acquaintance whom he had offended at a party or an intrusive stranger in a bar. He required as deadly a weapon as he could quickly fashion without looking far in the near darkness.

He was too squeamish to run a crude spear into a man's back from ambush, but *would* be capable of using a club. He fashioned the caveman type of bludgeon, lashing a hefty rock into the split end of a stout handle.

He had extinguished the fire with water long since. In a stand of dense-grown brush twenty yards from the lean-to he took up a post from which he could see both that structure and the place beyond the other end of the clearing where the woman was concealed. For a while, at the beginning of his vigil, he feared that the absence of all light would confine him to such sounds as he could detect, but in time two-thirds of a moon appeared in a half-clouded sky, and enough of its illumination reached the clearing to identify shapes with a night vision that seemed better than it should be, but perhaps that was due to the same will that kept him awake and alert till morning.

8

■

and heard only the noises made by the smaller nocturnal creatures, scurryings, flutterings, the hollow cry of an owl, and once the shriek of something obviously being killed, perhaps by the same bird that had hooted. He shivered in the thin shirt and could not take the warming measures he had used when on his own, so will was applied to that matter as well.

When dawn came, he went to the woman, taking care first to call out, so that she would not be frightened by the disturbance of the bushes.

She was awake. Her eyes were without luster.

"I hope you were able to sleep."

"It doesn't matter."

"Let's have a look at the wound." He was gratified to see that she had not only worn his jacket but had fastened the buttons all the way up.

She returned the garment to him now and pulled up the tails of the remaining clothing. The scab was even uglier. The antiseptic seemed to have fed the infection, but he told himself that it was the usual case with any kind of disorder of body that things got bad only as a means of gathering the requisite force to recapture good health—just as the reverse could be true, as with his mother, for whom each remission served as

159

prelude to a more desperate phase, until he got to the point at which he dreaded hearing bad news that posed as good.

"I'll get a fire started and heat some water, enough anyway to wash your face with. I know how to make a container of birch bark: you wouldn't think that could be put over flames, but it can. Water can actually be brought to a boil in it." He raised his eyebrows. But nothing served to lift her morale.

In fact, his own could have used a boost. He had not slept in twenty-four hours, and during the same period had eaten only the one tiny fish and the remainder of hers, and the larder was empty again. A worse problem was that he had no idea where they were. If they had passed the midpoint of the end of the lake, every step they took would bring them closer to where they had last seen evidence of the enemy's presence. The woods beyond the clearing, in the direction Crews believed was generally north, looked exceptionally dense. Not only would the going be rough, but straying a few feet per mile off the proper course could result in missing the river altogether.

He went to the lake to clean up a bit, splashing water on his hairy face and scrubbing his teeth with a forefinger. He was trying to work up the courage to look at himself in the mirror, something he had not done in days, when she came out on the grassy point to join him.

"This is it," she said. "This is where I took the swim. There's where I left my clothes, right over there."

"Then your camp must be nearby," said Crews, standing up. "Just point which way. I'll go and do what has to be done. You don't have to come."

She shook her head violently and set off on a diagonal course through a grove of young trees that within thirty yards opened into a little clearing, half the size of that in which they had spent the night but unlike the latter no dead end: a clearly defined trail led out of it toward the presumed north.

But there was no corpse in view, and in fact no camp, though it was obvious that one was not long gone. He poked a stick into the ashes of a cold campfire. On the earth beyond was a rectangular outline from which the normal top layer of nature's mulch had been cleaned. At each of the four corners the ground had been pierced for a tent peg; the holes were still neat and sharply cut.

The woman came to confront him, with her noble forehead and eloquent eyes. "We really did camp here, as you can see. But nobody came out of the woods and murdered my husband. I lied about that. I still don't want to admit it even to myself. *He* wasn't killed. It was he who tried to kill me. *He*'s the one I was running from. *He*'s got the gun."

Crews looked away. He had been so glad to see her that he had not questioned her original story, which only now seemed implausible. After his initial surprise, what immediately occurred to him at this moment was that his adversary was not some veteran backwoodsman to whom the lake and its environs were home turf, someone born with a rifle in his hand, but rather a soft, civilized city guy who except for the expensive equipment furnished by a sporting-goods outfitter would be at the mercy of the wilderness—as he himself had been, but *he* had proved his mettle. He could take this bastard. He longed to meet him.

But what he said to her was, "There's the trail. I'm assuming it leads to the river. Let's get going. The sooner we get to this Fort Judson, the sooner you can report him to the authorities."

But now that she had been able to confess the central truth, she had to say more. "I was ashamed. I still am. He was getting ready to do some target shooting with that pistol of his. He did that every time we made camp, coming down from Judson. He'd blaze away at knotholes in trees or whatever, but his favorite target was something living, a squirrel or even a bird in the air. I hate guns on general principles, but the loud noise is really awful, out here where sounds of that kind would never otherwise be heard, and the possibility that he would wound or kill some creature for no reason at all always infuriated me." She gasped for air. "I don't want to be phony about it. I eat meat and wear leather, but I can't stand the idea of needless destruction of—but here's what never made any sense to me: *he*'s the animal lover, even gives money to—oh Christ . . . " It was as if she were trying to breathe underwater.

"Take your time," Crews said. "I'm listening. I'm not going anywhere."

After a moment she shrugged and said, in mirthless irony, "What a time to start an argument: when the other guy has a loaded gun in his hand. Maybe I was being suicidal. It seems so dumb now, but that was then, and he had never been violent with me." She shook her head with force. "But if I start to think of my mistakes, I have to go back a lot further than that. I shouldn't have come on the trip—I *hate* camping and canoeing! But I was trying to be fair. That's always an error."

Crews was shocked. "It is?"

"Not *being* fair," she said. "But *trying* to be, which means the effort will be unnatural. I wanted a divorce, you see. His response was to beg me to come on a trip into the unspoiled wilderness, far from the corruptions of civilization, without which we could surely reconcile our differences. Of course, I didn't believe that would or could or even should happen. So why did I agree? Maybe it was rather to be *unfair*: to pretend that I might reconsider while having my mind made up." She gave Crews a vulnerable half-smile. "Nothing like being shot to stimulate self-examination."

"I'm a veteran of marital strife," said he. "But gunfire goes beyond my experience. Do you think it was his plan from the first to kill you?"

Her expression grew hard, even hateful. Her answer therefore was a surprise. "No," she said quickly. "I don't think that at all. I think the shooting was an impulse. I think the trip was a device to postpone doing anything about the breakup. That's his style. When things don't go your way, play for time, delay, postpone. Then regardless of what happens, pretend the delay has settled every question in your favor. My mistake was in making that point to him while he was holding a gun."

"You were hit by the first shot and then you ran and he fired again and missed? I'm sure I heard two shots."

"I can't remember those moments very clearly. I was in the thick woods back there, running as hard as I could. I had no idea of where I was going. I didn't even know I had been hit until I finally looked back for a second, still running, to see if he was chasing me, and turned and slammed my face against a tree and fell down. Only then did I feel a sort of itch at my side, and I looked and saw my shirt was full of blood. I took it off and cleaned the wound with it and threw it away when I stopped bleeding. My face hurt worse than the wound ever did. I kept going until some time later on I found that cave."

Now that he had learned more about his adversary, Crews saw no need for undue haste in locating the river. The man was no longer as sinister as he had once seemed. It made sense to stay awhile at this place at which fish could be caught and smoked to take along as rations should food be harder to find where they were going.

"I want to hear whatever you want to tell," he said. "But, as you will find before long, the problem of food becomes paramount out here, outranking all others: unless you are preoccupied with it, you'll never get any. And even if you're obsessed, you usually won't find enough. So I should go and catch more fish now. If you feel like it, you might look around for some edible form of plant life. It isn't healthy to only eat fish, but I haven't done well at finding much else. I haven't had the nerve to experiment much. Better to be malnourished than poisoned. But maybe you can do better."

He realized that she might be offended by his displacing matters of great moment with banal practicality, but felt there was quite as good a chance that she might rather be relieved. He was, after all, not a destroyer but rather a preserver. And taking the chance paid off. While he fished in the lake with no success, despite trying a variety of bait and moving from place to place along a hundred yards of shoreline, she returned from

163

the nearby grove with a shirttail full of little dark-green coils.

"I know what those are," he cried. "Fiddlehead ferns! It never occurred to me to look for them around here."

He went to cut a piece of birch bark. When he came back he demonstrated his pot-making technique. "It doesn't look like much, but you wait: it'll do the job without burning up." The woman meanwhile had picked up and assembled the firemaking bow and drill.

"Am I doing it right?" she asked, but by the time he had completed the making of the crude bark vessel and filled it with water from the thermos, she had a flame going.

The blanched fiddleheads were delicious, just at the edge of bitterness, more delicate in flavor than spinach, firmer in texture. They blew on the coils but ate them still too warm, handing the knife blade back and forth, sparing their fingers but not their tongues.

One was so hot that Crews spat it into his hand. He excused himself, remembering Ardis. "I had a wife one time who really hated it when I did that. A leopard doesn't change all its spots, even under these conditions." They were sitting side by side on a fallen log. Between them was the birch-bark box, from which he had poured the excess water. He ate the coiled frond from his hand and stood up. "Go ahead, finish the rest. I'm going to take a bath in the lake and then we'll hit the trail. You can heat enough water in the box for at least a little wash. Maybe it's too soon for full-immersion bathing, what with your wound. Also it's sure to be ice-cold out there."

"I'll collect more fiddleheads to take along," she said. "Maybe they won't be easy to find where we're going."

"Now you're talking like a survivor."

He went to the lake and stripped, but took all his clothes into the water and washed both them and his own face, hair, and hide as well as he could. The water felt gelid until he became habituated to it. When he emerged, he wrung as much water from his clothing as was possible and put it on damp. Scrubbing had not gone far to improve the chinos, which continued to display the many stains they had acquired from fish oils, rabbit blood, wood ashes, and other souvenirs of his experiences. Nor did washing make spotless the seersucker jacket, though it revealed new tears of which he had been ignorant.

He had been quicker with his ablutions than she. Forgetting that she had to wait for the water to heat, he was about to return too soon to the clearing when, en route, he saw, in fragmented form through the trees, the glimmerings of her nude body. He discreetly backpedaled to the beach, where he was chagrined to notice a sizable fish rise to snap at an insect, just offshore of one of the places where he had failed to get a bite an hour earlier. Could they really tell when the food had a hook in it? If that were true, no fish would ever be caught. Maybe like human beings they had their keen days, but no living thing could preserve itself forever.

He did not want to think of the woman's body, of which he had seen very little in any event. He could hardly remember the feeling of fleshly desire, yet had he become altogether asexual he would not, or anyway not so quickly, have acted to honor her modesty.

When he did at last rejoin her, her face was still wet. It was glisteningly lovely that way, but he expressed his regrets at being unable to provide a towel. Dark patches of damp were visible here and there on her clothing.

"It's a warm day," she said, fluffing her hair with her hands. "It feels good to get wet and let everything dry on its own."

Crews indicated his own still sopping garments. "I washed my extensive wardrobe while I was at it, something I might have done more when I was alone. But maybe cleanliness is mostly social, like conversation. I never talked to myself—I mean aloud, where you have to be fairly formal, don't you, in sentences or anyway complete phrases. No doubt I made noises, grunts, et cetera. And I once talked or rather chanted nonsense at a bear. He probably didn't mean me any harm. He left soon enough, but it's scary to have one come and stare into your face when you're lying half asleep. But in the end I guess I scared *him* or maybe just bored him. He hasn't been seen since."

He had hoped to amuse her with the reminiscence, but it served rather to evoke a grimmer association of her own. "That was why Michael said a gun might come in handy: there were potentially dangerous creatures in the woods, like bears." Emotion darkened her face, which except for the bruise had stayed pale from the scrubbing.

He made sure the little store of equipment was stowed away securely at the appropriate places on his person. He had re-filled the thermos in the lake. He tried hanging it in a new position on his belt so that it would be less likely to strike him as it swung with his stride.

He turned back to her. For an instant he saw the unsullied face of a young girl, but that was something of an illusion: the bruised area was still visible as if in shadow, though fading, and while not as old as he, she was an adult.

"Fine," he said. "That should do the trick. Now that we've got that trail, we should make better time. How far is it from here to the river?"

"We camped overnight where we left the canoe. We started next morning and got here in late afternoon." When asked for practical information, she was able to give it without evidence of the feeling it must invoke.

"Same rules apply: if you want to stop for any reason at all, sing out. I can't keep looking back."

She smiled. "But you do."

He was surprised to feel embarrassment. It must be the first such occasion in many years. "That was when I didn't know if you could make it. . . . Let me know when it looks to you as if we're getting near the river, if it seems like I'm unaware."

"You think he'll be waiting there?"

"That's a possibility. It's also possible that he's just run away. He's not a professional killer, is he? He doesn't have any special reason to think you and I have joined forces, but on the other hand, he knows there's somebody else in an area that he thought was deserted. Has he got the guts to murder two people? When he did such a bad job at trying to kill you?"

"Obviously, I'm the worst judge of what he's capable of," she said. "I hardly ever heard him raise his voice. What I always liked about him was his gentleness. He's so big, but in four years, until this, I never saw the least hint of brutality in anything he did or even said. He loves animals, for heaven's sake!"

"Big?" Crews asked. "Tall, heavy?"

"Both, but not fat. He's a weight-training nut. That's how he got into the health-club business. That's where we met, in fact."

"Let's go," Crews said, and started off.

They hiked through a seemingly endless forest of straight, tall, high-foliaged trees so regularly spaced that it was sentimentally inviting to pretend the planting thereof had been by design. The trees were home to a number of squirrels, not only the familiar gray but a smaller red species that Crews was seeing for the first time. Hitting one of either breed with a projectile, spear, arrow, or rock, would be unlikely. All were much quicker than those degenerated by life in city parks, and the red ones would be tiny targets.

As a drunk, Crews had especially despised people who did anything at all to make or keep themselves fit, and almost his favorite opponent for a fight was some big inflated guy who thought bulk and physical strength were determining factors in hand-to-hand. Had this been true, the boxing champions of the world would always be the men who had been the largest contenders. But Crews was not his old imprudent, headlong self: he was lost, emaciated, and tattered, and he was defending a woman to whom he had no claim, one furthermore who had seen nothing wrong with this bastard until he tried to murder her.

The tall trees eventually came to an end and were succeeded by an area of low, brushy growth from which twice within two hundred yards plump white-flecked brown fowl sprang up with commotion and flew frantically away to land somewhere ahead—probably these two were one and the same, and likely it was edible, being grouse or partridge or pheasant, all of which he had eaten in the dressed and cooked form, none of which he probably could have identified in a living bird. He still had no weapon with which to bring down such prey.

Up ahead, the forest began again, now with pines, on rising terrain. He liked to think that on the far side, the downward slope, glimpses could be seen of the river in the valley below, for they had hiked steadily for hours, covering much ground. Even so, it was considerably more probable that his hopes were without foundation. That kind of ambivalence seemed essential to prevailing over the destructive elements of not just the wilderness but of the self as well.

He stayed skeptical even after they had toiled up the ascending ground—more taxing than it looked, continuing for a mile or more—and, going down the more acute slope on the other side, he heard the sound of rushing water.

When they arrived at the bank of the stream he could confirm that however vigorous, a stream was all it could be called.

He asked her, "This doesn't look like where you left the canoe?"

She shook her head. "That was a real river, not so fast-moving, a lot wider. In fact, it's the Kinnemac." She raised her eyebrows as if the name might be familiar to him.

He shrugged. "Don't ask me. . . . Did you cross, or pass, a stream that looked like this on your hike to the lake?"

"No. I didn't see water in any form. And we were on the lookout. We only had canteens."

The ground at the bank seemed dry. Crews found a patch of grass to sit on, and the woman joined him. He was thirsty for fresh water but, with so much at hand, enjoyed the spartan suspense.

"We'll make camp here. It's still early, but that overcast looks like it will stay until the sun goes down, and in fact I have begun to smell rain. But the main thing is that we're apparently lost again. I remember a couple of places where it might have happened. Somewhere I made a bad decision, took the wrong choice of forks."

"I certainly didn't help," she said. "After all, I was the one who had been along that way before, and yet I couldn't recognize anything since we left the lake."

Crews smiled ruefully. "I've boasted about how I've coped out here, building the lean-to and the raft, and getting food. But I don't have any sense of direction at all unless the sun stays visible, and even then it's easy to be misled. The other day I went all around the lake with the idea I was going in a more or less straight line. I thought we were heading north when we started. But the slightest divergence, especially when you're never sure precisely where you are in the first place, the slightest deviation can grow with each mile."

"*He* had a map and a compass," she said. "You haven't done badly with no help at all."

That he was pleased to hear such sentiments did not lessen Crews's chagrin. He had taken what seemed to be the more obvious alternative when they went from the open field onto the long wooded slope: there was a much fainter trail to the left. But then the error might have come much earlier: back in the tall trees, long before they had emerged to disturb the game bird from its home in the brush, he had noticed, perhaps too idly, the suggestion of another trail leading away to the right. Tomorrow they would have to retrace their route to the nearer of the alternative trails, take it, and if by the end of that day they had no good reason to believe it the correct one, come all the way back and take the other.

He said as much to the woman. "And if neither of them is the right one, then we'll have to really start all over, go back to your old campsite." He looked downstream, where the water became shallow, splashing around protruding rocks, a mi-

169

nor rapids. "Meanwhile, this looks like a livable place." He crawled to the edge of the low bank and filled the thermos cup with water, wetting his hand. "It's ice-cold." He gave her the cup and went back to fill the bottle. "Should be trout in here."

She was standing. "I'd really like to take a whole bath," she said. "I can put with up the cold water."

Crews frowned. "I don't know . . . "

"I'll be okay. I really have to begin taking over my own care. Believe me, I *need* to. It's no reflection on you." She smiled. "I'm all right, really. You've saved my life."

"Well . . ."

"But I have to get hold of it."

"But let me just see how deep it is," he said, "and how fast the current is running." He took off his jacket and dropped it on the bank. He stepped down into knee-deep water, which was so cold as almost to cause his legs to buckle. It came only to his waist in midstream. The current was brisk but not as forceful as it had looked. By the time he had waded back he was over the shock of the initial chill. But as he scrambled out he could say quite truthfully, "It's even colder than I thought. I wish you'd at least let me make a fire first." He was so chilled he had to show his teeth. "It's icy even with your clothes on." He squeezed as much water from his own as he could while continuing to wear them. "I'll get going on the fire."

He went into the nearby trees. It took a while to cut a selection of branches from which to make the little firemaking bow. He had been improvident in abandoning the rig he had used at the lake but had foolishly counted on the sun to be available next time he needed fire, and it was inconvenient to tote anything that could not be contained in his pockets.

When he returned to the streamside, he saw the woman's dark-green knitted shirt, the one borrowed from him, was darker still because it was soaking wet.

"I see you washed the shirt."

"Actually I used it for a towel. I hope you don't mind. I didn't have anything else."

Crews knelt to assemble his apparatus. He needed her shoe-lace again, and this time asked her to take it out, if she would, herself. "You went in without your shirt?"

She gave him the lace, having removed it while balancing nicely on one foot. "I was naked. The freezing water seemed to help the wound, like an astringent, you know."

He quickly completed the construction of the rig and put the tinder in place around the socket of the drill.

She said, "I've got an idea I'd like to try. Could I borrow the tool with the knife blade? I waded down to the rapids before. There are lots of fish that swim through the rocks there. The water's fairly shallow. It really looks like you could catch them with your bare hands, but I tried and failed. I'm just not deft enough. But what about making a spear? What do you think? Didn't the Indians fish that way?"

"I tried it early on, in the pond, and got too impatient when it didn't work. I probably didn't keep at it long enough. Also I didn't make a very good spear. But, sure, go ahead."

"Any suggestions as to the design?"

He deliberated for a moment. "If you could make a barb of some kind, like a fishhook. You'll need something to keep the fish from slipping off after it's speared."

"How about a long stick that has a little cluster of three or more branches at one end, like a hand almost?"

"That's a great idea," Crews said.

"It's not original. I saw it in the movies or television. It was being done on some island, I think, by people in sarongs."

"Terrific," Crews said. "Just one minute. . . . " He needed the knife for a couple of small alterations to the end of the drill and the socket in which it would turn, having finished which he presented the tool to her.

He watched her tall, slender figure go into the edge of the woods. Her hair was still loose. He hoped he was right in his assumption that if they had gone astray en route to the river, her husband would not be anywhere nearby. Crews had noth-ing but contempt for the man, and knew no fear for his own

safety, but to shoot her in the back from a place of concealment would not be beyond the capacity of such a coward.
Besides, it was a pleasure, really a joy, to see her graceful
movements. She went too far in saying he had saved her life,
but it was gratifying to know he had served some purpose.

He started sawing away with the bow. The process asked for
more than muscle: making fire by this unlikely means required the intense concentration of all faculties.

Before he had succeeded in producing the first wisp of
smoke, she was back, carrying a serviceable spear. At one end
it had been cut just above the junction of three branches.

"How does this look?"

"That was quick," he said. "I've been getting nowhere."

"Should I try? And you go spear fishing?"

"The spear was your idea. The fire was mine. We should
stick with our specialties."

With the knife blade she sharpened the three branch ends
to points and returned the tool to him. He sawed violently
with the bow and drill until sweat from his forehead began to
fall on that which he wanted to ignite. Taking a breather, he
watched her walk along the bank to where the water rushed
through the rocks. Balancing on one foot and then the other,
she pulled off her shoes and socks, then bent to roll her jeans
to the knee. She stepped into the current, which swirled
around her calves. Soon she stabbed violently at something,
but the spear came up dripping and empty. She did much the
same several more times and then turned to look his way and
shrug. He waved.

Like everything else performed with primitive implements,
spear fishing was surely much trickier in practice than it
seemed in theory. But he probably should have accepted her
offer to swap jobs, having by now lost faith in the likelihood
that fire could come from his current apparatus. He needed a
base plate of drier wood. He looked up to see her raise the
spear end triumphantly. A wriggling silvery fish was impaled
on its points. She waded near enough to shore to deposit her

catch on the nearest land. Crews thought it possible that the fish might writhe to the edge of the bank and fall into the water, but he decided to let her learn by experience.

Meanwhile, inspired by her success, he returned with vigor to his own efforts, to which he applied himself so obsessively that at first he failed to register that the sky was brightening. He dropped the bow and focused the mirror on the tinder. The sun broke through the overcast just long enough to get an ember going. It was like a special favor to him. By the time the cloud cover closed in on its temporary rent, he had made a hot little blaze.

During the same period she had mastered the technique and caught fish after fish. At one point she signaled to him with all the fingers of one hand and then shifted the spear to the other so as to display two fingers more. Apparently she did not know the way to signal numbers greater than five using only one hand, or did only boys do that?

When the fire was in a condition to go unattended for a while, he went along the bank to where her catch lay flopping. Now there were nine, and she caught the tenth as he watched. She waded in to shore and presented it to him on the tines of the spear. He added the fish to the lot on the grassy bank.

He gave her a hand with which to pull herself from the water.

"See what I mean?" he asked. "You're the fisherman in this—in this partnership." He had almost said "family." "I was just lucky the sun came out briefly. And by the way, it was over *there*. Which would mean that what I thought was north was actually way to the east."

"But to be really sure about direction, just looking at the sun isn't enough, is it? You really need an additional point of reference."

"Good of you to mention that," he said. "But I still have a lousy sense of direction, the only sense that hasn't improved since I've been out here."

"Maybe because direction according to the compass is a

man-made concept. That is, there really is a magnetic pole and a force we call magnetism that affects metals, but what animals care about is light and heat and water and food. Your directional instincts have been fine about those things, even when the sun went in."

"Now you're buttering me up," he said, "so that I'll cook your fish on my fire." He had brought along her shoelace and was about to return it but thought of another use. "Do you mind if I string some of these fish on it, to carry back?"

"Let me. You've got enough to do as it is." She took the lace and began forthrightly to thread it through the gills and out the mouth of a fish that was still feebly twitching. "I can't decide what's more humane: letting them suffocate or killing them in some other way."

Crews had known the same feeling. "I'm a coward about that. I just don't decide, which means they drown in air. . . . I see you know how to do that. It took me a while to figure it out."

She sniffed. "Michael never caught anything. But he talked about stringing up his catch, and I remember a lot of stuff just from listening. Then I've cooked whole fish that you buy, and watched the fish-store guy clean them—I think you're supposed to call him the 'fishmonger,' but I'd probably laugh if I did."

"I'll bet you're a lot better cook than I," Crews said. "I have got into the habit of just boiling or burning the food as fast as I can and gobbling it up."

By now she had strung half the fish on the shoelace. "I can do one or two simple things, but *he* was the main cook: that is, when we weren't eating out, which we did a lot."

Crews uncoiled some of his fishline. "Here. I'll take the rest."

They walked back together, each with a sagging string of fish. He dropped his on the ground nearby and knelt to inspect the fire.

He looked up at her. "I've never before had this much food at my disposal. I think I'll go wild and try a new gastronomic treat. Do you know those Japanese restaurants where they bring a hot rock to the table and cook all sorts of things on it, fish, vegetables, thin slices of steak, and so on? I think I'll try that. Meanwhile I can put a lot of these fellows on to smoke."

"Can I get the rocks?" she asked. "Nice big smooth ones?"

Crews missed her terribly even on such a trivial separation, when she was in sight the entire time. He had not realized he was so lonely until his loneliness was relieved. But she did everything so effectively that he welcomed the help. The rocks she brought back were just what he had had in mind. He put them into the hot coals. He constructed a smoking rack above the fire, hung on it a spitful of eviscerated fish, and threw on the green branches she had gathered.

"I'll let the rocks get good and hot," he said. "You don't suppose you could find more fiddleheads?"

"I sure can look."

While she was gone he filleted the remaining fish. After a time she returned from the woods carrying something in the denim jacket used as a bag. She dumped it on the ground alongside him.

There was a mixture in the outspread jacket, representing everything but fiddlehead ferns: some broad green leaves; some slenderer fronds; some delicate shoots that terminated in little bulbs. But most conspicuous were the pale mushrooms.

"God almighty," Crews said, with more emotion than he would have expressed had he thought about it. "I'm not going to try those!" He paused. "You *do* know some are poisonous?"

"We—he had this book about stuff you could find to eat in the wild, I don't know why, because he didn't look for anything. We lived on those freeze-dried packets they make for campers. Anyway, these mushrooms look just like the pictures of the edible ones."

"I've always heard there are bad ones that are dead ringers for the good kind, and only experts can tell the difference. We can't take any chances at all—I mean, apart from those that are forced upon us."

175

"All right."

"I don't mean to be disagreeable," he said.

"You're just making your point." She said this straightforwardly, squatting there next to her jacketful of vegetables.

He smiled at her. "Do you realize we don't even know each other's name?" He put out his hand. "I'm Bob Crews."

Her handshake was warm, but the rest of her response came from a greater moral distance. "You're welcome to inspect my driver's license, there in the pocket." She nodded at the spread-eagled jacket. "But if you don't mind, I'd rather not hear my name. He kept yelling it while he was trying to kill me. He made me hate the sound of it, at least for now. So if you don't mind calling me something else. I don't care what."

"Of course," Crews said sympathetically. He was still concerned that he might have been too harsh with her about the mushrooms, even though he had been quite right. "Let's see. . . ." He smirked. "I've been married so often, all the women's names I can think of have been used up."

"How about 'Friday'?"

"Pardon?"

"As a name," she said.

"As in 'Thank God, it's . . . '?" He laughed. "Okay, Friday it is, then. Now, these greens, what do you think, should we cook them or eat them raw?"

"I've already tried a little of one of these." She held up the sheaf of bulbed shoots. "Some kind of wild onion, I believe."

"I remember those things from when I was a kid. I didn't think they were supposed to be edible."

"Maybe these are a different species. They're not bad."

"I'll chop them up and use them as a condiment," Crews said. He tore a fragment off one of the broad leaves in her collection and chewed it briefly. It had a mild flavor, in the area of romaine, but was fairly tough. "This should be cooked." After similar tests with the remaining greenery, he decided, "These will make an okay salad. Are they plants you saw in the book?"

"I wish I *had* read the whole thing. Unfortunately I only looked at the part on mushrooms."

"I'm sorry about them," said Crews. "We'll get back to civilization and find that they not only were edible but of a rare variety highly prized by gourmets, and I will be proved a fool."

"No, you won't!"

She said this with so much feeling that Crews hastily assured her he had been kidding. "It wouldn't be the first time I was wrong about food. You should be warned that among my distinctions is an unerring instinct to pick the worst establishment from a selection: I even managed on occasion to find lousy restaurants in France—which by the way were not tourist places but where French truck drivers ate. You see, my then wife—" But this was not the time for such reminiscences. "The stones should be hot enough by now. The fish will cook fast once they're started."

He used a pair of green sticks to probe for the rocks, which were buried just inside one edge of the fire above which the smoking rack was mounted. The embers were so hot that the sticks were immediately dried out and ignited, but, working quickly, he worried the two stones out to free ground. Their appearance had not changed, but he could feel the intense heat as high as his face. They were searing the sparse vegetation beneath them.

The waiting fillets were stacked on a clean rock nearer the woman than he. He tried her name on for size. No doubt it would take a while to sound natural. "Okay, Friday, if you'll hand me the fish, we'll have a go at this. Unfortunately, I don't have any oil or fat. I'm hoping the surface will just be so hot the food will seal up when it hits it."

She brought him the fillets, and he rapidly dropped three of them onto each stone, skin down, snapping his fingers back before they were singed by the ferocious heat. The fish cooked so vigorously, with loud sizzlings and copious smoke, that no sooner had he deposited the last than he returned to turn the first piece over. He had had the forethought to provide himself

177

with two crude spatulas, lengths of a broad branch, each shaved flat at one end.

The first fillet broke in two on his efforts to lift it, but no further, and it left most of its skin behind to blacken and burn. But perhaps it was the oil from that skin that cured the surface of the stone so that, when turned and charred on the reverse, the fish did not stick.

He grinned at Friday. "It actually works!"

They ate off two clean stones that were flat and broad enough to serve as plates, but Crews found reason to complain of his own lack of foresight.

"It didn't occur to me that these cold rocks would chill the food so quickly. I should have asked you to cut some bark for plates." He was gobbling the fish as fast as he could, before it lost all heat, and speaking between bites. "On the other hand, if it was too hot we wouldn't be able to pick it up. Forks would be nice, too. It shouldn't be hard to carve something that would do." This thought had never come to him when he was alone.

"I'll try," Friday said, eating much more deliberately, and so gracefully with her long fingers that silverware might have been an encumbrance. "Meanwhile, this is delicious. I wouldn't even use salt if we had any."

"I wonder if there's something in the stones, some minerals maybe, that give the salty effect, because it's there, or anyway the illusion thereof." He was eating the middle fillet from the stack of three: it was still warm. "This is as close to stark reality as I've ever come, and still I wonder what's real and what isn't. And the only way I've learned to do anything is by trial and error. You waste a lot of time and effort like that, but when you've got nobody around to teach you anything . . . Until now I haven't even had anyone with whom to compare notes."

The clear stream flowed vigorously just beyond them. It was sufficiently fast-moving to provide what were probably trout, yet shallow enough to wade across should the need or wish come to visit the forest on the far side. It was full of food, and its water was cold and sweet. Likely it flowed toward the same lake the shore of which they had left that morning. If they had not yet found the river, at least they were not really lost within their piece of wilderness. The route from the lake could always be retraced, and they could start over. Meanwhile dinner was very good, and he could see just the spot to construct a lean-to, for which the adjacent woods would provide excellent materials.

"If it's okay with you, we'll stay here for the night. There'll be enough time, for a change, to make a decent camp." He was even enthusiastic. "I've learned a few tricks on how to make things somewhat comfortable." He squinted at the sky. "The weather looks good, but I have a feeling rain's going to come along later on, and a good tight roof might be in order. . . . I'm about ready for salad."

He had not gotten around to boiling the big leaves, which Friday had pushed aside, along with the mushrooms. She had torn the rest of the greenery into pieces, sliced the wild onions over them, and tossed the mixture in her jacket.

"Not bad," Crews said, masticating. "It would only be ruined by oil and vinegar." The onion got stronger in the aftertaste, or perhaps it was just that his palate was no longer inured to strong flavors.

Friday ate every shred of her portion, then went to the bank of the stream, leaned down, and rinsed her hands. She crawled back on her knees, a movement he found endearing, something she might have done at a picnic.

But she did not return his smile. She stared across at the dark woods on the other side of the water. "Whenever I let myself think about it—which is just about every time I get close to accepting that it happened—I begin to worry about where he might be."

"I haven't forgotten him," Crews said hastily, though in fact he had been trying to do so. "But if he was where we saw that smoke yesterday—and we've spent the time since in veering away from due north—then we're farther from him than ever. On his side of the lake, there isn't any high ground for miles.

We made that little fire last evening, but he wouldn't have been able to see our smoke from wherever he was in the woods. He'd have had to come out to the shore to get the right perspective. He's unlikely to have followed us all day to here. If he's got a compass and map, he knows how to get back to the canoe. I believe that's where he'll head. I keep saying 'we,' though it's possible he doesn't know you've joined forces with me. Do you think he might just take the canoe and leave?"

"I would no longer be surprised by anything he did," Friday said bleakly. "Unless it succeeded."

Crews took a chance and asked, "Is that more or less what you were telling him when he took a shot at you?"

She stared sharply at him for a moment, but then softened and said, "More or less. I was wrong—and I don't mean just because of what subsequently happened. I said cruel things to him sometimes, but you have no idea of how hard it is to live with someone for whom you've lost all respect."

Crews sighed inwardly: he had certainly heard enough on that subject at second hand, but he was not violent with the women who told it to him. He got physical only with men, and then invariably with those capable of damaging him. At least he was not nearly so dishonorable as he could have been.

"After a while," Friday said, "the person you despise most is yourself. You shouldn't let it go that far."

Crews was uncomfortable. He could only mutter lamely, "Well . . ."

"We'd get to a campsite, and I'd gather firewood and fetch water, and he'd shoot his gun at things," Friday said. "That infuriated me more than his women ever did, because at least they paid for their fees. He owned a health club until, of course, it went under, taking most of my savings with it. The bank wouldn't lend him a cent. His typical response as business got worse was to expand, open another branch."

"I'll bet you have your own profession," Crews said.

"I'm with a brokerage, in sector analysis."

"And whatever that is, I'm sure you do well at it."

180

She modestly lowered her eyes. "Okay."

"No," he said, "better than okay."

"I'm a vice-president, but only one of several. Let's say I earn a living."

Crews picked up her denim jacket, which had served as tablecloth, and shook it out. He returned it to her. "Let me get this over with: I don't know anything much about any kind of work. A person like you will probably find it difficult to understand that somebody like me exists. About all I can say for myself is that I've never really lived off a woman—if that's any kind of criterion for anything. But I did live off my father until I was way beyond childhood, and in fact long after he died, so I can't call myself a model of independence." He was suddenly aware that he had always responded favorably to women who had made a go at a profession, while he resented successful men.

Friday stood up and put on her jacket. "I'm wasting good weather on my whining," she said, staring into the sky. "I think you're right about the coming rain."

"Can you smell it too?"

She smiled intimately at him. "I think so because you do, and you're usually right."

Crews realized that he should simply accept the commendation, but the experience was as yet too rare to accommodate readily. So he had to say, "Except when I'm wrong." But that sounded like a rebuke, so he quickly explained about using one's nose in the wilderness. "I think maybe smell has a lot to do when you think it's rather some sixth sense. I've learned to breathe harder, by which I mean both deeper and faster, but mostly it has to do with, as it were, *listening* to what the nose tells you. I've tried to take my cue from the animals. Did you notice that deer? For a split second before he took off, his nostrils quivered. He was trying to smell us, even though he could see us well enough, but we were downwind."

"You saw *that*? He was just a blur to me."

"Because you weren't prepared for it," Crews said. "When you're out here for a while on your own, you develop the state

181

of mind animals have: you expect to be surprised at any moment. You go about your business, but you're always on guard. Being alert is a thing of the nervous system. It doesn't affect you physically until the moment for action comes." He laughed. "I'd be amazed if you found any meaning at all in those remarks."

"I think I do know what you mean," she said. "It's like karate. Until you actually make a move, your mind and body are supposed to be in a state of utter relaxation. Then, even while a punch is in the process of traveling toward its target, during that millisecond the fist is resting serenely, only to become like steel at the instant of impact. I hadn't realized that technique has some basis in natural principles. So much of it seems artificial, the ritual and all."

"You do karate?"

"My purse was snatched. I resisted and got my wrist broken for my trouble. I was sure I could have fought him off if I had known how: he was not that big. So I took karate lessons when my arm was okay. . . . " She was looking at the fish smoking on the rack above the fire. "I wonder if the smoke wouldn't be more concentrated if a little enclosure was put around it? Maybe a little lean-to, closed in at the ends. Want me to collect the materials?"

On all previous occasions Crews had used an unenclosed fire, which meant that the fish had to be positioned so that the prevailing breeze blew the smoke their way. It was not that he had failed to think of erecting a wind barrier; it was rather that he had not taken the trouble, what with all else that always needed to be done. But he had a partner now.

In no time at all, Friday had surrounded and roofed the fire in green foliage, through the multifold interstices of which rose the fragrant smoke from the moist wood atop the hot coals, having first bathed the fish on the spit.

Crews meanwhile began to build the structure that would shelter them overnight, the grandest one yet, almost seven feet long, more than four feet high at the ridgepole, and at least five feet wide.

Friday pitched in when her own project was completed. She invariably volunteered for any job he would have, working alone, postponed as long as possible, such as sinking the uprights into the earth, which required dogged excavation with an improvised and inefficient trowel of wood, through roots and rocks, and then leveling them by eye, a miscalculation in which, however minor at the outset, would be magnified as the structure rose with each joint untrue. But she was also more patient than he in the interweaving, the rudimentary thatching, of the freshly cut pine boughs that would, not by luck but with care, make the roof-walls shed rain.

By twilight they had built a shelter sturdy enough to continue standing when Crews pushed firmly against its uprights. It was positively spacious inside, a good two and a half feet for each, with at least a symbolic barrier between them, suggested by the two additional uprights mounted along the center line to help hold the long ridgepole stretching from front to back posts. Outside, because the structure was erected on level ground, they ringed it with a shallow drainage ditch.

"We'll know how sound the roof is only when it starts to rain."

"You were right not to make it wider, because that would have flattened the pitch and exposed it more to the rain."

"That didn't occur to me," he confessed. "I was just concerned with how long such slender poles could be without bending under the weight of the boughs they supported. There's so damn many things to keep in mind." He heard a pattering above them and for a moment believed birds were hopping there, then identified the sound as rain. "There it is already. I was right about its coming but didn't know how soon. We finished just in time."

"The fish!" Friday cried, and before scrambling out, said, "Stay here. I'll get them."

She meant those from the smokehouse. Crews had declared them done some time earlier and doused the coals.

She returned promptly, bringing the spitted fish and the strong scent of the fire. He caught the end of the heavily loaded spit as, crawling in, she tried to extend it with one hand. He hooked its ends into the structure above them.

"I hope that'll hold. As long as it does, we've got a convenient larder. You get hungry, just reach up. Of course, the whole thing might come down on top of us. Or the bear might show up. But I'm counting on the weather to keep him in his own home."

She writhed a little. "With just the right position, this mattress isn't bad. You gave me the equivalent of a ten-inch innerspring."

"And still it won't be enough," Crews said. "It'll be completely flat by morning. I've done that night after night for myself, and never yet have piled them high enough. What I miss most is not roast beef or ice cream or even salt: it's a real bed with a real mattress and sheets and blankets." The fish, with their smoky fragrance, were tantalizing. He finally reached up and pulled one from the spit. "I'm hungry again, after all that work. Help yourself."

"No, thanks. If it keeps raining, we might need them."

He had already eaten half the fish. "You're right. I shouldn't—"

"No," she said hastily. "I didn't mean that. I meant that I'm just not that hungry yet, so I can wait."

He swallowed the remainder of his snack and licked his fingers. "If you do have any criticism of me at any time, don't worry about offending me. Just sound off. Out here a mistake could be deadly. I'm lucky I survived those I made when alone. It was especially tough in the early days. Looking back, I think I was half out of my mind. I would just curl up in a hole somewhere. I couldn't even find the wreck of the plane after a while."

The light was poor inside the shelter. Her face was in shadow. "I've been obsessed with my own troubles ever since we met," she said. "I'm sorry to say I just vaguely remember your mentioning the crash, I think back at the cave."

He related the essentials. "In the first few days a couple of search planes flew over, but I couldn't attract their attention by spelling out messages on the beach. I think one did come after I could make fire, but I didn't have a fire going at that moment and couldn't make one because everything was wet. There haven't been any airplanes since. The only explanation I can think of is that Dick was way off course for some reason. Maybe his instruments failed. I think that can happen by hundreds of miles, eventually. By now I can speak with considerable experience about being lost on land. It must be even easier to do that in the air, especially if there's trouble with the radio. I remember he was yelling into the mike."

"Did you say that was a week or so ago?"

"More like a few weeks," Crews said. "I guess I should have kept a calendar, but I never started one early enough and by now I've really lost track. It was late in May, anyhow."

"*May*? It's almost August now. That's two *months*."

"God almighty, can that be? Then I'm even more lost than I thought, in more ways than one. I don't have any idea where the time could have gone. Building the raft obviously took longer than I was aware, and then I had the eternal job of finding food. I tried making sandals and some other stuff, bow and arrow, et cetera. Maybe I was on the beach, out of it, longer than it seemed. God, *two months*."

"Wait a minute," she said. "I was back in town then. There *was* a plane crash in the news, I think. But there were more than two passengers, as I remember."

"How about *four*? Did I forget? Dick brought along a couple of other passengers, business associates."

"Four. That's possible. A prominent businessman, and his party . . . that's right. But that was over the ocean, or anyway that's my memory of where they were searching for them, along the coast. That's why I didn't make the connection at first. Could that have been your plane?"

The rain had slackened off a bit. The roof thus far had not been penetrated, a fact in which Crews, disturbed by learning of the derangement in a basic sense he had never doubted, that was concerned with the duration of time, tried to take comfort. "Could have been," he answered. "Probably was, if what you say is true. I didn't know we were supposed to be anywhere near the coast, either by design or accident. But then I didn't know anything at all. I was drunk. In fact, I had been more or less consistently drunk for years." No doubt that accounted for his disorientation after the crash: added to everything else, the shock and all, were the effects of the cold-turkey withdrawal from alcohol. "What you say would explain why there hasn't been much of a search around here. We're nowhere near the sea, are we? Do you know?"

"I think it's more than a hundred miles from Fort Judson."

The rain had stopped pattering above them. Looking out the end of the shelter beyond his feet, he could still see as far as the bank of the stream, but the light had begun to fail. That it was so dark inside was due to the dense weave of the roof, which had been mainly Friday's deft work. They were, of course, vulnerable to any enemy, supine, and blind to any approach not from the brook or from that portion of the woods he could see by rolling on his stomach and looking out the end behind his head, which in fact he had not yet done.

"It's really hit me hard, that I lost all track of time."

"But isn't it true of animals that they lack a sense of duration? If you've ever had a dog, you know he hates to be alone as much for five minutes as for all day, and will give you as wild a welcome if you just come back from mailing a letter at the corner as if you returned from a month in Europe. You were just telling me what you've learned from animals. Maybe you acquired their approach to time as well."

"It's something to tell myself, anyhow," said Crews. "Thanks. I used to have a great dog when I was a kid, by the way. A golden retriever named Walt. Thanks too for reminding me. I'm going to get another when I get back. I haven't owned a dog in years. Do you have one?"

"Not since I've lived in a city apartment. But sure, all the way through school, my brother and sisters and I had dogs. Sometimes they were supposed to belong to us all in common, sometimes to individuals, depending on how well we were getting along. We fought a lot, and when we'd be mad at somebody, we were officially mad at their dog too, but in fact never were. We'd actually spoil the other guy's dog to lure its affection away. This never worked. Dogs never turn against any members of the family to which they belong—at least they don't if *every* member spoils them."

The rain returned with a sudden rush. Crews put his fingertips to the boughs above him. He could not really believe that the roof would continue to shed water under this downpour. "I think I developed a block against thinking of the past, though I did it for a while until it just seemed to be weakening me."

"I was just making talk," Friday said.

"God, I welcome it! There was a time when I thought I might never hear another voice. I got used to talking to myself internally, without the responsibility of forming words, let alone connected thoughts. But then my conversation with myself tends to get enmired in one subject alone: my failures. My marriages, my father. I had to read in the paper that he put a gun into his mouth and pulled the trigger. We didn't get along, but that was my doing, not his. There was a lot of other stuff I didn't know, either, until he was dead. Some of it was good. He was a trial lawyer. His best-known clients were mobsters, but he did a whole lot of pro bono work too, for otherwise defenseless people, for no fee whatever, many of whom, unlike me, went to his funeral in tribute, I read, including the poor guy who served nine years in prison for a crime he did not commit, losing his business, home, and wife. My father got him out and sued the state and never took a cent of the big settlement. I never knew at the end my father had cancer of the throat and couldn't talk, and he had had this deep, rich baritone that no jury—and few women—could resist. . . . "

A drop of water struck his head from behind. He rolled over on his belly and looked out the near end of the shelter. A little pool had formed in a slight depression in the earth between the shelter and the encircling drainage trench, and the rain was splashing in it. He was struck on the forehead and in the eye as he watched. But he was relieved to see the pool had not yet extended as far as Friday's side.

"That's what happens when I take my mind off the here and now," he said. "It's coming in over here. I should have made end panels."

He crawled out of the shelter, backward, at just the moment the heavens lost all restraint and poured water down in great shimmering sheets, one of which immediately drenched him. Before he reached the line of woods he was struck twice again. He was searching his soaked pockets when, out of another swirl of wind and rain, Friday appeared.

Her hair was a tight-fitting, sodden cap. She handed him the multipurpose tool, which he had forgotten she had used last.

"You shouldn't have!" he shouted. "Now get back."

"Why? I couldn't get any wetter." She was smiling, water coursing down her face and into her mouth. "You cut. I'll carry."

He worked as fast as he could, though as she had pointed out, there was no need for haste. They were both drenched to the bone, with no means of drying out till the sun returned. He would not even be able to find dry materials from which to make fire by bow and drill. Even if their roof held tight against the cloudburst, they would soak the interior merely by reentering. But it was better to work than to lie passively in wet misery. He cut enough pine boughs to give each an armload.

They piled a supply at the head end of the shelter, then entered, inserting themselves backward, in the prone position, at the foot—which thereby became, and stayed, the head, for they had to close that entrance too against the rain, and to do so otherwise would have required their reversing themselves once inside, so as to reach out and pull up the pine boughs. It was Friday who had the foresight to design this maneuver.

The interior was darker than before, and by now the roof had in fact finally leaked, though not badly, considering the force of the rain. And at least the makeshift mattress, though wet, kept them off the ground. They had both now rolled to the supine.

"I don't see how any roof we could make would hold up perfectly against these conditions," Crews said. "This one's doing a better job than could have been expected." From time to time a drop fell on his face, and if he felt for the spot of penetration and poked around, rearranging the branches so that it was plugged, one or more leaks were thereby created in the area adjoining.

"One more layer," Friday said, "and it would be watertight. I know that now."

"Maybe a steeper pitch," said Crews. "But a certain amount of width would have to be sacrificed, the higher the ridgepole."

"How about making it longer, to compensate, with compartments end to end, railroad-style."

"It wouldn't be as companionable, though."

"That's true."

He stayed silent for a moment and had nothing to hear but the falling water. "Where's it leaking on your side?"

"Here and there. I'm twisted, to avoid what I can."

Crews sat up. "Switch with me. This side's better. There's only a little coming in down by my feet."

"No, thanks," she said. "Certainly not. We're in this together."

"You've still got that wound, haven't you?" He had asked about it when they were building the shelter and had given her the antiseptic can to keep.

"I told you it's coming along fine. Really. It doesn't hurt any more when I move, only if I touch it."

189

"We're stuck here until the rain stops. I never have figured out quite how to handle the problem of bad weather—except in the case of that cave. You know, I went in there to get out of the rain. I never asked you, did you hear me come in in the dark?"

"Of course. For a little while I thought it was him. But then, after the noises stopped, I believed it was some animal, some big animal by the sound of it. I didn't sleep all night. I was terrified. And then when morning came outside, and a little light penetrated, there near the entrance where you were, and I saw you, and I saw that knife near your hand, I got the idea, the crazy idea, he had sent you to kill me. I had a box of matches in my pocket. I had just made a campfire and was going to cook lunch when he began his target practice the day he shot me. I had found a piece of dead wood that I thought I might use to defend myself, and brought it along to the cave. When I first made out your form, I almost panicked and considered beating out your brains before you woke up. Fortunately, I decided I ought to see you better before doing that, and I used up all my matches getting that stick ignited."

The rain ceased to come in gusts and settled down to a steady fall of medium force, but that was worse for the roof, which at least on his side leaked more. He did not mention this or ask about hers, because there could be no help for it.

"Don't forget the fish," he said. "They must be all wet by now. We'll have to dry them out when we can. Otherwise they won't keep long. Of course, we could eat them all."

"I'll have one now," Friday said. It had grown darker outside, which meant he could hardly see her, a foot away. "Here's yours."

He accepted the fish, which had been wetted on but stayed crisp of skin. "I'm still so hungry I find this delicious. But we might think about varying our diet. We could use more bulk, and something starchy if that's possible. Too much protein isn't good for the system. For that matter, some fat would be in order."

She was still eating the same fish. She made more of her food than he did. Thus far he had continued the same gulping that had been his way when alone.

"I'll get on that in the morning," she said.

He bent his neck at another angle, to avoid the water drops that were falling on his forehead. "I think I now have an idea where we got off the right trail. To find it again, we shouldn't have to backtrack too far." New drips had found him, and he moved his head again, this time nearer the center line.

"Why don't we sleep on it?" she said, very near where his face was now, startling him.

He pulled away a little. "Look, I don't want to bring up unhappy memories, but something's been bothering me. *Before* I heard those gunshots, I found a footprint on the side of a cliff. It couldn't have been yours, either one of you. Of course, I don't know how long it had been there."

He waited for her reply, but none came. He felt better for having brought up the question, even if there might never be an answer. He was pleased that she could fall asleep under these conditions. The rain had not stopped but was no longer falling so loudly he could not hear the regular sound of Friday's breathing. He had not *slept* with a woman in ages. He had not slept at all since the night before last, in the cave. He was soaked to the skin, in a universe of dampness, lying on wet boughs above mud, water falling in his face. But he was not alone.

9

■

Heavy rain returned at dawn, and Crews was awakened not by light but by a leak that had gone from drops to a thin but continuous stream of water, which found his face wherever he put it.

Friday's back was to him. If she could continue to sleep under such conditions, good for her. He rolled over onto his stomach and crawled out of the shelter, pushing before him the pine-bough barricade, but before he was all the way out, there she was, sharing the task.

They compared notes on the night. The fact is that he had slept well until so rudely woken up, whereas her sleep had been fitful.

"I would say the leaks were diabolically precise in finding just the places that would disturb me most. But the truth is that there were so many, they couldn't help hitting every target."

"Do you realize," Crews asked, "that you are cruelly dismissing the theory that has always given me solace? That I am the victim of the malicious rain god, or anyway the deity who is supposed to protect all makeshift roofs."

They stood there smiling at each other, being rained on. But the weather was warmer than ever, and since they had been wet for so many hours anyway, he found standing far preferable to lying prone and passive.

Friday wrinkled her nose as the water streamed onto it from her high forehead. "I've been thinking about the firemaking rig. All that really has to be dry is the socket the drill goes into, and of course the tinder. No, I guess the drill too, or its end anyhow, which creates the friction. Maybe we could locate a big fallen tree trunk, or even a stump that's thick enough and not so rotten it's soaked like a sponge. Maybe if we could cut away enough of the wet wood to get down where it would be dry? What do you think?" Somehow, the longer he had known her, the wetter and more bedraggled she was, the more attractive she looked.

"We could try," he said. He was irked with himself for not having the idea. But then how long had he depended solely on the sun, going fireless on gray days, before making the first bow and drill? No phase of woodsmanship had come easily to him.

They had to hike some distance from the campsite to find a suitable fallen tree. The rain came and went all morning, but fell in such volume that the foliage continued to drip abundantly between cloudbursts. When they finally found their log, its wood was the toughest Crews had yet encountered, and he was afraid he might break the knife blade on it.

But finally the parts were fashioned and assembled, and using Friday's shoelace as bowstring, he was about to make fire when she asked, "Can I try that?"

Either this was the best bow and drill yet, or she was a more effective user thereof, for her time in getting a mature flame was half his quickest. Once the tinder was ignited, they added on shreds from the dry inner wood of the log from which they had made the apparatus, and when those were burning well, piled on dead evergreen rubbish with incendiary Christmas-tree needles, then wet but thin branches, and on top of all, several logs thick as his forearm: these last sizzled and steamed when the heat reached them, and did not genuinely catch fire until the fuel underneath had been replenished several times. The absence of rain at the most crucial stages helped enormously, for even though, acting on another idea of

Friday's, they had found even larger flat stones of the kind on which Crews had fried the fish the evening before and built a roofed structure around the fire, it would never have defied a downpour of the cloudburst kind that had made a mockery of their shelter during the night.

Once the rocky surround had been constructed and a small fire was going inside, it was self-evident that they also now had a workable stove, on the broad top slab of which, balanced on uprights Stonehenge-style, food could be cooked. It soon grew so hot that the drops from the occasional drizzle to which the rain had now been reduced evaporated on contact, sometimes so quickly as to leave no steam behind.

"I guess I'll catch some fresh fish," Crews said, glancing around for the pronged spear. "We might as well stay here until we get in better shape for traveling. It feels to me like the rain's going to stay for a while. We ought to take advantage of the interim periods to collect food and also we ought to thatch our roof tighter—if we spend another night here, and in my opinion, better that than to be caught somewhere else without any shelter at all."

"I agree," Friday said, smiling. How she kept her teeth so white under these conditions he could not explain, and was too delicate to ask. Her cheeks glowed, too. Each was discreet about hygiene, going into the woods or to the stream, depending on the purpose. He had washed various parts of himself the day before, but did not have her stomach for full immersion in the icy brook.

"Just where did you leave the spear? I'm going to give your technique a try."

She pointed past the sodden black-and-gray ashes of the campfire of the day before. "I thought it was over there. I could have sworn I brought it back, but maybe it's down by the rapids."

"Okay. I'm going there. . . . We might think about making a drying rack for our clothes, only not too close to the fire."

He walked along the bank of the stream. Even the drizzle

had ceased by now, but the sky still looked heavy with water, as if any provocation, a thunderclap or lightning bolt, might cause it to rupture and drop more. The ground was spongy-slick when there was grass and elsewhere muddy, squishing between his toes, but turned to grit and gravel as it sloped to meet the rocky, swift-watered, swirling shallows. No spear was in evidence. He returned to the campsite.

"It probably got into the water somehow while we were stringing up the fish. It's reached the lake by now." Friday was stoking the fire. He asked her for the tool. "I'll cut another."

She frowned, pushing back her hair. "I could have sworn . . ." She produced the implement from the back pocket of the jeans.

"You're continuing to use the antiseptic, right?"

"Of course." She grinned, an expression he was seeing for the first time.

"I feel responsible for you."

"I know you do. . . . How long would you say it's been since we got the ingredients together for the meal yesterday? That would have been late afternoon, right? And now it's midmorning."

"Yeah," Crews said. "More or less. Why does the time mean so much?"

She poked at the fire with a long stick. It was not green, and the tip caught fire almost immediately. She let it burn. "You're going to be angry again, as you were when I brought the mushrooms back. . . . I ate some of them, and—"

"You *didn't!*" he cried. "Aw, for God's sake . . . "

"That was back when I first found them. If they were toxic, wouldn't I have felt it by now? It must be eighteen hours ago."

"How would I know? For God's sake," he repeated. "What happens if the poison just takes longer to act?"

"I'll die," she said. "I know that. I knew that when I ate them. I'm not that attached to living, any more."

"Don't say that." He shook his head violently. "It isn't *right.*"

"It may not be right, but it's true." She plunged the burning

195

stick farther into the flames and left it there. "You have to allow me my defiance, which I've bought and paid for. It's not against you. You're a good person, a fine man. But I tell you what I wish: I wish that Michael's aim had been better. I could easily stand being dead, but I don't know what to do with a superficial wound."

"I won't protest further," Crews said. "I suddenly remember what people used to say to me when I was drinking, people who cared about me. I don't know what to say that wouldn't sound like them, and I found what they said unbearable, because of course it was true. But it's not true that everything true is *necessarily* unbearable. I used to believe it was, but I was wrong. I was dead wrong. Now I'm right because I'm alive, not because I'm wise or good. I grant your privilege to not care whether you live or die, but my business is survival. If you stay with me, I'm going to restrain you by any means at my disposal from doing something self-destructive. You say it wouldn't reflect on me, but it would. I won't put up with it. If you don't agree, then don't be here when I get back."

He was genuinely furious. He saw no good reason why the mushrooms could even yet be called harmless. He could not think of her sickening and dying, and still he could think of nothing else. She was addicted to the man who tried to kill her. The phenomenon was not unknown. He hoped she would be gone when he returned.

He roamed amid a forest containing hundreds of trees of all species, from lofty masts to midget saplings, and could not find a single one with the configuration of branches required to make a spear of the sort that Friday had wielded so profitably. With every problem to which she had thus far applied herself, she had done better than he, but then she was obviously a lot smarter. But that was small distinction. The only one of his wives he even approached in intelligence was Michelle, and then probably only when she was stoned. But there had been a day when each was fond of him.

He tripped on exposed roots, and was savagely whipped in

the face by wet branches. He trod painfully on pine cones. He was losing his woodsmanship, regressing to the spirit of his early days at the lake. His own survival was now one with hers. He had failed to save his companions in the fallen airplane. If he failed her as well . . .

He stopped and looked about him. He was lost again. The disorientation was now to the third power: after the crash he had been lost to the world; then they had got lost while searching for the river; now this, at the limits of absurdity. There could be no fourth stage but to perish.

He tried to remember what he could of the terrain as it affected him physically. Where had he been whipped by the recoiling branches, with a spray of droplets? What had been the sequence underfoot? The thick, wet leaf mold, then the pine cones, the moss in the shadow of the fallen tree with rotten bark, the rocky outcropping, the area at which the level ground began gently to slope upward.

He climbed another two hundred yards through thick woods, more in hope than in the sense that the long hill would soon reach its crest. Then all at once he had reached the last line of trees, beyond which there seemed to be nothing but air. He emerged from the forest to stand on a ridge from which he could see the water, far away in the valley below. He was so high above and distant from the lake that it appeared narrower than he had ever known it to be, and also of a different texture or hue . . . unless it was another lake altogether, or the river that in fact it was, as he recognized in the next instant. Nor was it so far away, probably no more than half a mile.

He had found the river. The discovery should have inspired exultation, but there could be little under the circumstances. Nor was he lost. His trail back would be easy to follow, given the damp ground over which he had traveled. There had been places so spongy that his tracks had filled with water as soon as his feet left them. It was simply that he did not want to return to the campsite and find she was dead or missing. He should have offered her better alternatives. He should have made it clear that he would not forsake her for any cause whatever. If his purpose was to dissuade her from self-damage, he had been quite as negative as she. In so doing he had withdrawn the protection he had furnished, which, aside from managing to keep alive for these weeks, was his sole achievement as a man.

He arrived at an awful explanation for the disappearance of the fishing spear she had used the day before: her husband had found them, had confiscated the potential weapon, had lain in concealment until Crews went into the woods.

He began to run. He did not trip now nor get lashed by low-hanging branches. He was swift and sure, and half the route was downhill. In the light of the new menace, he accepted her argument about the mushrooms: if she had felt nothing untoward in eighteen hours, then they probably were not poisonous. It might still have been foolish to risk eating them, but that was not his worry now. He must return to the campsite as quickly as possible, but when he got near he must do so with stealth. Not only was the man armed with a pistol, but he was apparently some sort of athlete. It had not mattered when a drunken Crews got the worst of brawls he had instigated: nothing was at stake. But this was a battle he must not lose.

When he had come within a quarter mile of the camp he paused to cut and trim a sapling an inch and a half in diameter and about a foot shorter than he was tall. To its end, with the fishing line from his pocket, he lashed the tool fast, its knife blade extended and locked open by means of a tiny wedge of wood. He now had a weapon. He had left to find a spear that would catch a fish and returned with one that could kill a man.

He could smell the campfire when he was still some distance from it: he was upwind, the superior position as to sound as well as scent, which might determine who was prey and who the hunter. When he got close enough, he stole from tree to tree, careful not to step where he might make noise.

Finally he could see most of the site. Friday had built the

198

clothes-drying rack near the fire, and on it were all of her few garments, including the shirt he had given her. And he could see the woman herself, alive and obviously unmenaced, or anyway her upper half, placidly bathing in the stream, white in the swirling water, pale against the dark woods beyond the opposite bank.

He was not embarrassed to find his fears unjustified, but he would have been disconcerted had she known of his presence now. He returned to the woods, and scarcely had he done so when he saw a hearty sapling with precisely the sort of tri-forked crotch he had looked for earlier. He dismantled the man-spear and, with the saw and knife blade of the tool, fashioned an implement for the catching of fish.

When he arrived at the clearing, Friday was sitting near the fire, drying her hair with spread fingers. She was wearing only his knitted shirt, which looked still somewhat damp but was long enough, her legs arranged as they were, to cover her decently.

"That looks like a good one," she said, her head angled so that her hair hung free on one side.

"It took me forever to find." He bided his time for the dramatic news.

"I got the chance to dry my stuff out. As long as it was wet anyway, I washed it first. I grabbed this when I heard you coming. It's not quite dry. I didn't want to put it so close it would burn." She straightened her head. "I'd be glad to do your clothes, maybe a piece or two at a time. It's warm enough."

"As it turns out, I wasn't as far off the trail as I thought." He pointed in the direction from which he had come. "A mile, mile and a half. Up a long slope, thickly wooded, but at the top it's clear, and from there you can see the river."

She took her fingers from her hair. "You saw it."

"I thought it was the lake at first. It's the river, all right, too big for a trout stream. Unless there's another sizable waterway in these parts, that's the one you came down from Fort Judson."

She was still staring at where he had pointed, though there was nothing to be seen but woods. She turned. "I know we could make the roof watertight if we did enough work. And the same thing is true with food. If that deer we saw gets enough to grow as big as a person, and the bear you told me about, who is bigger and fatter, I'm sure, there should be plenty to eat if we really look for it."

"Which reminds me," said Crews. "I'll bet you didn't throw the rest of those mushrooms away yesterday. Let's eat them now, to celebrate."

Her expression was both contrite and modestly triumphant, according to whether one looked at her eyes or her eyebrows. She was smiling with her lips. "I can't promise that a wait of twenty hours is enough! Maybe the poison takes longer to act. How could I know?"

"Who cares," Crews said. "We're a community. Think of its being the last on earth, as in one of those phony movies about the world after a nuclear war."

She scowled. "I don't think I ever saw any."

"We'll eat," he said. "Then we'll make plans, now that we know where we are situated geographically, more or less."

"The mushrooms are behind that big rock over there. . . . Oh, not that it matters now that you've made a nice spear of your own, but I found mine behind the hut. I am sorry you had to go to all that extra trouble."

"But that's the only reason why I found the river," Crews said brightly. "I never would have looked for it in that direction." He rubbed his hands together in a gesture he had rarely if ever used. He was startled by how hard-leathery his palms felt, and in fact sounded. "Let's eat."

He fetched the mushrooms and impaled them, three at a time, on the tines of the new spear and grilled them over coals at the edge of the fire. They would probably have been very good if eaten with knife and fork at a table. Here, plucked hot from the spit, they were celestial fare. He tried to recall some of the gastronomic jargon from his days with Ardis, then applied to cèpes and chanterelles, but drew a blank. Even his more recent life in civilization now felt as remote as if it had been not banally lived but rather exotically imagined.

"These are marvelous." He offered Friday the latest smoking spearful. "Take more. There are still lots here." He shook his head at her, as if in reproach. "You had a hidden supply. All I saw yesterday was a handful. You suspected I might resist?"

"I gathered more while you were gone just now. They're right inside the woods over there. A little farther along are a whole lot of those onions, too."

"Nice place," Crews said, chewing. He fitted more mushrooms on the long fork. "Now that it's stopped raining." He nodded at the stream. "Maybe that's a tributary of the river, and does not flow toward the lake. Though you can never tell theoretically. I've learned my lesson. Nature can't be trusted. For all I know, this stream could take a major turn somewhere along the line and head for neither river nor lake. Better play it safe and take the overland route. It's partly uphill and very likely the longest way, but at least I know where it goes."

Friday had retained her civilized manners. She held a mushroom in two fingers and ate it with more than one bite. "I saw a plump bird I think was maybe a grouse—somebody once gave one to my dad. I would be a sissy about killing it, but I wouldn't have any scruples against cooking and eating it under these conditions. In town I practically live on chicken. I can't see the moral difference."

"There isn't any," Crews said. "And we've been slaughtering as many fish as we can find, exchanging their lives to keep ours. I just have to figure out a way to get a bird, that's all. Even if I could make a decent bow and arrows, I think it would be only luck if I hit anything." He offered her the penultimate mushroom and ate the last himself. "I killed the rabbit with a club, but I had to lie in wait forever. When it came time to perform the act, I did it readily enough as if I had been killing warm-blooded creatures all my life." He immediately regretted saying as much, but it was too late.

"That's how it seemed with Michael when he turned the gun on me," Friday said. "As if it were routine. I keep remembering that." She controlled herself and put a hand on his forearm. "I didn't mean—"

"I know you didn't." He put his hand over hers and kept it there. "You meant you never had seen that side of him."

"If it could be called that, his Mr. Hyde mode, but I think it's something else, the lack thereof, but of what? Decency? Humanity? Anyway, it's not the positive quality of evil. Mr. Hyde could not exactly be called a weakling, could he?"

She was still trying to love the man. Crews knew something about that tendency in women, which was probably maternal. He had seen it in his mother, and in fact, at least at first, in all his wives. "Maybe not," he said. "But as I recall, it was Dr. Jekyll who won out in the end. Was it not he who killed Hyde?"

Friday withdrew her hand from under his and glared at him, but he was not the focus of her anger. "If I could once admit that my husband is nothing more than a criminal, there might be some hope for me."

Crews could not have put it better himself, but he was glad not to have done so. He rose to his feet. "Now that we've dined so sumptuously, I'm not going to fish right away. Instead, I believe I'll work on the shelter walls. We'll be spending at least another night here, don't you think? I'm sure it will rain again before morning."

"We should stay long enough to get a supply of food to take with us," Friday said firmly.

"I hadn't thought of that," Crews said, though of course he had. He hesitated. "You turned out to be right about the mushrooms. But please don't take any more avoidable risks. It's your right to do with yourself what you will, even to throw your life away, and it's probably preferable to do that all at once rather than stretch it out, the way I did for so long. But until we get out of here, I *need* you. I couldn't make it alone."

He did not want to offend her, and therefore sought to lighten his statement. "Could I have found the river without getting mad at you?"

She responded in the same tone. "But if I hadn't taken an unnecessary risk, you wouldn't have gotten mad and gone off in the first place."

"Go ahead, use your unfair advantage in logic. But can you grow as ugly a beard as me?"

"It's not ugly," said Friday. "It's the height of woodland fashion, and you know it. You cut a dashing figure. When you get back, the youth of America will throw away their shoes and go everywhere barefoot."

"And tattered seersucker and stained chinos will become the rage. I've finally accomplished something."

Friday stopped joking. "The fact is, you have. And you ought to take pleasure in it and stop brooding about me. I won't let you down. I promise." She got up and, as he turned away, put on the rest of her clothing, which she said was not altogether dry but at least was not singed. It also smelled of woodsmoke. "But that will be a nice memory on days we can't have a fire."

Crews spoke in earnest. "That's our biggest deficiency. Not even the bow and drill works when the parts are wet."

"We could build a kind of oven, a more elaborate version of the arrangement of rocks you used for the Japanese-style fish. The front part would be roofed over with the biggest flat stone we could haul here." She gestured. "Mounted on stone walls, stuck together with mud?"

"Clay would be better, if there's any around. I might look upstream, where the banks are higher. Each fire we built inside would harden it. Leave space at the back for the smoke to escape, or even build a little chimney. We could keep the fire banked, so it would never go out entirely during the night or if we were away from the campsite for long." He frowned at her. "The perfect idea. Trouble is, it wouldn't be portable, and we'd have to stay here to use it."

Friday shrugged and abruptly turned away. "Let's get going on the shelter."

"Hey," Crews said, "what about your shoes and socks?"

"Not dry enough yet. Besides, I ought to toughen up."

"How does the wound look today?" He had seen only her right profile when she was bathing in the stream.

"Fine. I'm beginning to worry now that I won't even have a scar to show."

"To the police?"

"No," she said. "I don't care about that. I meant, to show to myself as a souvenir of my happy marriage."

After some experimentation they decided that elaborate interweaving of the panels of the shelter, such as they both had envisioned, would never result in a surface that was absolutely watertight, and that their purpose would be better served by piling on pine boughs to three times the previous thickness, and making sure they were all aligned so that a drop of water might find it more natural continuously to run along them to the ground than to find an interstice through which to fall inside.

"If we were going to stay for any length of time," Crews said, "we could cut shingles from bark. I'd do it now if there were any birches around. But this is one area where I haven't seen any. Other kinds of bark are much thicker and harder to deal with."

Friday stood back to survey the results of their efforts, which had been strenuous, for the weightier walls had required the building of a sturdier frame.

Crews had left the final touches to her while with sharpened sticks he gouged out a deeper drainage ditch than the shallow furrow of the night before, which had overflowed during the heaviest downpour. "We need some poles to lean against the windward side," he said, raising his eyes. "They'll hold the thatch in place. That's another thing I've learned to do, to notice the wind. Storms usually come from the same direction, but there are a lot of variations with the normal breezes, and that's of concern because of how scents travel. It's always better to have them coming toward you whether you are prey or hunter. But on water, if you're trying to catch the wind in a sail, completely different laws apply—*look out!*"

He was too late. She had taken still another step backward at a point at which he had deepened the trench, which still was too narrow to accept a foot at right angles to it, so her heel went in while her toes were forced back unnaturally close to her ankle. She fell, her leg folding under her, the toes now turning to fit the trench longitudinally and so relieving their bend, but the damage had been done to her foot, and now the ankle and even her knee were twisted.

When Crews helped her up she could not put weight on her right leg. He lifted her in his arms. She was lighter than he expected. He carried her near the fire, where she first tried again to stand before being lowered to a sitting position on the ground.

She shook her head at him. "And you say *you* need *my* help!"

"As much as ever," he said. "This could just as easily have happened to me. Thank God it didn't: you're easier to carry than I would be."

She gingerly felt her extended right leg, wincing in anticipation, grimacing when her fingers reached her knee. "I maybe broke or tore something here, and my foot hurts too much to touch. *Damn it.* Of all things to happen."

"What can I do for you?" Crews asked.

"You ought to leave me here."

"You could blame me for not reminding you of the trench." He squatted next to her. "It's nobody's fault, and it doesn't have to change anything. I'll make you a crutch to get around on, and if we decide to head for the river before you feel better, I can carry you at least part of the way, horseback-style. If we find the canoe, well and good. If not, I'll make another raft." He stood up. "Or we can just stay until you can walk normally. We were just saying what a nice place this is."

"And I'm not totally incapacitated," Friday said earnestly.

"There's lot of things I can do sitting down: preparing food if you provide it, keeping the fire going, drying or smoking stuff." She looked around. "Would you mind handing me my left shoe and one sock? I won't be wearing the others for a while."

He brought them to her. "I think we should use splints to keep your knee and ankle from moving and making the damage worse. It's probably a sprain or torn ligaments. At least we don't have to set any broken long bones."

She pulled on the sock and grimaced. "I'm not all that fragile! You should have known me when—" She caught herself. "Sorry. You don't need any more of my whining."

"But I haven't heard *any*," said Crews. "You're the one who knows karate. Your good leg is probably still a lethal weapon."

He went into the trees before he said more. He had been almost at the point of confessing that he was in love with her, but she might have taken such a declaration as a response to her vulnerability, and perhaps it was. Crews did not understand himself since he had become honorable.

10

■

FRIDAY'S FOOT HAD TURNED BLACK BEFORE
the day was out. Crews built the splint arrangement only
around the knee, and since any other kind of fastening might
have been uncomfortable against her skin, he used strips torn
from the bottom of his T-shirt.

Employing the Y-topped crutch, she was more mobile than
she probably should have been. He performed the longer-
distance chores, the fetching of materials, the fishing, and the
collection of edible vegetables, but she did the cooking, much
of the on-site work of home improvement, and the laundering
of clothes. She displayed unfailing good humor. She was even
amused to reflect that this was as domestic as she had ever
been: in town, she and her husband had eaten most meals in
restaurants or by takeout.

In fact, though she apparently did not suspect as much,
Friday was not much of a cook under the prevailing conditions, tending either to overdo fish by whatever method or, if
using a spit, to burn it. She was better at construction work.
Sitting on the ground, bad leg extended, she fashioned doors
for either end of the shelter, Crews having provided the
branches and boughs and also some long tough grasses to use
as lashings, the fishline supply having dwindled to what might
be needed for its proper purposes. Friday's finished products,

intricate grillworks of intertwined twigs, evergreen foliage plugging the interstices, were neatly framed to fit the triangular openings.

Once the doors had been hung in place on hinges of twisted grass, and been much admired by her companion, she applied herself to the matter of better-designed beds.

"The same thing that was done with the doors," she said, "only with heavier stuff: a frame, crisscrossed with branches, supported off the ground on little Y-shaped stakes driven into the earth. The platforms can be crude so long as they're sturdy enough to bear the weight. On top we'll pile the same boughs we used before, but we'll be off the ground."

This work took several days. A moderate rain fell the first night of the new roof and not a drop penetrated to the interior, but it had not yet been tested in a real downpour. Then came a period of sunshine of such heartiness that after a while it seemed eternal. Fire could be made on demand with the magnifying mirror, and after a few sunny days everything inflammable had thoroughly dried.

In his rovings, Crews had at last found a cluster of birches, and from the bark Friday had made several vessels in which water could be fetched and drunk or used for cooking. They ate more fish, mushrooms, and wild onions, but the supplies of the last two were diminishing, and they both would have welcomed another main course than the first. Crews had eaten little else since the crash. So when he had filled the last of Friday's orders for building materials, he applied himself to the matter of diet.

"There used to be a guy who made a name for himself by finding edible things in the great outdoors. Do you remember him, and if so, anything he said? I guess it's too early in the year for nuts and even fruits: anyway, I haven't found any."

"Yeah," Friday said, "I think I do, but I was a kid then. . . . But wait a minute: you can make tea from pine needles."

"That's not what killed Socrates, was it?"

"Hardly. At least it didn't hurt my brother and me, though

208

we didn't like it much. But what did we know? We didn't like mussels either, nor even asparagus, and all kinds of other stuff."

"Your family will be looking for you now."

"It hasn't been that long yet. They all live in different parts of the country, and I sometimes don't get in touch for months."

He and she were lying side by side in the dark, in the new and improved lean-to. This had become their time for the conversation they could not always find room for during their daylight labors. "Dick Spurgeon's family and those of the other two fellows must be suffering," Crews said, "not knowing what happened. But maybe it's better that they continue to hope than know the truth. I'm not eager to get back with the bad news. I've got nobody of my own. That's not self-pity but simply a fact. I guess my next of kin are some cousins, but they cut me off years ago, for the best reasons."

"Michael's got nobody, either," Friday said. "He was raised in foster homes. He wouldn't talk about his parents. Maybe he never knew them. He made something of himself, you can't take that away from him. He got athletic scholarships for college, then he worked at a series of crappy coaching jobs before he could get the health club off the ground."

Crews writhed whenever he had to hear about her husband but was certain that any negative response of his own, however sympathetic to her, would be misguided. "Why don't we try the pine-needle tea tomorrow? I haven't had a hot drink since I got here."

Friday was quiet for a while. Then she asked, "Do you dream?"

"Once in a while I do, and it's almost always about food. But the details are sometimes odd. What I'm eating in the dream, with great relish, might be something I never cared for: chicken livers, for example, or shredded raw carrots."

"I don't dream at all," said Friday. "Not once. Never. I always used to dream a lot. I even had nightmares on occasion.

What's funny is that it seemed to happen when I was happiest, or thought I was."

He was sorry to hear this. He had begun to entertain the simpleminded hope that she was as happy now as he, and that her reluctance to leave their home behind was not based on physical infirmity. "It's the law of compensation," he told her. "If you've had a living nightmare, you don't need the make-believe for a while." What he did not mention was the possibility that she had had unconscious premonitions of disaster. She could live in a dreamless present now because she was looked after by someone who would lay down his life for her.

"Tomorrow I'm going to finally finish the spoon." She had been whittling at the utensil whenever he could spare the knife. "Should I start a second one or next try a fork? With one complete set, we could share them."

"The fork," Crews said. "Remember, my offer stays good. Anytime you feel like starting for the river, I can carry you piggyback."

"It won't be much longer." She had been saying that for a good week. The discoloration was fading from her foot, but to his observation she was as disabled as ever.

"I hope I did right in immobilizing your knee that way." He had finally removed the splints. "You don't think that made it worse?"

"Oh, no. I wouldn't be as far along as I am."

"Maybe you should try bending it a little. Hot compresses might help. It can't be right to let it stiffen up from disuse."

"It's getting better, really."

"I'm not in a hurry to get going," Crews assured her. "You must never think that."

"I don't," Friday said.

They exchanged good nights, but he stayed awake for a while. It was one of those nights that were so quiet he could hear each of her breaths.

Next morning he rose first, as usual, and went into the woods to relieve himself. With so much space available, this

210

still seemed preferable to fashioning a fixed latrine. He took his morning bath in the stream, the chilly waters of which he had never gotten used to. He was less modest than he had been earlier on, but that was mostly due to Friday's discretion in staying inside until he was done—to do which she had to look out eventually, and when he was late in drying himself and dressing, she probably saw him naked, as he so frequently had seen her. He never got really dry, because he had no proper towel, but he scraped off with the edge of his hand such visible drops as he could reach and walked about in the air, which was now usually warm and not humid.

He filled one of their birch-bark vessels with water and started a fire. By the time the water had come to a boil, Friday had limped about on her morning rituals, the forked crutch in her armpit, after which she gathered pine needles.

The tea on first sip was weaker than Crews had anticipated, so he let it steep longer, after which it was rather stronger than he wished, though the steaming liquid, only faintly colored, looked like so much hot water.

"Sort of like witch hazel."

Friday was not so quick to abuse the decoction. "I think it takes getting used to."

His third sip was more potable and less astringent, so perhaps she was right, and the warmth of the drink was ingratiating. He toasted her with his birch-bark cup. But she was preoccupied. "Are you still worried about not dreaming?"

"I didn't sleep that well," she said, holding her own cup in two hands. "I know I haven't fooled you: my leg has been okay for some time. It's another of those things I haven't been able to admit to myself."

"But you're doing it now."

"In words only. If I keep the crutch in place, I can actually put all my weight on the leg, and I can bend my knee all right, though it's a little stiff from lack of use. But I have to keep hold of the crutch, though not for support. I just have to know it's there."

"You've tried to walk without it?"

"I fell down."

He got to his feet and reached for her. She pulled herself up with the help of his hand. The crutch lay on the ground. "Leave it there. Start walking on both legs. You can always grab me."

Fingertips against his upper arm, she gingerly imposed weight on her right foot, which was still bare, though the inflammation had faded to a shadow. Crews had slipped his arm back to a position from which he could swoop it around her waist in an instant should she fall, an event that would not have made him despair, even though the exercise was his idea. But then he was at odds with himself in all that concerned Friday, whom he wanted to rescue but also to keep a kind of prisoner.

She walked carefully, no longer touching him, both hands out for balance. "I'm doing it," she said softly. She still had a slight limp, but that was due to the running shoe and sock on her left foot. Turning to smile at Crews, she faltered but did not fall. Nevertheless, he seized her in the crook of his elbow, with such force that she was lifted off the ground. He lowered her as quickly.

"Sorry," she said. "My knee's a little stiff." They resumed walking.

"I just thought of this," Crews said. "If that outfitter at Fort Judson rents out canoes, then other people than you and—" He refused to name her husband. "Other camping parties must sometimes come down the river."

"There was supposed to be a party that left the day before us," said Friday.

"It's likely we'll see some other people before we're on the river long. This should be the heart of the camping season."

Friday halted abruptly and stared at him. "Do you think he's still looking for me?"

"I wouldn't know. I stopped worrying about it after the first few days."

Tears welled from her eyes, and her shoulders were heav-

212

ing. Crews put both arms around her. Against his chest she said, "Maybe it was an accident. He wasn't deliberately trying to shoot me. He just turned with the gun in his hand and it went off. I panicked and ran, and he chased me not to do me harm but to catch me before I got lost in the woods. After all, he didn't shoot me again. He could have, but he didn't. He would have if he wanted me dead."

"I thought I heard two shots," Crews said. "I suppose the second could have been the echo of the first. I was on the lake at the time, and sounds are funny near water." Bolstering her new theory did not serve his own cause, but he would do what he could to assuage her pain, because not only did he love her but he had come to have some grasp on what that love entailed.

"I couldn't stand to have him arrested," Friday said.

"You're not serious?" Crews continued to enclose her supple body.

"It would just be my word against his."

"For God's sake, you're the one with the wound."

"It wasn't anyplace vital."

He hugged her more ardently. "It can't be right to let him—"

"But what would be gained if we went through some legal mess?"

"A would-be killer might be put away for a while."

Friday stepped just far enough back to look at him through accusatory blue eyes, she who had seemingly been about to pardon the real criminal. "You have to understand we're talking about somebody who's basically a helpless weakling."

Crews nodded. "Forgive me, but I really have to say this: you once saw something in him."

"There's nothing to be proud about," said Friday, "but I'm not ashamed either. I found him attractive! It's always hard to explain why to anyone else. He's handsome and he knew more than I did about something I was interested in learning at that time, and he seemed interested in and attracted to me, and—"

"Reasons enough," Crews said hastily. He was scarcely in a position from which to contest such points. What his wives had first seen in him would have been difficult to specify. He had brought the matter up only to dispose of it. Mutual attractions can seldom bear the scrutiny of persons uninvolved, whereas aversions are often immediately obvious to all. His resentment of a man better-looking and more physically fit than himself was so natural as to be impersonal.

"But what if he is stalking you, or us?"

"He isn't," she said firmly. "I was a coward for a while, but I realize now he wouldn't take *you* on."

"He stole my fishing tackle."

"You weren't there at the time." She shook her head. "He's gone back and told his own version, that the shooting was an accident and that I ran away and got lost."

"You're beginning to believe that now yourself," said Crews.

"So be it." She smiled sadly. "Maybe it's even true. He'll lead in a rescue expedition. He'll try to put a good face on it and maybe hope even to emerge as a sort of hero."

"But how could he count on you not to accuse him of attempted murder? This change of heart is new even to me."

"He knows me," Friday said. "I have to admit that. He knows in the end I always give him the benefit of the doubt on anything that pertains to his manhood."

"I've been counting on that myself," Crews said, and though pretending to levity he was serious enough.

"Your quality is not in doubt," she said tenderly. "People don't fuss over those who are strong! What a tiresome companion I've been! I think I've finally got it all straight. I'll do better now, I promise."

Crews was aware that he should be man enough to accept prestige gracefully, but he was still too new to it. "Good! Except when I'm hunting, I intend to lounge about camp while you do the menial chores. Isn't that the way the human race started out?" He could not keep the joke going. "You don't know about me. I'm almost forty and I've never really had a job. I've been married three times. I was drunk for years, and I lost all the money I ever had, none of which was earned. I don't understand how I was able to hang on out here by myself, but it was just barely. I instinctively saved myself in the plane crash. I didn't deliberately let the others drown—if they were still alive after the impact—but I was no help to them. It's only since meeting you that I've had any sense that I'm doing more than just keeping alive only because it is natural to fight against ceasing to exist."

"That's only what *you* say," Friday said, linking arms with him. "How would I know what truth is in it? Anyway, that's the past."

"But what's the future? What will I do when I get back?"

She sighed happily. "Write a book about how you survived here! Come on, let's celebrate by taking a walk down to the fishing hole."

"I've never done anything like that." Yet he felt exultant. "I guess I could tell it to somebody, who would do the actual—"

"No," said Friday. "That's not like you."

"The fact is, it's exactly like me. I'm trying to be realistic." She had succeeded in overcoming his initial restiveness and getting him in motion, but she still had to pull him along. "What I did here was an alternative to perishing. I was forced into it. What compulsion would I have back in town? It will be hard enough to keep off the booze."

She stepped in front of him. "I'll be there, won't I? You won't be able to let me down. *I'm a witness*: I know what you stand for."

He had never heard a statement like that from anybody his life long. He could only assume that her judgment was still quite as faulty as when she selected the ineffable Michael for a mate, and Crews was almost too devoted to her well-being to let her do it again; but not quite.

"Do you mind my asking where your husband will be, if you won't send him to jail?"

"Just because I don't intend to press charges," Friday said, "doesn't mean I intend to stay married to him."

They continued walking downstream, past the rapids, to an area where the banks gained in height as the water became less turbulent. During his weeks in the wilderness Crews had developed an attentiveness to practicalities that was unaffected by emotional preoccupations. At the moment his feelings were in what otherwise might have been a turmoil, yet he did not fail to notice a promising striation in the side of the bank beneath them.

He knelt and reached down. "Look at this." He held up a sample for Friday's inspection. "This feels like clay to me."

She rubbed it between her index finger and her thumb. "I only remember the stuff we had as kids. This is the wrong color, but the texture seems right."

He wiped his fingers on some weedy vegetation and ripped up a sheaf for her. "We can making things with that. Cups and plates, to go with your wooden silverware. If I get really ambitious, I think I could make that oven. Then we could bake and roast things. We might try some roots. Roasting's a sophisticated culinary technique. It might make all the difference."

She had taken his arm again. "Now that you've found the route out of here, you're in no hurry to use it."

"The hurry was for your sake," Crews said. "But I'm beginning to understand: you're going to let your husband stew in his own juice for a while. He won't know whether you're dead or alive, or what you'll say when found." He squeezed her hand between his elbow and ribs. "I was afraid, there for a few moments, that you were going to forgive him."

"I'm going to do my best to forgive him," said Friday, "at least for our time here." She lifted her face to take the sun on its fine surfaces. She closed her eyes and sniffed. "Rain is on its way."

Crews raised his nose. "Damned if I can smell it."

"Even though there's not a cloud in the sky."

"Are you making fun of me?"

"Only if it turns out I'm wrong," Friday said, swinging around to face him with sparkling eyes. "But we've still got time before it comes to improve our house, put on those birch-bark shingles. And you probably can even get the clay oven built. You know, a fire could be kept going in it throughout all kinds of weather."

"You won't be wrong," said Crews. "Sooner or later it always rains."

"When it does, we'll be nice and snug." She was laughing in the sunlight.

They walked to a point at which the woods swung away in favor of a sun-drenched meadow.

"My God," Friday cried. "Don't tell me those are blackber-ries!"

Her eyes were sharper than Crews's own for the middle distances. She ran ahead, and had plucked a handful by the time he arrived. She popped one in his mouth.

The berry was an explosion of sweetness against his palate. "They're at their peak," he said, accepting another from her and speaking through it. "And look at all the bushes. It's this whole part of the field!"

Friday had removed her denim jacket and was using it as a receptacle for the gathering of fruit. Crews helped fill it, but both were gobbling down more than they saved.

"After all," Friday said, chortling with berry-stained lips, "the only breakfast we had was that awful tea."

"I thought you liked it."

"I didn't want to hurt your feelings."

Crews groaned through a mouthful of blackberries. "The tea was *your* idea."

"It was?" Her eyes were disingenuously wide. "I could have sworn . . . " An insect had followed her latest handful of fruit, and in shooing it away from her face, she crushed a berry against her cheek. She mugged at Crews. "I must be painted like a clown."

He thought her more beautiful than ever. "Is my beard stained?"

"Not nearly enough!" She smeared him with her red hands.

He cupped a palm, scooped some loose berries from her jacket, and threatened her with them.

She screeched like a schoolgirl. "You wouldn't *dare.*"

"You're right. I wouldn't." He threw the berries back.

Friday's face fell. "I'm okay now," she said softly. "You don't have to take it easy on me."

"It's not you . . . "

"All of a sudden you're sad," said Friday. "Is there anything I can do?"

"I'm happier than I can ever remember being," he said. "I want you to know that, because it has to do with you. I'm sad because I can't just stay here being happy until we run out of berries or the weather gets so bad we can't protect ourselves from it—winter will come eventually—or until you get enough of my company. I really have to think of the families of those men on the airplane. It was self-serving to say they are better off in their ignorance. I ought to stop telling myself such lies." He paused. "Unless I go back, it might be years before the plane is found. Those bodies should be recovered."

"Of course. I always knew that."

"You did?"

"That's the kind of man you are." She quickly pushed some berries into his mouth. "Now don't say anything else on the subject. We know what we're going to do tomorrow. Let's make the most of what we have here today."

Ever since arriving in the wilderness, Crews had gone to bed when night came and, except for bears, mosquitoes, or bad weather, remained asleep until dawn, for a natural reason: without artificial interference, the human being is a diurnal animal. But on this last night in their home camp, he and Friday stayed near the glowing embers of the fire until the only natural illumination was a thin slice of moon amid a vast sparkling dome of stars.

He pointed to a constellation that was exceptionally vivid this evening. It was the only one he could identify. "Would you look at the Big Dipper? It's unmistakable. The two stars that make up the leading edge of the receptacle point directly at that bright one out there. That's the North Star, as everybody knows."

"I didn't, as it happens," said Friday, resting her tilted head on his shoulder, so as to study the heavens more comfortably.

"Well, I've known it since I was a kid. I think I saw it in the comics, not the ones with stories but those that inform you of certain facts, like what makes the tail of a comet, and so on. I remembered some other stuff about natural indicators of direction: moss tends to grow on the north side of trees and the bark is thicker, but there are so many exceptions to the rule, depending on other factors, that you can't really trust such things. But the North Star is never wrong. And I forgot to stay up and look for it when I was lost!"

"Would it have made much difference?" Friday asked, nestling her warm head against his neck.

"None, when I was on my own. But I would have found the river sooner when you and I were looking for it."

"But then we wouldn't have made this nice place."

"You're right," he said. "What do you think—when we've both done what we have to do, should we come back for a visit?"

"That won't be possible," Friday said. "Once the news is out, this will be a popular camping spot."

"I won't tell how to get here."

She sat up, his arm falling to her waist. "You're going to be a celebrity, whether you like it or not. You won't be allowed to keep any secrets."

"Especially since this can be called a love nest." He shuddered. "You're giving me every reason not to want to go back. Can't we just wait till we're found?"

"It's tempting," Friday said. "But we've got to take the initiative. You know that."

"I need you to remind me. . . . If we have to lose this, then we'll make another place, even nicer."

"There's no doubt about that," she murmured.

"Then that's settled."

"Now that we're going back," said Friday, "I'll have to start thinking again about what I tried to forget. My situation has gotten a lot more complicated than when it was just that my husband shot me."

"Under the circumstances," Crews said, "we *had* to live together. We can deny we were lovers."

"I don't know about you," said she, clasping the hand he had kept at her waist, "but I would find it humiliating to make such a statement when everybody looking at us would know it was a lie."

11

■

DESPITE THEIR DECISION TO JOIN THE
rest of humankind now that the route had been located,
Crews might have found it easy to procrastinate in doing as
much had Friday not convinced him, on arising next morning, that, if you thought about it, there was no good reason
to delay. *He* could have stayed in place at least until the
blackberries were exhausted, but she was right, and not only
in the obvious sense. Having command of oneself meant you
made decisions and acted on them: whatever the outcome,
you had completed a process. He had lived too long in fragments and spasms.

At the edge of the clearing they stopped to look fondly back
at the lean-to.

"Next time we'll do the birch-bark shingles," Friday said.

"And make the clay oven," said Crews. "And by then we'll
have done research on edible wild foods. There's probably all
kinds of stuff we missed now." He turned. "We're jumping the
gun. We've still got a long hike to Fort Judson."

"Yeah," Friday answered. "But this was a real home." Her
bruise was gone by now, and her face was of a flawless tan.
Her teeth were as white as ever.

"It wouldn't be quite the same if we really knew what we
were doing," said Crews. "So maybe we shouldn't try to repro-

duce it but rather tackle something new next time. Bathroom with shower."

"Heated towel rack and bidet!"

As always when a route was known, following this one took only a fraction of the time needed for its previous discovery. The hill from which the river could be seen now seemed to be only a mile or so from the campsite. But though it had been in sight from the crest of the hill, the waterway was no longer visible once they entered the trees on the downward slope, and because the trail from here on was entirely new, the travel took forever. They were still on descending ground when the sun had climbed to its high-noon position.

They paused to sit on a fallen log and eat the blackberries Friday had bagged in her denim jacket, which was lavishly stained thereby.

"Along with the other things I have learned," Crews said, "is a respect for the bygone explorers who first made maps. It takes me no time at all to get the feeling I don't know where I am. You don't think we've taken a wrong turn somewhere?"

"No," said Friday. "We're fine."

"Then where's the river? We should be there by now."

"Farther than it looked." She fed him several berries. "It has to be, doesn't it, if we saw where it was and then walked straight toward it?"

"But I don't know if we did walk straight. We had to skirt some fallen timber, and then remember that patch of thorny bushes."

Friday chewed and swallowed a blackberry. "Consider this: we're still going slightly downhill. Water seeks the lowest level, no? As long as the earth continues to slope downward, it isn't possible for the river to be there. When we reach level ground and don't find it soon thereafter, then I'll worry."

She was proved right within the next hour. There, beyond a strip of deciduous-treed bottomland, was the river, which, after the lively trout stream, looked broad and sluggish and the color of dull metal. He tossed a stick in and watched it slowly drift away. He had expected a more rapid current.

He asked Friday whether anything looked familiar. "Maybe we should look for the canoe. Paddling against the current might go faster than I thought. We'd probably make better time and also be more comfortable in a boat."

She stared upstream and down. "As usual, everything looks the same in any given area, and I'm only now beginning to try to notice particular distinctions. I wasn't doing that the last time I was here. I do remember that where we landed last, the bank was lower than this is. He pulled the canoe partway out of the water and then, when we had unloaded everything, all the way up and back into a grove of trees, where he turned it over and covered it with branches and brush. But that could have been anyplace."

"I guess we should start to walk it," Crews said, "staying right along the bank, which looks passable as far as I can see. Maybe we'll run across where you pulled in. With luck, it'll be upstream from here. If it's downstream, it can be written off. What do you think?"

"I defer to you."

"But you often have better ideas than I."

She seized his hand. "Usually it's when you begin to doubt your own judgment that you are struck by my brilliance. If I'm so smart, how did I get here?"

Perhaps it was seeing the river again that evoked the masochistic impulse. Crews averted his eyes from the sight of pain in hers. "I could say the same about life," he told her. "In fact, I used to say it all the time. But that was in the old days, when I shaved from time to time and changed my clothes and ordered from menus."

Squeezing his hand, she said anxiously, "Promise you won't go clean-shaven when we get back without warning me first."

"I promise."

"I don't mean asking my permission," Friday added, almost desperately. "I mean, just letting me know."

"You don't have to worry about that."

"I'm not necessarily stuck on beards," she said. "But everything is changing so much that—it's just that I know you that way."

"You're going to let me take off this jacket, I hope."

"Never!" But she was back to kidding again, and pushed amiably away.

This was the first time since taking off from the suburban airport, many weeks before, that Crews had had a known destination. At last he could be sure about something: except in the unlikely event that there was more than one river in the area, with this one he could count on going in the opposite direction to which the current flowed and eventually reaching Fort Judson. There could be no exception to this truth. The conviction brought with it a sense of adequacy simply not available when his position in space was in doubt. Had the accident not marooned him in trackless terrain he would probably have gone his life long without experiencing such literal disorientation, as opposed to the kind common to the drunk, which might be called sentimental, for it could be corrected only by a negative measure, i.e., ceasing to drink.

They hiked along the bank on nondemanding ground, for the most part level and grassy and five or six feet above the water. The other side of the river, probably a hundred yards away, had what looked like gravelly beach, anyway quite a wide lip of shore at water level. Over there, and not here, was the place to pull a boat in. And this was true mile after mile. He might have begun to question Friday's impression of where she and her husband had landed had he not quickly disciplined himself: that *Fort Judson was upstream of everywhere* was a truth as fixed as the position of the North Star that he had forgotten to look for.

Maintaining a regular pace, they did not exhaust themselves and needed no stops for rest. Occasionally they drank from the thermos, and at one point, continuing to walk, they ate smoked fish from the little supply Crews carried, wrapped in fresh leaves, in whichever pockets could accept them. They remained silent except on practical matters. It went without saying that real conversation was reserved for camp. Crews was no longer astonished at their compatibility, which by now seemed a matter of natural instinct.

By late afternoon the terrain had changed. The bank on their side had gradually dwindled in height and finally, at the beginning of a bend of the river, become a broad shingle, a beach of stones, but small ones, pebbles mainly, and rounded, so that walking on them would have been no problem had they not been heated by hours of sunshine. They were fiery to bare feet. Crews danced briefly before hopping down into the thin leading edge of the water. He moued over at Friday. "It seems I'm still a tenderfoot. About time to make camp. Everything we need should be in that grove up there. I don't know that we'll want shelter for the night. It's so warm, and no rain is coming. What do you think?"

"Still, it would be cozy."

He had hoped that she would say as much. But he pretended otherwise, saying dubiously, "Well, all right. Then *you* can get to work. Do you have the tool?" She pulled it out of a pocket and waved it smugly. "Good. Oh, here's the mirror. You might start the fire. I'm going to try some fishing, as long as I've already got my feet wet. And I want to reconnoiter the river down there around that point. Maybe I'll be able to see Fort Judson."

He was joking, but Friday frowned. She had come to take the mirror, standing at the edge of the dry pebbles. "Watch yourself down there. You'll be out of sight."

"Yes, ma'am. I'll try to keep out of trouble. If I run into a bear, I'll yell for you to come and handle him. Can you sing off-key?"

"One of my specialties! Or at least so I was told when I got rejected for glee club."

Her reminiscences were invariably of her schooldays. Crews spoke very little of his own past. As the days since meeting her went by, his memories were less and less applicable to the present. He continued to splash along in the shallows and watched Friday as their routes, at first parallel, diverged and she angled off across the pebbles, heading for the trees. He hoped she would look back before they could no longer see each other, and she did, at the last possible moment before he reached the point, waving merrily.

The stones gave way to a low bank, below which the water rapidly deepened. Crews scrambled out of the river and, mounting the rise, could see what was beyond: another pebble beach, though this one was narrower than that he had just left.

A dark-green canoe lay bottom up, back where the short slope up to the woods began.

He leaped down to the beach and ran across the stones, immune to their heat. At the canoe he bent to read the legend stencil-painted in yellow on the bow: "Scanlon's, Fort Judson," under which appeared a large number 3. But Friday had said that many campers who came downriver hired equipment in Judson. It had been a long time since she fled her husband, who by now had surely returned his own canoe to Scanlon's and given the authorities whatever story he had chosen. But if so, why had there been no sign of a search party?

Crews saw the top of the tent before he had run all the way up the bank, and gaining the crest, he saw Friday. She was being hugged by a man a head taller than she. It did not look as if she was resisting him.

12

■

BEFORE CREWS COULD ACT ON HIS COW-
ardly impulse to retreat in silence, Friday saw him and pushed
herself away from the big man and shouted and beckoned.
Crews went to them, though like a sleepwalker.

"Robert," Friday said when he got there, and her first use,
ever, of his name did little to restore him to real life. "This is
Michael."

The man was even larger than he had looked at a distance.
He was also wide of upper body and clean-shaven and dressed
in what, by contrast with any other clothing Crews had seen
in a season, looked like a brand-new khaki outdoorsman's
costume, of the sort favored by the late Dick Spurgeon. Everything about him was outsized, including his prominent jaw,
a head of dense dark hair, and the thick-fingered hand that,
after Friday's next words, he readily thrust forward.

What Friday said was, "I owe my life to this man."

In his coma Crews for an instant assumed she meant the
other and not himself. He allowed his hand to be shaken vigorously, though the grip was not as crushing as it occurred to
him he had expected.

The man was smiling. His voice was surprisingly boyish.
"Christ almighty," he said in his tenor. "How can I thank
you?" He sighed and his smile grew even wider. "But I'm sure

going to try." He let go of Crews's hand and turned a fond expression on his wife. "You must have done something right. El looks mighty healthy. And that tan is new. She was white as a ghost when we started out."

Crews had avoided looking at Friday all this while, but he did so now and simply asked, "El?"

"Ellen," Friday said. "But you—"

She was interrupted by her husband. "After the accident— which I guess you might know about—I searched for her the whole time. I ransacked the woods. I went around the lake and up and down miles of the river. I finally was running real low on food. Yesterday I used my second-to-last match. I was heading back to Judson. But I never gave up hope. It's warm weather, after all." He had begun to speed up his words. "I was coming back with reinforcements, boats, helicopters."

Crews was still looking at Friday. At last he asked, "Why were you hugging him?"

She winced. "I was *being* hugged."

Her husband meanwhile anxiously continued speaking, as if he had not heard the exchange. " . . . everyplace, my God! I was going out of my skull . . . "

"Didn't he shoot you?"

"Do you think I was lying?" she asked angrily.

Crews turned to Michael. "You stole my raft, and then you stole my fishing stuff."

The accusations brought the larger man out of his obsessive monologue. "Those were *yours*? I'll make it good, I'll make it *all* good. I was desperate. I had to make time. *She* was headed in that direction. As for the fishing rod, I thought I might run out of food, and that's just what did happen, not right away, maybe, but it's true now: I'm down to my last packet."

Crews said, "I'm taking your canoe in exchange."

Michael's instant of puzzled stare by stages became a crooked grin. "Why, sure," he said brightly. "We'll all fit in it, and you can take bow paddle."

"Not you," said Crews. "Just me."

The other chose either to ignore or simply not to acknowledge this statement. "Look," he said, "about the rod and stuff. I've still got it, right there." He thrust his square chin at the tent. "I wasn't going to keep it permanently. I'm no thief. I can see how you might be steamed, though." He chuckled for effect. "You might be interested to know I never could catch a damn thing with it. I admire the hell out of you trout-fly guys, but I guess I just don't have the patience to stand there for hours, casting away: not enough of a physical challenge. But maybe I should have tried harder, because I'm real low on rations."

Crews was studying Friday again. "Okay, *Ellen*, what are you going to say?"

She responded in anger. "What do you know about it?"

"Come on, man." It was Michael. "You can't stay mad forever. We're all out here together. I told you I'd make it good, and I will." He seemed to notice Crews's appearance for the first time, from hairy face to bare feet. "Do you *live* out here?" He shrugged his thick epauleted shoulders. His twill shirt-jacket had a special pocket on the upper right arm for sunglasses. "You must have been a godsend to El."

"I don't get it," Crews said to Friday. "Are you waiting for me to do it?"

Tears blurred her eyes. "Oh, hell," she cried softly. "Oh, the hell with you."

Crews was really fed up. "I meant what I said: I'm taking the canoe." He turned and started toward the beach.

"Now, just a minute, fella," said Michael. "You—"

Crews could hear nothing but Friday's interruption, though it should properly have been less audible than her husband's sudden bluster. "*No*," she said, "*you don't want to do that*. I'm getting ready. It isn't easy, you know."

Crews came back. "I know. But you can do it."

She looked levelly at her husband. "You shot me."

The big man twisted his thin mouth in exasperation. "You know damn well that was an accident. God almighty, El!" He turned to Crews. "I was reloading the gun. She panicked. I couldn't catch her. She ran like she was nuts." To Friday he said, "I can see it must have been a shock, and that's what you were in: shock. But Jesus, to run into the woods and get yourself lost? Come on, El! Shot? You say you were shot? I swear I didn't know it. Why didn't you say so at the time? How could I know? That makes it worse than ever. We had a first-aid kit, for God's sake. So you run off when you're bleeding? What kind of sense does that make? And you're supposed to be the smart one?"

Friday nodded judiciously. "That would explain why you didn't ask me about the wound just now."

"Why, sure it would," Michael cried, half-grinning back and forth between his wife and Crews. "How in the world could I have known about it if you ran away?"

"You fired twice," Friday said. Since wiping her eyes she had remained expressionless.

"Oh, you're wrong about that. If it was an accident, why would I keep shooting?" He smirked at Crews. "My finger got stuck in the trigger or something?"

"*I* heard the two shots," Crews said.

"You? Where were *you?*" The big man looked as though he was about to become hostile, but then caught himself and whined instead. "You know how echoes sound across water."

"You saw me on the raft."

"Did I not just apologize for borrowing it? What more can I say? I wanted to make time getting to the other end of the lake. By then El had such a head start, and I was worrying about her getting lost. I didn't know anything about her getting shot." He stopped abruptly and raised his eyebrows at his wife. "I've been looking for you ever since! Are you giving me the works on this business? I mean, okay, so I deserve it for scaring you, maybe, but this is a serious accusation. And then, how do I know you *were* hit? Where's the so-called wound to prove it?"

Friday smiled genially at him. "I've had a lot of time to think about this, Michael, and I ask myself just what it is that makes you such a special case. For a while I thought it was stupidity. But then I realized that I must be dumber than you, because I'm the one who went camping, and I'm the one who got shot for my pains."

Michael was at last displaying some slight evidence of authentic emotion as opposed to the bogus, even feckless indignation he had shown thus far. His right cheek twitched as though he were trying to suck a fragment of food from between the underlying teeth. "You going to start that again? Leave it to you. . . . Do you mind not embarrassing this gentleman? We can go into all of it when we get home."

"*We* are not getting home together," Friday said. "And I think I can speak for 'this gentleman' when I say he won't ever be embarrassed by me."

Her husband glared at her for a moment, nose twitching. Then he looked at Crews with a stage sneer. *"Him?"*

In the vodka days Crews would already have tangled with the man, whom he would have disliked on sight, and not necessarily for the best motives, and would very likely have been painfully thrashed by him, because say what you might, it was physically unreasonable that, barring elaborate conditions, he could have held his own against a healthy opponent six inches taller and at least fifty pounds heavier in what looked like only muscle. By now, Michael must outweigh him by a hundred.

"He's the finest man I've ever known," Friday said fiercely. "Don't you touch him."

As it happened, Crews had not been all that offended by her husband's sneer, but he *was* humiliated by her defense of him. To maintain any semblance of pride, he now believed he might have to go up against this giant athlete who ran a gym.

Michael displayed the palms of his large hands. "Far be it from me," he said. "He looks like that guy who sleeps in the shoe-store doorway, down the street from my place. I give him a couple quarters every morning."

Crews must have shown some beginning belligerence even though he was not yet fully conscious of such, for Friday clutched him and pleaded, "Robert, *don't!* He's a black belt."

Now there was no doubt what Crews had to do. In a way, the two of them, husband and wife, were collaborating in his moral ruin. He undid himself from her grasp.

"You have to let me do something here, Friday."

"*What* did he call you, El? *What?*" Michael was still on his second derisive "what?" when Crews stepped in and threw a punch with maximum force. The blow had been directed to the left side of the jaw, but the man reacted so quickly to the approaching fist that it missed all of his meaty face except the very tip of an earlobe.

In counterattack he simply covered Crews's entire forehead and nose with one big hand and pushed. Crews was projected backward too violently to keep his balance for long, and he sprawled on the earth.

"Stay right there," Michael commanded, but still in his jeering boyish tone. "Next time I'll break something of yours, and you haven't got anything you could afford to lose." He grinned toothily at Friday. "Sorry, El. I had to touch him because he touched me first. It wasn't any pleasure, I can tell you, but at least I avoided that scummy beard. But then I guess it's not that repulsive to you, crummy as you yourself are, and by the way, you both *stink*. Fish and burned stuff and God knows what all else."

There was no way Crews could have taken this guy by legitimate means even on two months of square meals, daily showers, and nights on innersprings. In the current circumstances there was no reason he should try.

Friday raised the hem of her shirt, the shirt Crews had given her. "I've got a wound where you shot a gun at me. If you do anything more to him, I'll swear out a warrant for your arrest when I get to Fort Judson."

Crews climbed to his feet despite the warning. "Don't make bargains with a man like that." He was almost as annoyed with her as when she had first tried the mushrooms.

Friday ignored him. "The canoe is on *my* credit card," she

told her husband. "It's mine, and we're taking it—or are you going to shoot me again?"

Michael had hardly glanced at the scar below her ribs, but he did show some chastening. "You can't get away with that. If I hit you at all—and you'll need more evidence than that little scratch—it was an accident, and you know damn well it was. But how do I know this bum didn't do something to you? Who *is* your bodyguard, anyhow? Somebody you found in a hobo jungle?" His laughter was a hoot.

Crews was conscious of a loathsome desire: he wished he had a drink, in fact a whole bottle. Meanwhile Friday had stepped between him and her husband. He was in fact hiding behind a woman's stained denim jacket and jeans, both much the worse for wear.

"Get going," she said, her head half turned, to Crews. "Go find the canoe. I'll take care of him."

Crews was so startled by this command, and so frozen in shame, that for an instant he did nothing but watch her go into a combat stance, one foot forward, knees bent, fists raised.

Her husband asked incredulously, "Are you forgetting who taught you karate in the first place?"

"I haven't forgotten *anything*," Friday said. "I'm just surprised you haven't gone and got your gun, yellowbelly."

Michael winced in exasperation. "You're hooked on that gun." He grinned. "You need it to prove your virility? . . . I'll say it again: I don't think you even got hit. Anyway, you certainly weren't hurt badly, if that scratch is all. So kindly stop clowning and we'll let bygones be bygones. Bright and early tomorrow morning we'll head for Judson. If you owe this guy something, we'll leave him a sleeping bag."

"Which also was rented on my credit card," Friday said. Over her shoulder she cried, "Go *on*, Robert, find the canoe. It should be down there someplace."

"I saw it," Crews said, finding his tongue. "Don't worry

about the canoe." He stepped out from behind her. "Be reasonable, Friday. You're not going to take him on."

"You might just be surprised," she said. "For a change I want to be the one who hands out the punishment."

"You've certainly got it coming. But justice has nothing to do with these things. Believe me, not because I'm a man, but because I have experience at such matters."

"How about both of you at once?" Michael asked derisively. "And I'll use only my left hand."

Friday launched her attack, a graceful-looking high kick, which missed, followed by a straight punch to Michael's face. Without bothering to assume a karate posture, he deflected the latter so forcefully as to throw her off balance, then slapped her head with such violence that she was knocked to the ground.

Before Crews could offer her assistance she was back on her feet. "Please stop it," he said. "It's not going to work."

"I don't care," Friday screamed. She lowered her head and shook it. She had taken a savage blow.

"He's making sense," said Michael, standing away. "I guess I never made it clear to you that karate is effective when used by a smaller person on a larger one only when the larger person hasn't been trained in it. Do you get it through your thick head, El? How *could* it work if the bigger fighter is himself a black belt?"

"You're going to fight me with respect!" Friday shouted.

"No, I'm not," Michael said, laughing, and stepped in with his usual blinding speed and slapped her again, this time with the left hand, then for good measure hurled Crews to the ground once more.

Friday had not fallen this time. She was annoyed with Crews—so much so, he believed at first, that her cheek was suffused with blood. But then he recognized that the discoloration came from the second slap. She grimaced down at him. "Are you going to keep out of this?"

"All right," he groaned, laboriously rising. "But only if you quit too. He's too much for us. We'll end up getting hurt badly, and who needs that? Come on, let him go. Sometimes you've got to lose."

She stared at him in disbelief. Her husband said, "Hey, the old tramp knows what he's doing. He's not all bad. Just take him and leave while you both can still move. I *was* going to share my last food with you people, but I withdraw the offer. You're filth."

Friday said to Crews, "I never thought I'd hear *you* talk like this."

"Kiddo," Crews mumbled wearily, "the secret to successful survival is to know when to quit against overwhelming odds." He avoided her importunate eyes. "He's right: we should go while we can still walk." He demonstrated the limp he had acquired already, which brought him to a collection of firewood that had obviously been chopped by Michael with the neat little belt-ax that lay nearby. Unlike himself, the man was well equipped for a sojourn in the woods.

Crews seized the heftiest log, which must have required some muscle to chop through, and taking her husband by surprise while the strong man was still sneering at Friday, hit him in the side of the head with such force that a splintering sound was heard, whether from wood or skull. Michael toppled as though he were a tree being felled.

Friday rushed to the fallen man, else Crews might have, animal-like, taken advantage of his opponent's helplessness and done him further damage. Kneeling, she cried her husband's name aloud. Michael made an incoherent noise.

"Water!" she screamed at Crews. "Get some water!"

The thermos hung at his belt, but why waste their supply? He looked for the expensive canteen the other guy was sure to have and soon found it hanging from the leading tentpole.

When he returned with it, Friday looked up reproachfully. "Why did you have to be so rough?"

Had she been one of his wives he would probably have pointed out that only a moment earlier she had thought him a coward. But he gave a rancorless answer. "With somebody his size, you've got to put him out of action as decisively as possible. He's lucky I didn't use the ax."

Friday unscrewed the top of the canteen and, having filled her right hand with water, patted Michael's face. "He's actually sort of fragile," she said. "He gets lots of colds, and he always seems to hurt himself in odd ways, like when adjusting exercise machines."

The big man's eyes opened. He recovered so quickly that Crews could not believe he had been actually unconscious at any time. He sat up. "*You*," he said to Friday, with venom. "I'm charging you and your boyfriend with assault with intent to kill."

"Let me hit him again," Crews said, pretending to reach for the log he had tossed aside. He was not serious. He just wanted to see the man flinch.

And Michael did so, but seeing that Crews did not follow through on the threat, became hateful to Friday again, stupidly rejecting the sympathy she had just bestowed on him. "I've said it before, and I'll say it again: you couldn't have done so well at your company except on your knees, under the boardroom table."

Friday made no reply. She deposited the canteen at his side and stood up.

Her husband made no attempt to rise. He addressed her back. "And as anybody can plainly see, you survived in the wilderness the same way." Apparently his skull had not been seriously damaged: he had yet to finger the affected side of his head or favor it in any fashion.

"You want to get your fishing rod?" Friday asked Crews. "I'm taking whatever food's left. It's mine. I'm paying the rental on the tent too, and the rest, but he can keep them. Tomorrow we'll be in Judson."

"You two puny characters are going to paddle upstream?" Michael shouted derisively. "You got a sucker punch in on me, but you're not going to put one over on Nature."

"I've been doing that for weeks," Crews said. "There doesn't seem to be much of a current. If it's too strong we can always try poling, along the shore. I'm tired of walking."

The big man continued to rant, but he stayed where he was, sitting on the earth. Probably he had been hurt more substantially in the spirit than in the flesh.

Crews retrieved the cased rod and tackle box from amidst the other things inside the tent, and then he went through the fancy backpack, with its aluminum frame, until he found the pistol and an accompanying box of shells, only a few of which remained. The weapon was of the six-shooter type and felt heavier than it looked.

Michael was in the process of rising, but when he saw the gun in Crews's possession he sank back to the ground and, cowering behind crossed forearms, cried, "Hey man, wait a minute. Don't do it!"

And even Friday, holding what looked like some kind of camp cooking kit, nested pots within a canvas pouch, recoiled and said, "Oh, *no*. Throw that thing away!"

"Take it all," Michael pleaded. "But don't kill me. You got no reason to. I'm not resisting! It would be cold-blooded—"

"Will you stop sniveling?" Crews said. "Am I even pointing it at you?"

"Please get *rid* of it." Friday made forceful gestures. "I don't want it in existence."

But Crews candidly defied her on this matter. "We'll hold on to it, in case you need it for evidence. It's insurance." The pistol was too heavy for any of his pockets. Finally he put it and the extra ammunition on top of the gear in the tackle box, closed the box, and slung the strap at his shoulder.

Michael now asked, in a howl, "You're leaving me here, with no food and no means of protection?"

Friday sighed and rooted in another canvas bag, coming up with a little pouch of shiny plastic. She read aloud the legend printed on it. " 'Chicken-and-noodle soup.' Here you go." She tossed it to him, but he refused to catch it, and it fell near his elbow.

Crews was interested to note that when it came to violence or the threat thereof, Friday's sympathy went immediately to the putative victim. But at other times she could be uncompromising.

"So I've got a temper," Michael wailed. "You ought to know better than to needle someone holding a loaded gun."

Crews asked Friday, "Is he still trying to explain how you got wounded?"

"Yes," said she. "And about that he's right. I'll never do it again."

"But you just took him on at karate."

Her expression was reproachful. "That was something else entirely. Can't you see that?"

"I'll try." The tackle box was growing oppressively heavy, with the added weight. He shifted it to his other shoulder and hung the rod case from the free one. "We'd better get going before it's too late to see what we're doing."

"Call me about your possessions when we get back to town," Friday said to her husband. "I'm changing the locks at home. What you do with your car is up to you, but I'm not going to make any more payments on it."

Crews dawdled before setting off down to the beach, should Michael be stung into some sort of action, but the big man's morale was not quick to recover. All that he had left was spite.

"You're pathetic," Michael said. "You're getting old and you're losing your muscle tone. All of you is about ready to slide south. You just got a short reprieve, eating acorns and deer droppings or whatever old Dan'l Boone here provided. But you'll put the blubber on when you get back. You know it, and I know it." He cackled with laughter. "Hey, buddy, did she tell you what she weighed when she first waddled into my club? I used to work with her in private, otherwise it would have been bad for business: drive people away, you know? What you see there is *my* doing, not hers. On her own, she'd still be the Queen of Lardland."

Crews asked her, "Do you want me to give him another taste of the log?"

"Now you know all that's worth knowing about me," Friday said, managing a wry smile. "Once again, though, he's right. But let's go. I've heard enough bitter truths for one season." She tossed her head for practical reasons: a strand of hair had swung across her eye. She brandished the bag of food. "He lied about the provisions: there's a lot left. Cocoa and dehydrated beef stew and all. *And* almost a whole little box of matches. I'm taking a couple of pots and pans too. Can you carry the paddles? They're leaning against the far side of the tent." Her husband had prudently brought them up from the beach, so as to deny them to thieves of his own ilk.

Before leaving, Crews asked the sitting man, "You're not thinking of doing anything to stop us, are you?"

Michael made a keening sound, but in simulated glee. "Stop you? Brother, I'd do anything I could to hasten you on your way. You're hauling away a load of garbage that otherwise I'd be stuck with. I'm grateful to you. I love you for it."

"I'm fond of you too," said Crews. "But I'm sticking to the one with the career."

When he and Friday reached the canoe, Crews said, "I haven't been in one of these since I was a kid. You've had more recent experience. You want the boss paddle? That's the rear one, right?"

"No, thanks," said Friday. "I had a hard time getting the hang of it when I tried, and that was downstream. Anyway, the guy in front can complain about what the steerer is doing back there. My sense of self has taken enough for one day. . . . I really ought to say this: there was a time when we, when we . . . "

"When you liked each other better," Crews said. "I'm sure that that is just as true as any of the negative things. And a balanced memory is easier to carry. Give me a hand here, will you?"

The canoe was light enough for him to turn over and for both to carry if they put their undernourished backs to a

weight that her husband had surely toted with no effort at all.
It had given Crews enormous satisfaction to deck such a man.
No doubt this was a shameful feeling, not to be shared with
decent human beings, but it had been sufficient to stifle his
brief, craven urge for a drink.

Floating the vessel in the shallows, they tossed their burdens
therein, and Friday climbed on board. Crews restrained the
stern from rising as she crawled to the bow seat with her paddle, then splashed aboard himself from the thigh-deep water.

Friday looked over her shoulder. "I can't absolutely guar-
antee that I won't get fat again."

Crews shrugged. "If that happens, and I start boozing, we
can always come out here again, with no supplies and bare
feet." The current, while not so strong as utterly to frustrate
their intent to go against it, was stronger than it had looked
from shore, and the first strokes of their paddles, not yet in
coordination, swung the craft to face downstream.

A hoot of derision came from the bluff. "Don't mind him,"
said Crews. "If he starts throwing stones, remember I've got
the gun. . . . Now, let's get organized. Keep your paddle on the
right, and I'll put mine on the left for the moment, but I think
it's the back paddle that usually does the switching if necessary. What we need in the bow is stability."

Friday glanced back again. "That's what you'll get."

"I hope you'll keep calling me Robert. Nobody else ever has."

She was already too busy, digging into the swirl with the
paddle, to answer except with a saucy upthrust of her shoulder cap.

After several more fits and starts, and even one near mis-
carriage in which the left gunwale dipped within a hair of the
roiling water, they at last brought the canoe to the optimum
attitude to head for civilization. About an hour remained before they would pull into shore, start a fire with matches, eat
beef stew and wash it down with hot chocolate, and, one more
night, sleep under the stars.